DEATH IN NONNA'S KITCHEN

Also by Alex Coombs

The Old Forge Café Mysteries
Murder on the Menu

The Hanlon PI Series
Silenced for Good
Missing for Good
Buried for Good

The DCI Hanlon Series
The Stolen Child
The Innocent Girl
The Missing Husband
The Silent Victims

DEATH IN NONNA'S KITCHEN

ALEX COOMBS

NO EXIT PRESS

First published in the UK in 2024 by No Exit Press,
an imprint of Bedford Square Publishers Ltd,
London, UK

noexit.co.uk
@noexitpress

ISBN
978-1-915798-74-9 (Paperback)
978-1-915798-75-6 (eBook)

2 4 6 8 10 9 7 5 3

Typeset in Janson Text
by Palimpsest Book Production Ltd, Falkirk, Stirlingshire

Printed in Great Britain by CPI Group (UK) Ltd, Croydon CR0 4YY

'Good food is the foundation of genuine happiness.'

Auguste Escoffier

For Mike Boyce
Great chef, great guy, great friend

Chapter One

It was the end of May when, on my morning run, I turned onto the path that bordered one of the many fields near the village of Hampden Green where I live. I'm a Londoner; I moved out here to the Chilterns and opened a restaurant and I've been here six months.

Business was going well. But despite – maybe because of – favourable reviews and bums on seats, I was tired. I was short of money and short of breath, but I ran on. I might die exhausted, penniless and in pain but at least I'd die fit and lean. If it was an open-casket funeral people would say, 'She's looking good, so slim.'

There was a sheet of blue paper, laminated against the weather and secured to a bush. It was the third such notice I'd seen. Instead of ignoring it and simply wondering what it said, as I had the first two times, I did something clever. I actually stopped and read it. It was a change of usage notification from the council for the field. For three weeks in July the field would host an open-air event with licensed bars. I shrugged and jogged on – it was nothing to do with me.

I lengthened my stride and picked up the pace. It was good to be running on a day like this in the Bucks countryside. The fields bordered with neatly trimmed beech hedges looked great, the trees giving a wonderful canopy of green overhead. It beat being in the kitchen.

All too soon I was back there. Work, frantic prep for the day ahead, then the first trickle of orders coming in shortly after twelve, that like a river in full spate crashed around my ears with a vengeance from quarter to one onwards.

Later, during a lull in the lunchtime service, a brief respite from the heat of the stove and the pass and the clatter of pans on metal and the roar of the fans – I asked Francis my kitchen porter/chef (in a kitchen as small as mine the distinctions get blurred), a man as strong as an ox and somewhat less intellectual – if he knew anything about the event.

'Of course, everyone does.' He looked genuinely astonished at my ignorance. He scratched his head in perplexity.

Everyone except me.

'It's the Marlow House Festival,' he explained.

'Cheque on,' Jess my waitress said as she handed a ticket to me over the pass. 'Two parmesan crust chicken, one confit tomato linguine and a grilled aubergine with Provençale ratatouille.'

'Cheers Jess.' My hands automatically opened fridges, put another couple of pans on for the order. I turned back to Francis.

'The Marlow House Festival?' I repeated.

'Opera, Chef,' he said. Anyone else might have added

this in a condescending way, but not Francis. He was condescension-free. He not only wouldn't be able to spell it, he wouldn't know what it meant.

'Opera?' I said, somewhat stupidly.

'Yeah, opera, singing. . .' He looked at me, puzzled, as he started work on a dessert cheque: a strawberry pavlova with Chantilly cream. It's not uncommon for kitchen porters, or kps as we call them, to do relatively simple tasks like puddings. I had never quite lost hope too, that one day I might make a chef out of Francis – although this hope often seemed optimistic, if not forlorn.

'I know what opera is, Francis.' I said tetchily.

He finished what he was doing. 'That OK, Chef?' he said anxiously, showing me the finished result.

'Yeah sure,' I said. I could have done it better but it was acceptable.

'Service,' he called out to summon Jess, then walking over to the sink and, starting to load plates and cutlery into the enormous Hobart dishwasher, he continued. 'The Earl puts on a big event every year for about a fortnight. The first two or three weeks of July. There'll be a huge marquee there, about three hundred people per night, fireworks. . . It's mega.'

'Is that the Earl's opera event you two are talking about?'

It was Jess who had just walked in. I know very little about opera – it certainly didn't feature much on Beech Tree FM. That was the radio station we listened to in the kitchen, playing undemanding, uncontroversial pop classics. Their DJs had a permanent air of sunny mindlessness and inane links. One came on at this moment, '. . . *and now, here's a song about numbers, yes it's a former Number One, it's "Two in a Million" by S Club 7!. . .'*

'Yes,' I said, 'maybe we'll pick up some custom from it.'

Jess shook her head. 'No, you won't – it's fully catered.' She scowled at the radio. 'Do we have to listen to this?'

'It's S Club 7,' I said. 'I think it's high art. . .'

Jess pursed her lips; she hated my plebby taste in music. She left with the dessert and I hummed along to the music as I seared the chicken breasts.

An opera, eh?

What I didn't know was that the Earl's opera event was like the tossed pebble that starts the avalanche that would ultimately lead to several deaths and a scandal.

Chapter Two

Strickland was in a bad mood. He was on a split shift from his restaurant where he was head chef and was allowing himself a lunchtime drink before he went back to work.

'French bastards!' he said irritably. There had been an article on the Michelin system of awards in the trade press that had sparked his ire. This was a sore point. Strickland was aggrieved as he'd just narrowly missed out on his coveted Michelin star. He still had his four rosettes but boy, did he want that final accolade.

'Bloody Michelin Guide. . .' he grumbled. 'Bastards. . .' He would have chewed his arm off for a star.

It was Friday and we were in one of Hampden Green's two pubs. The grotty one. The Three Bells. The Three Bells was certainly in no danger of featuring in the Michelin Guide, or any other guide you might care to mention. Grotty décor, grotty toilets, grotty furniture. It was a beautiful day outside but not in here; in here it was genteel gloom. The sun never shone in the Three Bells. It was a wonder we came here at all, but it was quiet, and handy, and that suited us.

What the pub lacked in desirability, it made up for geographically. It was a five-minute walk from both our restaurants and as we both spend six days a week shackled to our respective stoves morning, noon and night, it was a blessed relief from our respective workplaces.

'What are you up to?' he asked. 'You look a bit down in the dumps.'

'I'm knackered,' I said. 'Jess is going off on holiday in August. I've got no one to cover for her, and a couple of my regular customers have said my wine list is unadventurous.'

I drank some Diet Coke; I wouldn't be drinking wine in here. I'd tried once, it was like paint-stripper. The Three Bell's wine list wasn't simply unadventurous, it was potentially lethal.

'You couldn't lend me your maître d' could you, Graeme?' I knew he was French, he had to know something about wine, which I didn't. I like drinking the stuff but I know very little about it. I desperately needed guidance.

He shook his head. 'No,' he said. Something in the way he said it made me wonder if there was some kind of problem there. He didn't elaborate. 'You could always try Malcolm.' I gave a tight, sarcastic smile.

Behind the bar, resplendent in a moth-eaten grey cardigan, Malcolm, the taciturn landlord with the very red face, like a God of the Undead, stood tall, cadaverous and silent, the grotty lord of all he surveyed. He was a discouraging presence. There was no hint of welcome or eagerness to serve, to spring into action should a customer appear; it was more as if he were guarding the bar from anyone who might be rash enough to try to get a drink.

My fellow chef was vibrating with energy. He had just come back from his third visit to the toilet. He might have had bladder problems, but his suspiciously wide eyes and frequent sniffs, as loud as they were frantic, told a different story.

His restaurant, the King's Head, was the other pub in Hampden Green. It had been turned into a restaurant and Strickland had firmly dragged it by the scruff of its countrified neck, from pork pies, filled baps and ploughman's lunches into the world of fine dining. He was highly successful. Now, if you wanted to eat there it was a three-week wait, unless there was a cancellation.

I changed the subject. 'And how about you – how are things at the King's Head?'

He took a mouthful of lager, and shook his head regretfully. 'It's Jean-Claude, the maître d'' he said. 'He's inefficient, but it's never that bloody obvious that I can sack him for it.' He sniffed loudly again and stared at me through his slightly glazed eyes. So that was why Strickland had looked so sour a moment ago.

He continued. 'And he's hitting on the waitresses. . . Anyway, one of these days he'll go too far and commit a sackable offence.'

I'd had enough of restaurant gossip. I changed the subject.

'Do you know about the Earl's opera thing?'

Strickland nodded. 'Yeah, and I know who's doing the catering too.' He smiled at me.

'Who's that then?' I asked.

His smile broadened. 'Have a guess. . .'

7

'I really don't know. . .'

He sat back in his chair. 'Matteo McCleish!'

'What, *Nonna's Kitchen* Matteo McCleish?'

'The one and only,' he said.

Chapter Three

Strickland's pet peeve might have been the Michelin Guide, mine was TV chefs. Everyone knows Matteo and his bloody TV programme, *Nonna's Kitchen*.

McCleish had worked his way up from being a chef who cropped up on *Saturday Kitchen* and an appearance on *MasterChef: The Professionals*, to having his own TV series on BBC2. That was *Nonna's Kitchen*. The story behind it, everything has to have a back-story these days, was that his Nonna (Italian for Granny) had fostered his love of cooking. Matteo's mother had been of Italian parentage but brought up in Scotland, his father Scottish – and at the age of ten his family had relocated to Italy, where he had been brought up. His parents worked long hours and he'd basically been looked after by his beloved Nonna, spending long hours with her in the kitchen where she showed him the rudiments of cooking. She'd been a decent, simple cook, and he showed how with his expertise, the simplest of ingredients and ideas could be transformed into restaurant style food.

The most obvious thing about Matteo, other than his

ability to cook, was his extreme good looks. He had a seductive, half-Italian, half-Scottish pronunciation, and a model wife. She was Italian, completely so – the kind of woman you think of if someone says hot, Italian babe. She was, *naturalmente*, also an influencer with a sizeable following on Instagram and TikTok where she appeared often, usually wearing very little, some consumer product artfully placed, very much in the foreground.

So, Nonna's kitchen had something for everyone. Matteo made women swoon, Graziana attracted a male audience. Some people maybe learned a bit about cooking.

Strickland nodded. 'Yeah, thought that would surprise you.'

I smiled grimly, baring my teeth; surprises are not always welcome.

Oblivious, he carried on. 'He's going to be running a pop-up restaurant for the Earl's opera in a fancy marquee. What do you make of that then?'

I tried not to be churlish. The village could do with some excitement. Since January when there had been a murder nearby – in which I had unwittingly been involved – things had been remarkably quiet.

The arrival of a bona fide famous person, a chef in the same league as Gordon Ramsay or Tom Kerridge or Rick Stein, would most certainly be the topic of conversation around here for the next month.

Strickland had some more information. 'Not only is he running the pop-up, he has even moved here.'

Now that did surprise me. I knew he had a restaurant in London, I guess like many successful chefs he was starting

10

to empire build. 'So, Matteo McCleish has moved to the village? Where?' I asked.

'Yep, into the Old Vicarage,' Strickland replied, raising his eyebrows, 'well temporarily at least. He arrived a few days ago.'

I knew of the house. The Old Vicarage was massive, built back in the day when the clergy had money and bling. Not like today. It belonged to a shady businessman who had needed to leave the village quickly, address unknown. That had been a hot topic locally too. It was currently on AirBnB, so someone had said, for a massive sum of money. Well, it looked like the shady businessman had found a client.

Strickland pulled a face and drank some of his lager. 'What do you think of him?'

I paused for thought. I didn't want to say that I had to confess, I didn't like him. I suddenly thought, maybe the root problem lay not with him and the cliched Nonna figure, but me. I guess I was envious. I wanted the freedom from financial worry that Matteo had. I bet he didn't wake up in the morning concerned about his unpaid bills. If I was honest, that was probably why I didn't like him; he was successful and I resented it. I wished that I could go through life like he did, not a care in the world.

I didn't realise I was about to learn a lot more about Matteo McCleish than either of us expected.

Chapter Four

Speak of the devil and he will come. The very next day, on Saturday lunchtime, I met both Matteo and his wife, the beautiful Graziana.

Jess had announced their presence. Normally, Jess does her job running my restaurant with a mixture of good-natured efficiency and ironic detachment. For her, it's a well-paid holiday job, a distraction from studying IT, which is where her future lies. She rarely gets excited – why should she? Working in the hospitality business is not her dream. Unlike most people in kitchens who aren't passionate about food, she's not crazy, unqualified or desperate. But today was different.

She had come running into the kitchen an hour earlier.

'It's Matteo McCleish, and his wife, in our restaurant!'

I had never seen her so excited. She was wide-eyed; her hair, unruly at the best of times, stood up like she'd been electrocuted. Francis stared at her, a parody of amazement.

'Gordon Bennett!' he said. That, for Francis, constitutes great excitement. It was a measure too, of Matteo McCleish's fame, that Francis knew who he was. His knowledge of people is usually confined to cricketers and rugby players.

'Can everyone just calm down,' I said, calmly. In reality I was feeling anything but relaxed. I seemed to have forgotten my earlier reservations about the McCleishes. You hypocrite, Charlie, I told myself sternly. But it was no good. I was as bad as my staff. My heart was thundering with adrenaline. It's Matteo McCleish, and HIS WIFE, in MY restaurant! Feigning nonchalance, 'They're just customers.'

But of course they weren't just customers, they were culinary royalty, and when I got their orders I cooked their food as if it was going out to the King.

Matteo had lamb fillet with an anchovy and caper dressing garnished with a mint sauce and rösti potatoes, and Graziana, a chicken Caesar salad. I scrutinised every single ingredient on their plates as if I were performing brain surgery.

Jess kept us updated every time she came into the kitchen.

'They've started, they look happy!'

Then:

'They are loving the sourdough bread.'

'He just said, "Compliments to the chef". Oh, God, this is so exciting!'

A bit later: 'They're halfway through, they still look happy and there are three paparazzi outside on the green! And they've parked illegally!'

She was a true child of Hampden Green. If the Four Horsemen of the Apocalypse turned up, someone would point to the sign, 'Oi, you, that means you – War, Famine,

Pestilence and you, Death! No Riding On The Common (£100 fine)'.

When the plates came back we all stared at them like doctors looking at a life or death X-ray.

'Blimey, clean plates!' said Francis.

I shrugged. Feigned nonchalance again. They liked it!

'Don't sound so surprised, Francis.' My voice was dismissive. Inside, I was shouting to myself, 'He ate everything!'

They had dessert.

Cue another update from my waitress: 'Matteo's having the strawberry bavarois and Graziana's having the lemon and lime posset with almond shortbread.' She added, 'God she's even more beautiful in real life than on Instagram.'

Then, more clean plates, compliments to the chef and the following bombshell: 'He wants to meet you!' Jess looked at me adoringly. Normally she treats me as if I were slightly half-witted, like a dotty aunt who needs to be humoured. Now I was transmuted from lead to gold by the alchemical hand of Matteo McCleish, sprinkled with his TV stardust.

The gods had come down from Olympus. Or at least out of *Nonna's Kitchen*. Matteo was here in high resolution and 3D. And so it was that towards the end of service, I found myself shaking the McCleish hand, wondering what to call him. It was a problem that I would never have thought I would ever have. Matteo sounded too presumptuous, Mr McCleish far too formal.

He was the first really famous person I had ever met. I've cooked for a fair few, but they've never come in the kitchen, why would they? It was a strange sensation. I couldn't help but scrutinise him as intensely as I had his food when I'd sent it out from the kitchen half an hour earlier. It was hard work not staring at him too obviously.

In the flesh he was smaller than I had expected – shorter than me – and surprisingly slender. TV gives little indication of size unless people are helpfully standing next to something that has a recognisable benchmark height, a post-box for example, or a Labrador. Matteo was also more handsome in real life than he was on the screen – he certainly didn't disappoint there. He was ridiculously good-looking in an Italian way.

He looked very stylish and had an even bronze tan. I'm normally quite happy with the way I look, but he was so high wattage that standing next to him, I felt very plain. I also felt my hair was letting me down. It doesn't normally. It's red-brown, shoulder length, plaited today to make sure none of it went in the food, but it looked dowdy next to Matteo's luxuriant locks that reached to his shoulders. He was like a Seventies rock star but one dressed by Henry Holland.

He put an arm around me in a friendly way as Jess took our picture together on her phone.

It was unusual for Jess to rave about anyone; normally she treated people and events with a healthy scepticism.

The McCleishes had been a big hit with all concerned. Damn, I thought, Matteo even smelt good. I had just finished a busy service in the forty-degree heat of the kitchen and I suspected that I exuded an aroma of sweat, strain, and food.

I gawped silently at him, bereft of the power of speech.

'I enjoyed my lamb,' he said, encouragingly. He had quite a strong accent, that heady mix of Scottish and Italian. I should have known this from the few times I had seen him on TV, but it had never occurred to me he would actually talk like that. 'And the bavarois was excellent.'

Thank God I hadn't known it was destined for him when I had originally made it, I thought. There is something very unnerving about cooking for a celebrity chef or a food critic. You feel every little thing is going to be inspected to the nth degree. Graeme Strickland would have laughed at my nervousness, but I wasn't an insanely overconfident megalomaniac like he was (or coked out of my brains) nor was I as good a chef. Strickland was touched with the hand of genius.

But, I thought smugly to myself, Matteo McCleish wasn't in his restaurant right now, was he? He was here.

I smiled confidently, or tried to anyway. My lips certainly twitched.

Matteo gave my kitchen a cursory glance. I was very proud of it, but a kitchen is a kitchen. What was I going to say?

'Could we, erm, have a quiet word somewhere?' Matteo said, nodding his head to the side.

That was a harder question to answer than it sounded.

The downstairs of the Old Forge Café was taken up by the kitchen, dry store (a glorified cupboard) and the restaurant. My office was a space under the stairs. Upstairs was my accommodation. To say it was spartan was to oversell it. There was virtually nothing up there at all.

16

Virtually, though, was better than nothing at all.

I had bought a bed, a huge step up from sleeping on a mattress on the floor, and the sizeable living room did have a TV balanced on a beer crate, and a secondary beer crate (or IT suite as I liked to call it) where my laptop sat. Matteo might think I was merely eccentric. He might think that I viewed the accumulation of material objects, like furniture, with scorn. Or he might realise the truth – that I was embarrassingly poor and that all my money had gone into kitchen equipment.

I wasn't going to have him know that.

So, upstairs was out of the question. No one likes revealing how boracic they are. Anyway, it was a bit too intimate, I didn't want Matteo getting any ideas. For all I knew he had some kink thing going on about female chefs.

'Let's go outside and I'll show you my walk-in fridge,' I suggested. 'It's new!' I added proudly, instantly regretting it. Matteo wouldn't have boasted about his fridge; the company would have given him one for free and then paid him a fortune to endorse it.

Matteo brightened. 'Good idea!' he said. We walked out of the kitchen into the little yard, which, luckily, I keep immaculate. I've even started growing herbs in large terra-cotta pots, which seems to be working well. In the afternoon sun it looked rather beautiful. Matteo nodded his approval and then we disappeared into the walk-in. I pulled the door to behind us and said with a polite gesture, 'Take a seat. . .'

Matteo looked around the fridge, about the length of a shipping container with racking inside. He sat down on a sack of Yukon Gold potatoes and looked up at me. I leaned against the fridge door, smiling politely. I wondered what this was all about. You don't go and have a conversation in an industrial fridge to make idle chit-chat. It's chilly, but it has the advantage of privacy and nobody can eavesdrop.

Matteo looked up at me and brushed his long hair back from his face. There was a smattering of designer stubble on his upper lip and chin.

'I was talking to Danny Ward, the head chef at the Cloisters – remember him?'

I nodded. Danny – a tubby, lecherous Scot with a look of infinite cunning, pebble-thick glasses, balding red hair and a whiny Fife accent – was the proud possessor of a Michelin star (Strickland would be extremely jealous) and I'd worked for him as a chef de partie in charge of his sauces.

The restaurant was in St Albans in an expensive hotel and the kitchen fronted onto the staff car park that was covered in pea shingle. What really stuck in my mind wasn't the food but Danny's personal life. Danny was having an affair with a married woman, and her husband, who was a roofer as solidly built as St Albans Cathedral but slightly larger (according to Danny), had vowed bloody revenge.

One of my jobs, aside from the sauces, was to check every time we heard the scrunch of tyres in the staff car park, that it wasn't the jealous roofer hellbent on GBH. Whenever a car or a van arrived, Danny would go and find something to do in the cellar until I told him the coast was clear.

'He told me about you and the builder. . .' Matteo said, looking at me expectantly.

'Oh,' I said, disappointed. I had hoped Danny would have praised me for my exceptional *saucier* abilities, not for dealing with some psychotic workman.

'He said that you beat him up.'

I shook my head. 'No, well, I reasoned with him.'

I remembered the incident well. One day the builder had actually arrived. I was beginning to think that maybe he was a figment of Danny's imagination. One item that Danny had bought for the cheese board was called Stinking Bishop. It's a soft cow's cheese, and it reeks to high heaven. He'd bought a 1.8 kilo wheel of it, that's a lot of cheese, and two or three weeks later we'd still got a fair bit left. I'd cling filmed it, put it in a plastic container with a lid and it still stank. I cling filmed the container, it still stank. Every time you opened the fridge door a waft, no, it was far more than a waft, a torrent of ripe cheese stench smacked you in the face. 'Danny, I love you,' I had said, 'but it's either the cheese or me, one of us has to go.'

I got my way. I was carrying it out to the bins on a paper plate, reverentially, like a head on a platter, to put in the organic waste when I saw the builder's van pulling in. Danny had shrieked out of the kitchen window, 'It's him, it's him, I'm deid. . . Quick, do something, woman!' and went to hide. The builder parked his van and jumped out; he marched over to me. He was short, stocky, aggrieved, and wearing a plaid shirt. What is it with builders and plaid shirts? Judging by the expression on his face, he'd come looking for trouble.

'I'm sorry,' I had said politely, ostentatiously blocking his way, 'this car park is reserved for staff.'

He ignored my parking advice. There was a stiff breeze blowing towards the hotel, the builder was upwind of the Stinking Bishop that I was holding behind my back.

'Where's the Scottish bastard!' he demanded.

'Hiding' would have sounded disloyal. I told him he couldn't go into the kitchen (a health and safety issue, I'd said) and to go away, and he replied, 'Out of my way, bitch!' I raised my eyebrows theatrically at his rudeness.

'Don't call me names, baby cakes,' I said, warningly. That's when he went ballistic. Maybe he didn't like being called baby cakes. Maybe it was all too much, one chef knocking his missus off, and here was a lady chef giving him lip. He went very red in the face.

'You asked for it!' he snarled.

In fairness, he didn't try to hit me with his fist (what a gentleman!), he tried to slap me. That was a bad idea on his part. I'd got the Stinking Bishop on its plate behind me. I've also got very quick reactions. I ducked under his hand, straightened up and slammed the putrid, squishy cheese into his face. Like a clown driving a custard pie into another clown's face.

As a weapon it was unbelievably effective.

He stopped dead in his tracks. The stench was overwhelming. The cheese which had been bubbling and sweating in its container for ages, was now runny and liquid. It was in his eyes, up his nose, in his mouth and to top it all he must have suffered some kind of allergic reaction.

He sank to his knees, hands clawing at his face, swearing, rubbing his eyes.

'Help me. . .' he moaned. How are the mighty fallen.

'You big baby,' I said, staring at my handiwork in awed fascination. The cheese was all over his face, like he was wearing incredibly thick yellow clown pancake makeup of a gruesome kind. He was a figure out of a horror film.

'Aaaa. . . Aaargh. . . what the fff? It's horrible. . . ' Then, 'Pah, pahhh. . .' It had gone in his mouth when he'd opened it to speak and he was retching, spitting out rancid cheese juice.

I got him a bucket of water from the tap by the kitchen door. He plunged his head into it, scrubbing off the cheese as best he could. That had been it.

When his vision was slightly restored, he'd sworn at me, but feebly, got back into his van (well, staggered back really) and driven off, and that was the end of it. The affair fizzled out, my contract ended – I was covering for someone who was on extended leave – and we went our separate ways. I'd all but forgotten about it until today.

'Well, whatever,' said Matteo, clearly disbelieving my statement about reasoning with him. He made a mildly Italian gesture with his hands to indicate this. I suppose I hadn't done that much reasoning, the Bishop had done the heavy lifting.

He carried on: 'He also said that you were a woman who could be relied on to keep her mouth shut.'

I shrugged. 'Well, I suppose I didn't tell his brigade about the affair he was having.'

Matteo said, 'No, you didn't.'

He looked at me admiringly, I guess justifiably so. Sharing a cramped kitchen space with other chefs for ten hours a day, you do tend to gossip. To have kept my mouth shut, especially about something so beefy, as Jess would put it, did show a great deal of self-control. Matteo carried on.

'And I heard on the grapevine about you solving that murder that happened around here, earlier this year.'

I didn't know what to say, so I tried to look enigmatic. Matteo made his offer. 'How would you like to come and work for me for a while?'

I blinked in disbelief, and Matteo must have misread this as reluctance. He carried on in an encouraging tone.

'It'd look good on your CV.'

He was really serious. I blinked again, in surprise this time. It most certainly would look good on my CV. Better than that, it would be great for business. It was a job offer to die for.

Word would get around that I had been hired by one of the most famous TV chefs in Britain and it would have a dramatic effect on bookings. People would say, 'That Charlie Hunter, she's working for that guy from the TV show *Nonna's Kitchen*.' My reputation would soar. Oh, brave new world! Then reality bit. Savagely.

'Well, Matteo, I'd love to,' I said reluctantly, 'but I haven't got anyone to take care of my restaurant – there's only me. I just can't.'

Matteo shook his head confidently. A BAFTA award nomination and a prime slot on BBC2, plus high viewing figures had obviously done wonders for his self-esteem. People didn't say no to him.

22

'That's not a problem, I'll lend you one of mine. He'll fill in for you while you're gone. I've seen your menu; it's nice, but let's face it, it's not rocket science.'

That was a bit uncalled for, I thought.

'And I'll pay well.'

I was thoroughly confused. Then I got suspicious. Why did he want me to work for him? There were plenty of other, better qualified chefs around?

'Why do you need my help?' I asked.

He suddenly looked away, as if he had gone unaccountably shy. Then he turned his head back to me.

'Because I'm being blackmailed,' he said.

Chapter Five

I looked at him in astonishment. It certainly wasn't the answer that I had been expecting.

Blackmailed! Surely not the wholesome star of *Nonna's Kitchen*. What could he have been up to? Lurid possibilities swirled around my head.

'Oh, right.' I didn't know what else to say. I stared blankly at him, sitting there looking poised, elegant and successful on the sack of potatoes.

'Could you be a bit more specific?' I asked.

Matteo looked around the fridge as if seeking inspiration. Thank God everything was labelled and day-dotted. I am so tidy it verges on the obsessional, which is a good quality in a chef. He picked up a plastic tub that said 'smoked hadok' in Francis's wonky, child-like, writing. He opened it, peered inside and absent-mindedly sniffed it, obviously checking it hadn't gone off. Force of habit.

Either he was very interested in fish and fish storage or the blackmail story was a sensitive one.

'It's for Cullen Skink,' I said helpfully.

He looked bewildered. 'Cullen Skink?'

'It's a Scottish fish soup,' I said, slightly desperately, 'not unlike a chowder.'

'Oh, right.' He put the fish back on the shelf and looked at me. 'I should know that really, I'm betraying my Scottish roots.' He smiled. 'Nonna only ever taught me Italian food. . .' He sighed and got back to the main point.

'It's Graziana. . . she did something unprofessional in her youth and it's come back to haunt her. . .' he finally said.

'Oh, right.' My turn now. I felt like reaching for the box with the haddock. There's that thing isn't there, in Men's Liberation Movements where they have a Talking Stick? Whoever has the Stick gets to speak. They pass it around. We could do that with the smoked haddock. Pick it up as an indication that it was my turn to hold the floor and nobody would be allowed to interrupt.

'It's sexual,' he finally said. 'She did this thing in Italy, like Only Fans.' He sighed. 'She was young and naïve and pressured into it. She had another name online, Gemma Moravia. . .'

He smiled at the memory, 'we did that thing to find your porn name, your first pet, she had a dog called Gemma, and your street as a kid, Via Moravia. So. . .'

He shook his head, 'we thought it was ancient history. But someone got hold of it. . .' Then he added, softly, 'And, to make it worse, I think it's someone I know. It's one of my brigade.'

'Oh,' I said. I felt for him, but what was I supposed to do about it?

He continued. 'I really want to know who's behind it, and of course, it goes without saying I want it stopped.'

'It sounds like you should go to the police,' I said helpfully. Matteo looked at me sadly and shook his head.

'I can't,' he said. 'I can't trust the police to keep this quiet. If it gets out, it could wreck my career. The TV people are very twitchy about anything involving sex these days, particularly with mainstream, family oriented talent. As well as that,' he added angrily, 'I don't want naked pictures of my wife in compromising positions plastered all over the internet.'

'Point taken,' I said. 'So no police.'

'No police.'

'Private detectives?' I suggested, brightly.

'Exactly, Charlie. The problem is, I don't know any private detectives.' Then he smiled, 'But I do know chefs and how resourceful they can be. We're innate problem solvers, Charlie,' (I thought of Francis – how true) 'you're the one I need to help me.'

'Me!' I said, disbelievingly.

'Yes, you, Charlie.' He warmed to his theme. 'You can handle tough people, and I heard you solved a murder. You've proved you can do it. So I want you to help me find out who is blackmailing me. It's one of my brigade, it has to be, and I need to know which one and I need to know soon. It's tearing me apart.'

The penny dropped. It had taken a while – it should have been obvious from the word go. Matteo didn't want me around for my cooking skills. He wanted an investigator who could also be his minder. In all honesty, I felt a bit deflated. I had been so excited thinking that he rated me for my cooking abilities when all he really wanted was someone who could push cheese in people's faces or whack them with whatever came to hand and was, above all, discreet.

I didn't know what to say. I sat there in disappointed silence.

'Please,' he said. It was the heart-breaking gentleness with which he spoke that did it. I'm an easy touch for a sob story. I think it was then that I finally decided I didn't dislike him; on the contrary.

As I looked into his sincere, pleading brown eyes I knew I would help him.

I did some swift calculating. If I agreed to help him, I'd get help in the kitchen, and I could treat my new job – tracking down the blackmailer – as a paid mini-break. It had to be better than working a hundred plus hours a week slaving over the stove.

'OK,' I said. I would still be working for one of Britain's leading chefs; nobody would need to know exactly why. Everyone would think he'd hired me because I was a great chef and not because Matteo wanted help of a very different kind.

We shook hands and he embraced me. Damn, he smelt good! Lucky old Graziana.

I thought back to a conversation I had been having a few days ago with Jess. I had said it was going to take a miracle to get another chef. And lo, the miracle had happened.

I just hadn't expected it to happen the way it did. But, I guess, that's the way of miracles.

Face it, Lazarus must have been as surprised as everyone else when he was led out of the tomb.

Chapter Six

'We'll need a cover story,' I said. Matteo was still comfortably perched on the potato sack looking very pleased with the way this conversation had gone.

He smiled. 'I was thinking that I would tell them I'm doing a cookbook on British pub and restaurant cooking and you would be my helper, as someone who is used to relatively simple menus.'

Was there an implied slight there? Me and my 'relatively simple' menu? I decided to ignore it. I told myself, concentrate on the fact that you're being paid and you'll get a free chef thrown in.

'What,' I asked innocuously, 'to keep you grounded – no foams or emulsions. . .'

'Exactly. And you need to understand how I work, so you'll be working with my chefs.'

'Will they believe that?'

Matteo snorted. 'I'm the head chef. They'll believe what they're told to believe.'

'Fair enough,' I said. Who was going to question him? The head chef, like God, was almighty and worked in mysterious ways. 'Who's going to be looking after my kitchen?'

'I'll lend you Giorgio, my sous chef. He's good.'

I nodded. The sous chef deputises for the head chef in the kitchen, covers for them when they're on holiday or ill. If I wasn't in my kitchen, I would need someone of sous chef ability to replace me.

'What if he's the blackmailer?' I asked.

'He might well be,' Matteo said. 'That's what makes the whole thing so awful, they're all closer than family. Knowing that one of them has got it in for me is unbelievably depressing, and stressful, Charlie. I can't trust anyone and it's wearing me down.'

My heart went out to him. He continued: 'Well, you can see what you think of the others first and keep him in mind for later. Besides, they'll talk more freely if he's not there – he's quite a forceful character.'

Hmm, I thought. I heard the faint sound of alarm bells ringing. Forceful character? That could cover a multitude of sins. Oh well, I thought, I'm sure Matteo knows what he's doing.

And so, a couple of days later, on the Wednesday morning, I found myself in Matteo's rented property, being introduced to Matteo's team. I'd been shown in by the back door, there'd been some sort of photo shoot going on at the front. We were still a fortnight away from the team taking over the kitchens at the Earl's house for their ten day preparatory run before the opera began. During those ten days they would feed the performers and orchestra as they rehearsed, plus the backstage staff, getting a feel of their new kitchen and the menu before the paying customers arrived. Today the brigade were being given a tour of the area, and I had become one of the attractions.

They looked distinctly underwhelmed to meet me.

'Hello, everybody.' Matteo McCleish was all smiles as he introduced me to the assembled group. 'This is Charlie Hunter, the chef I've told you about, who'll be joining our team soon. . .' He turned to me, waving a proprietorial arm. 'There are other people on the books but these are my key players. . .'

I smiled winningly. I was excited despite my misgivings about my crime-solving ability. Possibly one of them was the blackmailer ?

We were in the dining room of the Old Vicarage where Matteo had just finished a briefing to his kitchen team. There would be other agency chefs working alongside them, but this was the core group and therefore they made up my main suspects.

The 'key players' looked far from overjoyed at the news that I was joining them. Perhaps they hadn't read the Bucks Free Press when it had described the Old Forge Café as a welcome addition to eating in the Chilterns.

Never mind, I'd email them the link. I'm sure they could hardly wait.

Introductions were made.

'This is Giorgio, my sous.' Matteo pointed out the 'quite forceful' chef to me. 'He'll be the one looking after your kitchen. . .'

As I studied his face, I hoped for my kitchen's sake that

he was nicer than he looked. 'Quite forceful' was probably one of those euphemisms like, 'he's a bit of a character', usually shorthand for a total nightmare.

Giorgio shook my proffered hand with little enthusiasm. He was tall and thin with a downturned mouth like a shark, which made him look both bad-tempered and dangerous at the same time.

I was then introduced to Tom, his development chef, a quiet, tough-looking guy in his mid-thirties with a hipster beard.

'Pleased to meet you.'

'Likewise.'

Tom's grip was vice-like, powerful, as we shook hands. He was wearing an Iron Man hoodie to proclaim how fit he was. I was suitably impressed. I couldn't swim three miles, cycle a hundred-odd kilometres and then run a marathon, much less one after another. I half-turned and noticed Giorgio run his eyes over me in a considered, evaluating way. Bet he does that with all the ladies, I thought to myself as he obviously awarded me quality points the way you might a piece of meat. As if to confirm the thought, he smirked and stroked his chin, nodding to himself. I didn't smirk back.

'This is Attila, my pastry chef.' I didn't think Attila was Iron Man material. He was medium height, slightly over-weight, as befits a pastry chef, and worried-looking, with an incipient double chin and a lot of black stubble. He was one of those men who I guessed had to shave twice a day. He nodded at me, obviously unimpressed by what he was looking at. He didn't look like the kind of man who would have enough get up and go to blackmail someone, and pastry is probably the least fraught areas of working in a kitchen. Then I reflected that a good pastry chef, and he had to be good or he wouldn't be working for Matteo, had to be a meticulous planner, be analytic and be patient. All of these qualities would be ideal for a blackmailer to possess.

I had two more chefs to meet, two more chief suspects. I quickly added adjectives to the faces to help me remember them: Giorgio was Grumpy; Tom, Sporty; Attila, Unhappy.

There was Octavia, who wasn't Italian but, judging by her voice, simply very, very upper-class. She was the intern. She was tall, blonde, and I'd guess in her early twenties. She smiled at me with glacial contempt.

She went on my mental list as Arrogant.

And lastly there was Murdo, a young Scottish chef, also tall but gangly as opposed to the willowy Octavia. He had a mop of curly ginger hair, some of it skywards-pointing in a poorly assembled top-knot – he reminded me of an overgrown schoolboy. He was the only one who showed any enthusiasm at all to be introduced to me.

His jacket was partially unbuttoned. There was a black T-shirt with red lettering – 'Cannibal Corpse', it said. I hoped that was the name of some rock band, and not the name of a restaurant he had worked in.

Well, if it was a band, it probably wouldn't get much airplay on Beech Tree FM. Rick Astley's 'Never Gonna Give You Up' had been playing on my journey over. I guessed that Cannibal Corpse probably would not be covering it. (Later I looked them up. I'd liked Murdo. I somewhat doubted Rick Astley would be covering 'A Skull Full of Maggots' in the foreseeable future.)

'Hi,' he said and blushed furiously.

Bashful.

Well, those were the prime suspects, and bringing up the rear were the two others in the McCleish entourage. I knew Matteo suspected his brigade, I wasn't sure if the management qualified as potential suspects. There was his agent/manager, Charlotte, a short, buxom woman with thick glasses and unruly brown hair tied back in a bun. Wisps of it stuck out here and there in an untidy way. She smiled politely as she shook my hand. She looked intelligent and hard as nails. There was something slightly intimidating about her, maybe in the way she projected an air of supreme self-confidence like a forcefield.

'And this is my assistant, Douglas,' Charlotte said.

By way of contrast, Douglas was skinny and angular with horn-rimmed glasses, a bald spot clearly visible under thinning hair, and a prominent Adam's apple. He was one of those people whose looks never seem to change throughout their lives. He was probably in his early twenties but looked about forty in a paradoxically ageless way. He had probably looked forty when he was at school and he would probably look forty when he was drawing his pension.

He appeared nervous, like a skittish horse. He practically twitched as she introduced him to me. I smiled sympathetically, as I reflected that it must have been tough for him to deal with Matteo's kitchen team. Chefs are poorly paid, grossly overworked and, in general, have an awful life. But what they do have, and this has evolved like a protective carapace, is an aggressive sense of their own importance.

Douglas, the non-chef, would have been viewed with

borderline contempt. He had certainly been born with the face of someone unhappy with his lot.

I filed the two non-chefs in my mind as Pushy and Twitchy.

The chefs were all wearing whites. Douglas wore an ill-judged short-sleeved shirt that accentuated his thin arms, and unfortunate blue polyester trousers. He looked like his mum had dressed him.

Giorgio, as if he had been reading my thoughts, turned his head to look at Douglas and gave him a hostile stare. Douglas caught his glance and visibly quailed. I saw his knuckles whiten as they tightened around a clipboard he was holding. He gave Giorgio a subservient smile, the way a dog might to a larger dog. I guessed that Giorgio probably made his life hell.

The chefs looked at me with suspicion. Whether or not they liked each other, they were used to working as a unit. It would take a while before they accepted me and relaxed long enough to talk freely.

But Matteo was right. They wouldn't suspect me of anything. And crucially, neither would the blackmailer.

I looked at Matteo's team and said winningly, 'I'm sure it'll be an education working with all of you.' I took my phone out. 'Can I have a picture, to savour the moment I met a star of the present' – I nodded at Matteo – 'and stars of the future!'

How glib was that, I thought. I'm Ms Suave. Nobody looked impressed or flattered but they all obligingly shuffled into position, as I held the phone up and checked all of my suspects were in the frame.

Click.

I put my phone away.

The door opened and a tall figure stood framed in it – another one of Matteo's team?

'Matteo! I heard you were all here. . .' He looked like he had been auditioning for a part in *The Three Musketeers*, and sounded like it too. His accent was very French and he had shoulder-length hair, a large nose and a Van Dyke-style combination of moustache and goatee.

'Jean-Claude!' Matteo put his arms around him and they kissed on both cheeks. Giorgio's face brightened. He walked up to Jean-Claude (d'Artagnan, I thought to myself) and kissed him as well. I managed to restrain myself. They started speaking to each other in French.

'Charlie,' said Matteo eventually, 'this is Jean-Claude Touraine. He used to work for us at the restaurant in London before. . . well, before he moved on.'

We shook hands. Jean-Claude smiled politely, while Matteo grinned around at his team.

'And now if you will excuse me, I need to speak to Charlie. You'll all get the chance to get to know her better once we start work in the pop-up kitchen over at the Earl's. I'm very excited and I know you are too.'

They were so well disciplined they managed to conceal their excitement well. Giorgio even managed a yawn.

As Matteo took me by the arm and led me away to his study, I took a last look back at his brigade and my new workmates. I wondered which one of them, d'Artagnan, Arrogant, Sporty, Grumpy, Bashful, Unhappy, Pushy or Twitchy, was the Judas figure who was blackmailing Matteo.

They all looked plausible as suspects to me.

Chapter Seven

'*Ma dai*! But who is this. . . Matteo, you should have told me that the new chef was coming this morning. . .'

It was Graziana who came into the study just after us.

'Darling,' said Matteo. They kissed each other's cheeks and they briefly spoke together in machine-gun-like Italian. Graziana moved over to me and shook my hand.

She was wearing a strappy white cropped top that showed off her body, and tight low-cut hipster jeans to reveal her TikTok/Instagram famous tattoo of the swan rising from the waistband of the very dark blue fabric, its head and beak coiling around her pierced navel, the wings rising upwards towards her ribs. The top had the word *Liar* emblazoned on it.

The overall effect of meeting Graziana was like being hit by a truckload of sensuality. I'm not that way inclined, but 'Wow' I thought.

'It's Charlie, isn't it?'

There was certainly no danger of my forgetting her name.

'It certainly is, Graziana,' I said warmly. She smiled back at me and kissed me on the cheek.

On her social media accounts she came across as overtly sexual, flirting with the camera, skin-tight gym-wear, provocative yoga poses, pouting, artfully disarranged clothing – the usual. I'm sick of people trout-mouthing at the camera, that and insanely white teeth. I was fully prepared to dislike her, but the reality was mitigated by a very heartfelt welcome and an immediate feeling of warmth.

'And how is Jess?' she asked.

How sweet of her to remember, I thought. 'She's fine,' I said.

'You are a lucky woman to have such a talented girl to work for you, as lovely as she is intelligent.' She smiled brightly at me.

'Thank you.' I would tell Jess later. My estimation of Graziana went up another notch. I turned my attention away from her and looked around the study. The Old Vicarage had been extensively renovated many years ago and it still bore the hallmarks of its absentee owner, the shady businessman. I was pleased to see that the study was furnished in true old-fashioned gangster style from the 1970s. Retro villainy.

I inventoried: a white shag-pile carpet, a large black desk with those clicky metallic balls that bang into each other in an annoying, metronomic way, black leather sofas and a glass-and-chrome coffee table. There were even a couple of enormous nude portraits of women done in pastels on a black background. I know very little about art, but they were awful. At least, I assumed this kitsch tat wasn't Matteo's doing – it would have been retro gone mad, or a shocking lapse of taste. There was also a canvas rifle bag leaning against the wall; the shady businessman with his organised crime connections would have approved. Perhaps he'd forgotten it in his rush to flee the country.

As it was, in his ripped jeans, shoulder-length hair and ornate jewellery, Matteo clashed horribly with his own furniture. He had a latte in front of him and had pulled a Diet Coke for me from a small fridge under the desk.

Matteo leaned forward and lifted one of the silver metal balls and released it. The two of us watched in fascination as it banged into the others and they clicked metronomically back and forth.

'Tasteful, eh,' he said, grinning at me. 'I've got an intercom too.' He pointed at a teak box with a silver mesh speaker and three switches. He pressed one and spoke into it. 'Send him in, Miss Jones.'

Another grin.

He said, 'There's a speaker on the desk out there in the hall so a secretary can sit there and do whatever you tell her to do. It's weird how things used to work.'

I nodded, as we both contemplated the past. The days of secretaries and intercoms. The last time I had seen an intercom was when I was a kid at school outside the headmaster's office. Longer ago than I cared to think about. I'd often been in trouble. It was an attitude thing.

I pointed at the gun bag. I had grown used to seeing things like that in the countryside, they're not so common in Kentish Town, where I used to live in London. Most of the firearms there tend to be illegal and concealed.

'Do you shoot, Matteo?' I asked.

He laughed. 'God, no. That's Douglas's. He leaves it in here when he brings it with him to go shooting.'

'Douglas shoots?' I was kind of surprised, he didn't look the outdoorsy type.

'Not pheasant,' Matteo said, 'smallbore. It's a .22 target rifle, small bore; he shoots at a club near Farnham.'

'Oh, I see.' That made more sense; target shooting is quite geeky. And solitary. That figured.

We got down to business.

'What do you make of Matteo's team, Charlie?' asked Graziana taking a seat next to him behind the big desk. 'Which one is the blackmailer?'

She leaned over and kissed him affectionately. Matteo ruffled her hair. I felt a pang of envy – I had nobody's hair to ruffle. The best I could muster was to pat Francis on the back. I shifted in my chair. It was a leather Chesterfield and fiendishly uncomfortable. It made a kind of squeaky, farty noise every time I moved or shifted my weight. I sat bolt upright, immobile.

'One big, happy family,' I said.

Graziana laughed scornfully. She pushed her hair back imperiously. 'Wait until you get to know them,' she said. 'Attila's a moody depressive, Murdo's heavily into drugs, Octavia's man-mad, Tom's violent and Giorgio harasses the waitresses.'

She had my attention with the last comment. I didn't want anyone like that working in my restaurant. 'What does Giorgio do?' I asked.

'Nothing really,' said Matteo quickly.

'He pesters waitresses,' said Graziana. 'We've had to warn him about it.'

'I've told him to be on his best behaviour at your place,

Charlie. There won't be any trouble.' Matteo was looking at me imploringly. He made an equivocal gesture with his hand.

I sat upright and narrowed my eyes. 'I hope not, Matteo, for his sake. No one harasses my staff,' I warned. I was thinking of Jess and Katie.

'Nobody will; now, if we can move on. . .?'

I tore my mind away from potential unpleasant scenarios involving Giorgio.

'What about the management?' I asked. 'Do you suspect Charlotte or Douglas?'

Matteo shook his head,

'Charlotte takes a healthy percentage of my earnings as it is, she's very solicitous of my welfare, maybe overly so.' He laughed. 'I wouldn't like to be in the blackmailer's shoes if she found out who he was, God knows what she'd do.'

'And Douglas?' I asked.

'He's terrified of Charlotte. Besides, just look at him, does he look like a blackmailer to you?' Even though blackmail could be done by anyone, I conceded the point. Douglas looked too stressed for crime, as well as too ineffectual. Then I moved the conversation along.

'Blackmail,' I said, bringing us to the business in hand, 'and that involves you, Graziana?'

She nodded unhappily. 'Si.' Matteo looked uncomfortable, shifting his weight in his Eames-style executive chair.

Silence fell.

'Would you like to elaborate?' I asked.

He sighed and said, 'We were living in Milan. I was working at a restaurant that would get a Michelin Star soon

40

after I joined. It was an amazing place to work, but money was tight. We wanted to come back to Britain and open a place over here, we needed seed money.' He looked at Graziana and smiled sadly. 'There's this porn site in Italy, "Per I Tifosi".'

'For the fans,' explained Graziana. 'I stripped. . . did some other things. . . you know. . . sexy things. . .'

I could imagine. I moved back in my leather seat. It farted again, inappropriately.

'I don't need to know the details,' I said, primly. 'Are these images of you still available online or on the site?'

She shook her head. 'No, it was a live feed. You weren't supposed to record it but they must have filmed the screen with another camera.'

'So what are they threatening?' I asked.

She said slowly, 'If we don't pay up, they are going to upload about five minutes of me doing. . .' here she blushed, 'doing. . . stuff. . . to the internet.'

'Would that harm your career?' I asked Matteo. It was a stupid question, I realised it as soon as I had said it.

He looked at me angrily. 'Who cares what it would do to my career, what would it do to Graziana and me!' he said.

'You're right, I apologise,' I said.

'That's OK,' he said, with a hint of despair. 'She didn't do it very long, just long enough.' Then he moved back to my original question. 'And yes, it would harm my career. You can't be a beloved public figure on TV and be involved in sex scandals. There have been several incidents lately of public figures blowing their careers for inappropriate behaviour.'

41

'We were desperate,' Graziana said, simply, 'we had no money. And like Matteo just said, he's a housewife's favourite, he goes on morning TV shows, he can't have a wife who is a porn whore. Sexy yes, slutty no.'

That made sense.

'So tell me the mechanics of the blackmail,' I said. I wanted to move the questions on to something less personal. 'How do they get the money?'

Matteo handed me a piece of paper. 'These are the instructions for paying the cash.'

I examined it with interest. I had never seen a blackmail note before and I imagined something luridly old-fashioned, like words cut out of newspapers and magazines then stuck to a sheet of paper. How hopelessly out of date that was.

Of course, it was nothing like that at all. It was prosaically boring.

It was a piece of A4, the words printed in some nondescript font, telling Matteo that he should take four thousand in cash in a plain brown envelope, go to the EROS SHOP in Vantry's Alley off Greek Street in Soho on the second Monday of every month just after opening and ask to speak to Greg. He was to hand it over saying, 'This is for Mick,' and then leave.

'How many times have you done this?' I asked.

'Three,' said Matteo. 'In three months,' he added.

'That's a thousand pounds a week,' I said helpfully, for once managing a quick calculation.

'It is indeed,' he said before draining his latte.

'Twelve thousand pounds!' I marvelled.

'You can certainly do maths,' said Matteo, drily.

42

'And this place is a porn shop?' I said. It had to be one of the last. The porn shops of Soho, like the bookshops of Charing Cross Road, have been largely put out of business by online streaming. But one or two still survived.

A thought struck me.

'What makes you think your blackmailer is someone you know? Surely they could just be someone who was an early fan of Graziana, kept a recording of her and recognised her again when she became famous? Why do you think it's someone from your brigade?'

'Because the first letter that I got had been put in my locker at work. So it has to be someone I work with. And the worst thing is, they must have known I would know that, so it's like I am being taunted.'

'I see.' I returned to the time frame. 'So the next drop is this coming Monday.'

'It is indeed.'

'Ok, I'll be there to see who collects it. Hopefully they won't be using an accomplice. Either way, we'll see what happens.'

There was a knock on the door and Charlotte, his manager, came in.

'Sorry to interrupt,' she said.

'No, it's OK, we'd finished,' Matteo said. She nodded. She looked as brisk and efficient as ever.

'Can I just have a word, Charlie, there's some admin stuff to go through.'

'Sure,' I stood up, said my farewells to the McCleishes and followed Charlotte outside and down the hall to her office.

She sat me down opposite her and looked at me.

'So now you know about the blackmail,' she said.

I nodded. 'But would it really matter in this day and age?' I asked. Despite what Matteo and Graziana had said, I thought surely to God, really, in this day and age, would anyone care?

'How do you mean?' She frowned.

'Posing on the internet on a porn site, would anyone mind that much?'

'They would,' she said, decisively. 'Matteo is synonymous with *Nonna's Kitchen*, he's not edgy or out there – he stands for decency and integrity. *Nonna's Kitchen* viewers are not cool teenagers, they are middle-aged and elderly, they're respectable and they don't want slutty behaviour.'

'I see,' I said. But she wasn't done yet.

'You're old enough to remember these people,' she said the names of a couple of ex BBC presenters and a more recent one from ITV who had been involved in erotic scandals. 'It killed their careers stone dead. I don't want anything like that happening to my Matteo.'

I noted the possessive pronoun, 'my' Matteo. She was genuinely worked up now, I could see what he had meant about her being so protective. Of course he was the goose that kept laying golden eggs and she was taking a healthy cut.

'Who do you think is behind it?' I asked.

'One of the brigade, has to be. He told you the blackmail note was in his locker? Well, they're the only ones with access to the changing room.'

'How about you or Douglas?' I said provocatively.

44

For a moment I thought she was going to physically attack me. Her face literally reddened with rage and she half rose in her seat.

'Don't you ever dare question my loyalty to Matteo. . .' she said very quietly. There was an unspoken 'or else' that I didn't want to investigate. I made a placatory gesture with my hands.

'Who do you suspect then?' I asked, backing down.

'If I knew, I would act, and we wouldn't have a problem. I'm ex-Army, I've got a legal background, Charlie, before I became an agent. Not only did I do legal work in the services, I prosecuted people for the CPS. I know how to deal with criminals, believe me.'

She opened her briefcase and produced some papers.

'Sign here,' she said. I looked at her questioningly.

'It's a standard confidentiality agreement to stop you talking to the media at any level about anything connected about Matteo and Graziana.'

I signed. 'And if I did?'

Charlotte smiled coldly, it was a frightening smile. 'I wouldn't, Charlie. I would bury you alive,' the smile vanished, 'and piss on your grave.'

I thought as I drove away from the house, I would not like to have Charlotte as an enemy.

Chapter Eight

The following day I was selling Giorgio to my unenthusiastic staff. It was a Thursday and we were gearing up for a busy weekend. Selling Giorgio was harder than selling food. It was proving to be an uphill task. They didn't want him to be there, and neither did he, that much was blindingly obvious.

'There's a lot going on in a Bakewell tart,' I said to Giorgio as we stood in the kitchen of the Old Forge Café, while he bit dubiously into a slice. I looked at his sour, thin face (thinner than a normal face should be in my opinion, it kind of reminded me of a shark's fin for some reason) and wished that Matteo had employed a more amenable sous chef. I could quite understand him lending me the most competent of his brigade but on reflection I think I would have preferred just about anyone to Giorgio. He chewed, swallowed and said, '*Non è male*. Not too bad.'

It wasn't as if I'd given him a piece of dung to eat, but the look on his face was far from ecstatic.

Giorgio looked around my kitchen with grudging respect. It was a very pleasant kitchen to work in. Airy, large, pride of place given to my double Hobart combi oven, which had been more than just ruinously financially expensive, it had nearly cost me my life.

Giorgio performed well. No surprise there, given his pedigree. He was remorselessly efficient, but without any joy in his work, like some sort of savage machine. A bad-tempered robot. One had that been poorly designed and programmed, or gone rogue like a cheffy terminator. We'd had a busy lunch, and I let him get on with cooking all the mains while I hovered by the pass, helping Francis with the starters and plating things up for the various dishes, taking pictures so Giorgio would be able to replicate layout, with Francis doing the vegetables.

With three people, the job was euphorically easy – normally it was just the two of us. We chatted while we worked.

Well, I chatted.

'So, what's Matteo like to work with?'

Silence. Banter, the oil that makes the engine of the kitchen bearable, was conspicuous by its absence.

'Here's the lamb. . .' Slam. Giorgio's movements by the stove were jerky, and rather odd. He was like a life-sized marionette moved by invisible strings. His thin face, with its dark five-o'clock shadow, expressed a discontent with life in general and me in particular.

Maybe he thought that having to work here, in the hell-hole of the Old Forge Café, was an insult, a demotion, a cruel punishment visited upon him by Matteo.

I quickly sliced up the lamb fillet, placed it on its bed of wilted rocket and drizzled some rosemary-infused jus over it, then added a little spoon of cranberry and port jelly. Giorgio had cooked it to perfection.

'Service, please!' I called, asking for it to be taken away.

Jessica came into the kitchen and I said, 'Table 12 please, Jessica.'

She glared over my shoulder at Giorgio. I turned towards him. By now I was studiously avoiding looking at him. I had hoped that he was a rough diamond, that when you got to know him you'd think he was actually quite nice. But Jess was a good judge of character, and when I saw the expression on her face, I knew that I had been deluding myself. The scales fell from my eyes. He was a bloody good chef but I suddenly realised the truth. He was horrible.

Giorgio came over to the pass to introduce himself to Jess, a sickly smile on his face. Maybe that's what he felt passed for charm. To be honest I preferred the scowl.

'Allo, my name is Giorgio, I work for Matteo McCleish' – in case there were any chance of mistaking the fact that he was too good to work for me – 'but I will be here for the next few weeks. . . and you are?'

This speech would maybe have gone down a little better if he had been talking to Jess's face rather than where it said 'Old Forge Café' on her apron.

She looked at Giorgio with as much enthusiasm as he had me earlier, and he returned to his position at the stove. Jess shook her head. 'What an a-hole,' she said dismissively to me.

The rest of the service passed by in a pleasantly hectic blur.

Despite his defective, lecherous, personality, it was a

delight having a competent grill cook. All I had to do was plate up and help Francis whenever he stumbled, which was often, with a starter or a vegetable accompaniment. Jess had been right, he underlined her point – I really did need another chef.

I tried once or twice to get him to talk about life with Matteo, to try and get some feel of their relationship, but it was useless. Any idea of getting useful clues from Giorgio rapidly disappeared.

The last dessert cheque was done at about half past two and we started cleaning down the kitchen. Giorgio disappeared outside to have a cigarette, and I took the opportunity to explain to Jess that she would have to put up with him for a bit.

'But he's so creepy,' she grumbled, 'and he keeps staring at me.'

'It won't be for long,' I promised her.

'How long?' she demanded.

I decided to be honest with Jess as to why Matteo had employed me.

'Well, the situation is this. . .'

I briefly sketched in the background, and Jess's expression became one of tender concern.

'So he doesn't want you for your cooking ability?' Jess patted me sorrowfully on the shoulder.

I shook my head. Her large eyes regarded me sympathetically, which was nice on one level but added to my sense of inadequacy. My waitress seemed to have made it her duty to try and protect me from life and its hardships, which was great but a little demeaning.

'That won't take too long? Are you sure?' asked Jess. 'I mean, your last out-of-the-kitchen activity was hardly a resounding success, was it?'

That was certainly true. I had tried to discover the identity of a killer and had very nearly become another of his victims. So technically it had been a success. . . I had found out who the murderer was, but my technique had been flawed. Nearly fatally so.

'Anyway, the only good thing to come out of that was your getting to see Andrea again,' she said, referring to my ex. Andrea was Italian, they seemed to be ubiquitous these days. Wait years for one Italian to come along. . .

'I dare say, but he's engaged – and not to me.' That was certainly sub-optimal as far as our relationship was concerned.

'He gave you his new phone number. . .' she pointed out.

'Matteo has every faith in me. I'm sure he knows what he is doing,' I said, emphatically, shutting down the Andrea conversation.

'You're an idiot.' Jess shook her head, but in a nice way.

'Anyway,' I tried to cheer her up, 'you're in charge of the kitchen while I'm away. Remember, Giorgio is working for you, not vice versa.'

'Oh, how consoling,' Jess said sarcastically. We left it there.

Chapter Nine

As I boarded a London train early on Monday morning, I was feeling a mixture of emotions: the thrill of the chase (which one of Matteo's team would turn up to collect the money?), apprehension (there was obviously going to be a confrontation, possibly violent, certainly abusive) and a certain sense of worry (that the whole thing might be absolutely futile and nobody would show up, or that a third party I didn't know would come to collect the money).

I had got up early that day and driven to Wycombe, the nearest big town, about half an hour by car from my restaurant. I was at the station by half past seven. It was more or less an hour to Marylebone although there were faster trains that did it in 40 minutes. The platform was already filling up with bleary-looking commuters, less than excited by the prospect of a day's work in London.

On balance, I suspected that the blackmailer, him or herself, would come to collect the money. The fact that the payment was made on a Monday, a day that everyone in the team had off, was a strong indicator that he or she would come to pick up the cash rather than an accomplice.

And it was a lot of money. What successful blackmailer would be able to resist going straightaway to grab that cash-stuffed envelope? Or so my hopeful reasoning ran.

The alley, off Greek Street in Soho in the centre of London, was an area that I knew relatively well. Not because I used to buy porn there, but because I used to work round the corner in an airless basement kitchen of a forty-cover restaurant that did steak and very little else.

I would stand, hunched over a chargrill in the tiny room, while the ticket machine spooled out infinite requests for fillet, ribeye and sirloin and the commis endlessly fried thin chips, or '*pommes allumettes*' as they were rather pretentiously described on the menu, and plated up garnishes for me. After a week in there, no matter how much I showered and scrubbed myself raw, a faint, pervasive odour of charred meat clung to me wherever I went. My boyfriend at the time didn't like it, but if I went anywhere that had cats or dogs, be it friends' flats, parks or pubs, I attracted an interested animal audience.

Swings and roundabouts, I guess.

The shop front was whited out, the legend 'EROS SHOP ADULT BOOKS, DVDS AND MAGS' emblazoned in blue across the top. I wondered how it was surviving in this age of downloadable or streamed porn. I guessed it must have a predominantly elderly clientele. It was half past nine and the place had only just opened. There was a small independent café opposite with a window overlooking the sleaze emporium. I sat there with a good view of the door and ordered a cup of tea. I surreptitiously pointed the camera of my phone towards the entrance. I would take photos of anyone coming in after Matteo had been for an hour or so, just in case someone other than a member of the brigade collected the money. Someone that Matteo might recognise. For all I knew, the owner was in on it, a stranger might collect it or someone might turn up at six in the evening, but for now my plan would have to suffice.

At 10 o'clock I saw Matteo enter the alley and stride into the shop. He was wearing a hoodie to hide his long hair and sunglasses to help disguise his face. It would be ironic if he were papped going into a porn shop while paying money to avoid being linked with the sex trade. I waited, and a couple of minutes later he exited the shop.

Time passed. I ordered more tea and watched several men enter the shop opposite. I took their photos just in case. If necessary I would show them to Matteo later in case he recognised any of them. The customers fell into two groups: either furtive, looking around guiltily before going in, or feigning nonchalance. I had got the age group about right, none of them were exactly young. Nobody really wants to be seen to be going into a porn shop – it's not something to feel proud about. I pondered this too. I was getting to do a lot of thinking today.

I drank another three cups of tea and played with my phone. The girl behind the counter must have wondered what I was doing in there. Staring avidly at the frontage of EROS Adult Books. Maybe she thought I was a jealous girlfriend with a boyfriend who was into porn. Or, I mused, maybe a former erotic actor fallen on hard times, reliving her past somehow by staring at where she had formerly reigned supreme. An R rated version of *Sunset Boulevard*. It would add a new twist to the famous lines, 'I'm ready for my close-up now, Mr DeMille.'

A few more guilty-looking men entered the shop, each leaving shortly afterwards with a plain blue plastic bag in hand.

I ordered another tea; my bladder was perilously full but I worried that the moment I used the café's loo would be the moment my quarry walked into the shop.

I shifted uneasily on my stool then took my phone out and scrolled through the photo album to look again at the selfie I had taken of myself and Matteo's brigade.

There they all were, the suspects.

I knew their routine, Charlotte had described it for me.

Right now, they were engaged in the run-up to the Earl's opera fortnight, which in practice ran to nearly three weeks. The pop-up restaurant would keep them busy for the last ten days of June, which would be the setting-up time. That would be in under ten days from now. Then came the actual festival which was the first three weeks of July. The Marylebone restaurant which was the place that had won awards was still very much going. It regularly cropped up in guides to eating in London and also was a favourite with celebrities and actors. I guess by now it had a well-worn groove and didn't need constant attention, it could coast along, its wheels oiled by Matteo's growing fame.

I had asked Charlotte how they spent their time when there wasn't such a gig available. As well as the restaurant, their usual work was in the development kitchen for a forthcoming TV series. That was the bulk of it. I gathered that there were public cookery displays at gastro-fairs and exhibitions, and TV appearances, mainly on daytime shows. Even a five-minute Matteo slot involved quite a few hours' prep to make sure that everything was seamless and there were no glitches.

Charlotte ran everything behind the scenes while Douglas, her timid sidekick, did all the humdrum but time-consuming work, mainly involving numbers. He seemed to be indispensable. He worked out not only staff costings, expenses and the like, but also liaised with Tom on dish costs. When a dish appeared in a magazine, it was Douglas who would tot up how many calories it contained and how much it would cost, down to the last spurt of balsamic vinegar. I had to do this for my own restaurant and knew what a chore it could be. Boring and time-consuming.

I wondered idly if he might be the one turning the screws on Matteo. He was obviously good at organising things; I couldn't imagine Charlotte hiring him otherwise. But he seemed such an unlikely criminal. I doubted he'd have the nerve. But he had the same reasons as Charlotte for ensuring that Matteo was a success, his job depended on it.

And that got me thinking about Mrs McCleish, the beautiful Graziana.

I didn't need a picture of her to remember her. That imperious, beautiful face, the oval brown eyes, the lustrous, silky-looking dark hair cut in an artful, tousled boyish way, the very full sensual lips, the hint of an amazing body under the T-shirt that had shown her swan tattoo. Could envy of Matteo's good fortune in having her cause someone in the team to want to poison Matteo's happiness, to bring him down even more? You could do considerable jail time for blackmail.

And it was then that I saw Matteo's blackmailer turn into the alley and head straight for the shop door.

Chapter Ten

I called Matteo immediately.

'It's me.' My voice was tense. I should have been elated that it had all gone so well, but I wondered what I was now supposed to do.

'I know, any news?' he sounded breathless, excited and apprehensive, all at the same time.

At that moment, Giorgio left the shop and stood for a moment, holding one of its plain blue carrier bags. He looked around him with the same cold distaste that he had used in my kitchen. I had to hand it to him, there was no furtive scuttling away or the fixed look of determination on his face that the shop's other customers had, the kind of look that was supposed to indicate that no, they hadn't been in the sex shop, that they'd just happened to have passed it.

Giorgio, by contrast, had his usual scowl in place. His expression said, yes, I have just bought a load of porn, what are you going to do about it?

Part of me was relieved that it was him, that it wasn't someone I'd liked – Murdo, for example – but part of me was also disappointed. I didn't like Giorgio, but he hadn't struck me as the blackmailing sort. Blackmail was kind of sneaky, and my feelings about Giorgio was that he was horrible, but upfront. My feelings weren't important though. I had done the most important part of my job.

'It's Giorgio,' I said. 'What do you want me to do?'

'Nothing, I need to think.' Matteo sounded confused, panic-stricken almost. I think, like me, he was wondering what to do now he knew who it was. I wondered if like quite a few men, he had grown used to letting the women in his life, Graziana or more probably his manager, make the decisions. Probably the latter. I suspected 'I need to think' was code for 'I need to speak to Charlotte.'

The phone crackled in that way mobiles do when reception is poor or compromised and then went dead. I stared at it in irritation and then I looked at Giorgio out of the coffee-shop window. My heart was thundering in my chest, I wasn't sure what to do, but I felt I had to do something.

Giorgio lit a cigarette – no vaping for him – and walked out of the alley into Greek Street. There was no time to call Matteo back, for want of any instructions I decided to follow him.

So I walked behind him, hoping he wouldn't turn around and recognise me. The narrow streets of Soho were no place for an argument that might get physical.

He strode along with me in tow, my phone still pressed to my ear. I think I had some kind of half-baked idea that I could hide behind it, like people in the old days used to behind a newspaper. You can't see me, I'm invisible, I have an iPhone pressed to my ear.

Fortunately he didn't turn around. I kept about twenty metres back. Soho was quiet at that time. The creative types who worked in film and advertising were shut up in their offices and workplaces, and it was too early for the crowds who would flock here to eat and drink at lunchtime in the long, thin, fashionable streets.

The morning that day in Soho was warm and the air hung still and heavy. Giorgio was dressed for the occasion in skin-tight white jeans and a form-fitting T-shirt. I wondered how much space four thousand pounds in notes would take up. Not a great deal probably, but he had to be carrying it in the plastic bag; there would be no room in those jeans.

I hid in a doorway while Giorgio checked out the menu of a restaurant in Greek Street. Well, mate, I thought to myself, as of today, you'll be looking for another job. Very soon you'll be back breaking your balls doing 70-hour weeks in Soho. Maybe the Greek place has got a vacancy, I'm certainly not employing you.

I fiddled with my phone and checked my messages and emails. Then I read a text from Jess and I switched my phone off. I felt a boiling rage surge in me. Any fear I might have had of dealing with Giorgio evaporated in my incandescent fury. We close early on a Sunday after lunch and I hadn't been around for that service. I had left Giorgio to get on with it by himself. This was the first time I'd communicated with Jess since the previous morning.

We continued our walk through Soho until we reached Soho Square. I was more than ready for a confrontation now; I felt like a tigress whose cub has been threatened.

The square is a small, rectangular garden surrounded by offices that used to be residential houses, and a couple of churches. Despite the proximity to Oxford Street and Charing Cross Road, it's often pleasantly quiet. The area in the centre is mainly grass, with some kind of hut in it and a statue of King Charles II. A moth-eaten looking statue.

It was here that Giorgio turned around and recognised me. He walked quickly over to me. There was no point running away. Not that I wanted to. I stood there and waited for him.

'What are you doing here?' He scowled at me. 'Are you following me?'

I reflected that the Italian accent, generally so charming, was conspicuously not so pleasant coming from the sous chef.

'You've been harassing my staff,' I said quietly. I was furious with him, and it had nothing to do with him blackmailing Matteo McCleish.

There was, in all fairness to Giorgio, no feigned indignation, no pantomime of incredulity. He knew what I meant immediately.

'So, what did that bitch say then? I just tried to play with her *tette*.' He sneered.

He mimed, or started to mime, holding a pair of breasts.

I glared at him. He glared at me. Two angry chefs snarling at each other in a square in Soho.

I made the first move. I suddenly snatched the plastic bag off him. He hadn't been expecting that. He stared at me with incredulity.

'What do you think you're doing?' he said angrily, almost incredulously. 'Give me that back!'

'Go away before I shove this up your skinny, non-existent arse,' I said, pleasantly.

He raised a hand threateningly, I really think that he would have struck me but he never got the chance.

There was a loud, dull thud and Giorgio's head rocked forward as he gasped in pain and put his hand to the back of his head like he'd been struck by something. What the hell? I thought. Then my eyes noticed the round, red ball at his feet. He had been struck by this missile. I recognised it immediately as a cricket ball. Wtf, I thought, where's that come from?

'*Che cazzo*. . .' I heard him say. He was as confused as me. He looked up at the sky, then at me angrily, stepped forward – then he gasped again. Two huge hands had pinned his arms to his sides from behind. He struggled, but he was no match for Francis who had come up silently and grabbed hold of him.

'Say sorry to Chef,' a calm voice instructed him.

Giorgio tried to break free and I saw his face whiten as Francis inexorably increased the pressure. He was hugely strong. The two of them stood absolutely motionless. How much did Francis weigh, I wondered. Maybe 120 kilos plus of mostly muscle. Francis's face behind the Italian's shoulder looked as though he was concentrating on a slightly difficult puzzle, he was frowning gently but otherwise fairly expressionless. Giorgio looked as though he were trying not to scream.

'You'd better do as he says,' I said, warningly, 'he might break your arms. . .'

He didn't want to but I saw Francis's thumbs sink into

his flesh like iron hooks. Giorgio paled with agony then could resist no longer.

'*Mi dispiace*. . .' he said through gritted teeth.

'Don't ever come near my restaurant again,' I said, threateningly. 'Oh, and by the way,' I added, insouciantly, 'Matteo says he knows what you've been up to, and as of this moment, you're sacked. By him and by me.' I paused. 'Doubly sacked.'

I wasn't sure if I had the authority to do this, and quite frankly I didn't care. I did know that I loathed this rude, sex-obsessed blackmailer with all my heart, and never wanted to see him again as long as I lived. Arrivederci Giorgio.

I nodded to my kp and Francis let him go, bent and retrieved his cricket ball. He stood there smiling contentedly to himself.

Giorgio shook himself angrily, like a cat. He rubbed his arms, restoring the circulation.

'Matteo knows what?' he demanded.

'About your stupid extortion. It stops now, ok?' I said.

He shook his head. 'You are one crazy fucking lady.'

'I'll take that as a compliment,' I said. Haughtily, as befits a lady, albeit one with a screw loose.

Giorgio scowled. 'Tell Matteo, *vaffanculo*.'

He made an Italian gesture by grabbing his right bicep with his left hand and fist pumping the air. He then turned on his heel and strode off in the direction of Oxford Street with his characteristic, jerky, high-shouldered walk.

'I hope I did OK, Chef?' Francis asked; he looked worried now. I leaned forward and kissed him on the cheek. He turned a beetroot shade of red.

'Francis, you were fantastic,' I said, 'but how. . .'

'Jess told me to follow you,' he said. 'She said you might need help.'

How right she was. Then he asked, curious, 'What's in the bag?'

'Matteo McCleish's property,' I said, opening the blue plastic bag I had confiscated from Giorgio and taking out a manila A4 envelope. I opened it and we both stared in astonishment. Francis blushed an even deeper red than he had when I had kissed him.

Not four thousand pounds in banknotes.

Two DVDs – *Schoolgirl Super Sluts 3*, and *Office Orgy Secretaries* – fell into my hand, their front covers lavishly, luridly illustrated.

'Oo, er, crikey!' Francis said.

It wasn't quite how I'd have put it, but oo, er, crikey indeed.

Chapter Eleven

'So it was Giorgio all along,' I said. I was back in Hampden Green in the afternoon after the excitement of the morning, reporting back to Matteo and, inevitably, Charlotte. There were just the three of us in the Old Vicarage, Graziana was up in London somewhere.

Matteo nodded. 'It's weird,' he said, slowly.

'Why do you say that?' Charlotte said angrily. 'He was a nasty piece of work, is a nasty piece of work, I should say. What's weird about it being him?'

'And he was most likely to be a viewer of Per I Tifosi,' I pointed out, 'as it's like an Italian OnlyFans and he is a porn fan, well. . . there you are.'

Personally I was pleased that it was Giorgio. I felt that being exposed as a blackmailer, losing his job and, cherry on the cake, being brained by Francis with a cricket ball (those thing are hard, when it struck his head it must have been like a hammer blow), all these things came as some kind of divine punishment for grabbing Jess.

'I know,' Matteo said, slowly, 'it's just, well, I would have thought Giorgio would have been more direct, that he'd have done it face to face rather than anonymously.'

I didn't think that now was the time to worry about what had been going on in his head.

'Surely the whys and wherefores don't matter,' I said. Then a horrible thought struck me. 'How do we know he is the blackmailer?'

The two of them stared at me like I had gone completely crazy.

'Of course he is the blackmailer,' Charlotte said angrily. 'What are the chances that one of the major suspects should turn up at the exact time and place of the money drop simply by chance? Practically zero, I would have thought.'

'And he hasn't called me to protest about being sacked by you in my name,' added Matteo. 'That's hardly the action of an innocent man.'

'Well, now you put it like that,' I said. I was relieved that they had dismissed my fears. 'So, that's the end of the matter then.'

'No it's not,' Charlotte shook her head. 'He might just go public with what he knows and then Matteo will lose his TV contract. Major public broadcasters do not take kindly to their talent being involved in sex scandals.'

'I hadn't thought of that,' Matteo said. He suddenly looked very worried.

'Don't worry.' Charlotte leaned forward and patted him on the knee, like you would a small child to reassure them. 'I won't let anything happen to you, I'll go and see him tomorrow, make sure that your secret is safe.'

Then she turned to me. 'We'll keep you on for a couple of weeks, Charlie, until the opera proper starts.'

'What, maintaining the fiction?' I said.

'Exactly. No need for any of the brigade to know about any of this,' Charlotte said, as she stood up. She smiled enigmatically. 'I think it's all worked out quite well.'

Chapter Twelve

'And what time did this alleged incident take place?'

It was 10 o'clock on Tuesday. Here in Hampden Green, it was all so very different from the narrow, cosmopolitan streets of Soho. Outside the Old Forge Café, it was a beautiful summer's morning. The village common that my restaurant fronted onto was lush and verdant. The sound of families with their small children in the playground diagonally opposite carried clearly in the warm air. I could hear a tractor in the large field behind the green.

I had been busy with my morning prep, Francis hadn't arrived yet and I was alone in the kitchen when my work had been interrupted by the arrival of two policemen.

Giorgio was dead, stabbed seemingly, in his flat in London, and DI Slattery, a policeman whose paths had crossed with mine before, was helping out the Met who were keen to know about his relationship with me. Slattery was accompanied by a colleague with acne whose name I hadn't caught when we had been introduced. DS somebody or other. He looked ridiculously young to be a policeman. The three of us were sitting in my empty restaurant, Slattery opposite me.

'Oh, about ten or eleven yesterday.'

My mind replayed the previous morning's scenario. The wait in the café opposite EROS, following Giorgio through Soho, the fight in the park. Up until then it had all been, well, not exactly light-hearted – Giorgio had revealed himself as an unpleasant, sex-obsessed predator, not to mention a blackmailer, but nothing as alarming as this.

Murder. It could hardly be more serious.

'Mm-hmm.' Slattery consulted his notebook and read back '. . . I had received a text message that Giorgio Lombardi had sexually harassed one of my waitresses, Jessica Turner, and when challenged about it, he became abusive, both verbally and physically.' He gave me a sharp look. 'And that's all that happened?'

I nodded. 'That's it.'

'And your other staff ?' he asked.

'He left Katie alone,' I said. Katie Dodds was my other waitress, a quiet, efficient girl who also lived in the village.

I didn't want to involve Francis; I had studiously kept his name out of my account. I was concerned that an unscrupulous policeman – and I did not fully trust Slattery – could get him to confess to just about anything, PACE and solicitors notwithstanding.

When Slattery turned up at my place asking if I knew anything about the murder of Giorgio – I straightaway told him about our argument in the park. No need, I thought, to bring Francis into it.

Now I was beginning to relax a little. I am no stranger to being questioned by the police and at the moment I was perfectly prepared to be as cooperative as possible. I had nothing to hide personally, nothing to feel guilty about. The shock was beginning to wear off. And it had been a shock, the thought that this strong, vital, if unpleasant man, was now lying in a refrigerator in a morgue somewhere. Then again, I suddenly thought, as a chef he had spent a great deal of his life in refrigerators, so maybe he would feel somewhat at home.

Slattery pushed a hand through his thick, salt and pepper hair. He glanced at his colleague, a look that seemed to say, 'we're wasting our time here'. I certainly hoped that's what it meant.

Slattery was a big, burly man. He looked like a game-keeper with a weathered, tanned face and very powerful forearms. He was actually, I thought as I studied him, quite good-looking. The thought was so random it surprised me. He lived in Hampden Green and had a reputation in the village for possibly being a bent cop, and certainly no stranger to violence. I could well believe it. People were very wary around him. That was one of the reasons I was keeping quiet about Francis.

I gathered that the reason he was here interviewing me was to save his London colleague in charge of the investigation the journey to question his workmates, when they had a detective more or less in situ.

'So, he came on to Jess Turner and you raised this issue with him.' Slattery's tone of voice was sympathetic, kind of, we've all been there. . .

'Rather more than "came on to her",' I said, angrily. 'He grabbed hold of her, that's assault in my book, but in a nutshell, yes. And that did the trick. He left me, perfectly alive and well and that was the end of the matter.'

The youthful colleague leaned forward. I had never seen him before and I wondered if maybe he was part of the Met Police's investigative team.

'And you didn't follow him back to Acton?'

'Acton?' I said incredulously, 'why would I go to Acton?'

I was born in the Highgate area of North London. To me Acton was like way out in the sticks with an air of railway sidings hiding over it. Hicksville. I apologise to anyone from there but you know what it's like in London, you get very insular and intolerant.

'That's where he lived,' said the young policeman with a hint of asperity.

'Oh.'

He carried on, aggressively, 'What bothers us is, what were you doing up in London anyway? How did you know that Mr Lombardi would be up there? Were you following him?'

I also had absolutely no intention of telling them anything about the business with Matteo McCleish. That was Matteo's business.

I smiled sweetly. 'How could I be following him? I don't know where he lived.' Slattery nodded approvingly as if I had scored a valuable point. His colleague frowned. My explanation was irrefutable.

'Well, what were you doing in London then?' persisted the detective.

What was I doing in London? I tried to come up with a plausible explanation.

'I was going to visit Denny's in Dean Street,' I said.

The kid-cop seized on this remark. 'Who is Denny?' He managed to make the name sound suspicious, fraught with criminality.

'Could you go and wait in the car, Detective Sergeant?' said Slattery with a tone of exasperated impatience. His colleague blinked angrily as if Slattery had slapped him in the face. The DI added for his benefit: 'Denny's is a shop; it sells catering equipment. It's in Soho.'

Paul stood up, gave me a final glare and slunk away, out of the kitchen.

Slattery said casually, 'You do know that Denny's in Dean Street has been closed for a while now?'

I stared at him. 'No I didn't.'

'Well,' he said in a kindly way, 'it has, so what you probably meant to say was, you went there and it was gone and you were wandering around in a kind of daze when you encountered the deceased.'

I stared at him some more, this time in surprised gratitude.

'That's exactly what I meant to say, DI Slattery.' I looked at Slattery, my new-found saviour. We both knew I had nothing to do with his death.

'So what exactly happened to Giorgio?' I asked.

'He was found by his flatmate at two o'clock in the afternoon.' Slattery looked at me with interest. 'Someone had stabbed him, in the back. Repeatedly. It was a cold and calculated attack, nothing half-hearted there.'

I digested this information.

'Almost professional,' he said, with a note of almost grudging admiration.

71

I could honestly say that I wasn't heartbroken.

'Well, that's too bad,' I said. 'I guess that you're going to have a pretty long list of suspects.'

'And why is that then?' asked Slattery. 'By the way, I'll have that coffee that you've forgotten to offer me. Americano, no milk.'

I nodded. I could hardly say no, got up, went over to the bar and switched on the coffee machine. Slattery followed. For a big man he was light on his feet. While I was making Slattery his coffee I explained about Giorgio's reputation as told to me by Matteo. A 'ladies' man' in Giorgio's eyes, a sex pest in the eyes of the rest of the world.

'I'd look into aggrieved husbands and boyfriends if I were you, and maybe work-colleagues, waiters and wait-resses in particular. I'll bet he was universally hated by Front of House.' I didn't need to guess, I just knew he'd have been horrible to the waiting staff.

Slattery nodded and made a note. 'You've had him working here, I believe. What was he like?'

I shook my head in amazement at the village grapevine.

'Well,' I said, 'he was rude, a pain in the arse, charmless. He assaulted Jess.'

'How exactly ?' Slattery asked sharply. I handed Slattery his coffee.

I said. 'He grabbed Jess from behind, her backside to be precise. And then travelled upwards. So when she apprised me of the situation and I encountered him. . . well. . .' I shrugged. 'You know the rest.'

'And you didn't go back to his flat in Acton and kill

72

him?' Slattery's tone wasn't accusing, more wistful, as if he really had been hoping that was the case but was prepared to accept the fact that it wasn't.

'No, of course I didn't. What makes you think I did?'

He smiled. 'Cherchez la femme? As they say. My colleague had heard about your reputation locally as a hard-ass.'

Part of me was flattered, part of me alarmed. Hard-ass eh? Maybe I should wear pink or something floral more often to soften my hard-edged reputation.

I decided to ask Slattery for some clarification as to who his colleague was.

'What exactly is your colleague's interest in me?' I raised my eyebrows questioningly.

'The Met are investigating the murder, it happened on their patch and he's a junior member of the team. You're not a suspect, Charlie' – he smiled – 'despite your past behaviour, I think he just got a bit carried away.'

That reassured me. I said by way of further explanation, 'I'd already made my point, hadn't I? I'd sacked him. Good chef, mind you, no gripes about his actual work.' Why not give the devil his due. 'I didn't need to kill him.'

'I suppose so,' said Slattery. We both fell silent for a while. I spoke first.

'Acton! Was that really where he was living?'

I don't know why I was so surprised but it seemed an odd choice for an Italian chef to live. I would have expected somewhere more cosmopolitan. Well, he had to live some-where I suppose.

'It was indeed.' Slattery looked grim. He fell silent and

73

drank his coffee. 'How was Giorgio viewed by his fellow chefs?' he asked.

I shrugged. 'How on earth would I know?'

'You've met them. You've been working with them. Giorgio obviously knew his killer – he must have invited them in. Whoever it was that killed him had a pretty hefty grudge against him. You don't stab someone in their own flat on a whim. There were no signs of a struggle or an argument. It was all very clinical.'

It was a good question. I hesitated.

'I haven't started to work with any of them yet – they move in to the Earl's kitchen in about a week's time and I'm joining them then, so I really don't know.' I looked at him questioningly. 'So you really do think one of Giorgio's colleagues killed him?'

Slattery folded his arms and said, 'It's not my investigation but from what my colleagues have told me, Giorgio Lombardi worked from ten in the morning until ten at night five days a week, usually six. He went to his local pub, the Crown, in Acton and got pissed on his day off. He didn't have a regular girlfriend that we know of, but he did have a huge amount of porn, mainly in DVD form. His laptop was clean. He didn't have any friends or family that we can see. We found some drugs, coke, some weed, nothing unusual. He had a healthy bank balance with no signs of unusual activity. So, in the absence of any obvious suspects, work colleagues are the most likely pool of suspects.'

'Well, that's all very logical, DI Slattery.'

'So, I'm asking you. . .' Slattery's teeth weren't gritted

but they might as well have been, asking me to help him was a sure sign of desperation. 'If you were to choose a candidate from the small pool of suspects, who would it be?'

'I really don't know,' I said, 'but I promise that if I learn anything you will be the first to know.'

Slattery drained his coffee cup.

'Well' – his tone was sarcastic – 'I do find that most reassuring indeed.'

He stood up. 'I'll see myself out.'

He adjusted his jacket and moved towards the door, then he stopped and turned. To say that the look he gave me was icy would have done a disservice to frozen water. 'I do hope that you've been fully frank with me, Ms Hunter.'

'Call me, Charlie, please.'

He nodded but didn't say anything and the door closed firmly behind him.

I let out a big sigh of relief now that he was gone. Matteo's blackmail secret was still a secret.

Chapter Thirteen

It would be a mistake to think that all my life was tied up with Matteo. I was still an independent woman. I still had my own restaurant to run and my own life in the village. One person who figured in both of those was a lady called Esther Bartlett. She was prominent in Hampden Green. She was a parish councillor, she led the village litter clean-up days and she sang in the local church choir – she had a great voice. Despite this C of E affiliation, she was also the local white witch, High Priestess of the local coven and the Chair of SoBuNPag (the acronym stood for South Bucks Neo Pagans). Esther also liked her food – she was a regular customer of mine and used me for catering for her parties, both secular and religious.

So, a couple of days after Slattery's visit, I was at Esther's house to discuss a catering project with an associate of hers. Historically I had done quite well out of witches' parties. They liked their food and they seemed to have quite a lot of money. Worshipping the Great Mother obviously paid off financially. I stress they were white witches, not Satanists. I'm sure they existed in Bucks as well, but maybe they were less foodie – which is why I had never come across them. They were probably more inclined to sacrifice and/or worship goats than go for goat's cheese and chicory crostini which were on my menu.

'More tea?' asked Esther. She had kind, blunt features resting on top of her several chins and a pair of very shrewd blue eyes. She was a big lady, who tended to favour voluminous flowing caftans. She was wearing one today, a riot of crimson paisley.

I nodded. 'Please.'

She poured and smiled at me.

She was one of my favourite customers and her homemade jam made my Bakewell tarts all the better in my opinion. Though it still rankled that Giorgio hadn't noticed. Still, he was beyond the reach of jam now, poor man.

'I hear that you're working with *the* Matteo McCleish!' said Esther. 'We're all very impressed. I'm a huge fan of *Nonna's Kitchen*. What's he like?'

'Very nice,' I said. 'He's doing a book on English gastro-pub food and wants my input, which is very flattering.' I thought I'd establish the reasons for my being there early on. 'So I'll be with him and his team up at the Earl's place, helping out, to get a sense of his cooking style.'

'What's his wife like?' said Chris Reynolds, eagerly. He was the other person at the table, another devotee of the Craft.

Chris was far more occult-looking than Esther, with wiry, purple hair and hawkish features; he occasionally favoured eye makeup. He was an ageing Goth: think Robert Smith from The Cure but devoid of any talent. He certainly stood out when you saw him in the village when he came to visit Esther, which was often. Wandering around in his black clothes and pixie boots.

He was the Chair of NoBWic, North Bucks Wiccans, a sister organisation to SoBuNPag, based in Milton Keynes of all places, which was where he lived.

'Graziana is very nice,' I said.

'I heard she was a bit of a bitch,' Chris said with a glint in his eye, and more than a hint of a leer. 'Man-mad, they say.'

I looked at Chris in his black clothes and silver skull jewellery. Don't get your hopes up mate, I thought.

I shook my head. 'I think that's just the TV marketing people – they want her to float around looking gorgeous to attract male viewers – she's actually not like that. She seems very sweet-natured. Very grounded.'

She had also made good on her promise to hire Jess to improve her computer skills. Jess was in raptures.

I said firmly, shutting Chris down, 'Anyway. . . food. . .'

We turned to business. Chris was keen on hiring me to do the catering for the NoBWic Midsummer Festival. He may have had poor taste in fashion but excellent taste in hiring chefs. I politely listened as he droned on about the summer solstice.

'So when exactly is the solstice?' I asked.

Chris answered, 'It's the twenty-first of June, in six days' time. But we can't get the cricket pavilion, where we're having the Festival, until a month later in July. So that's when the feast will take place. It's not ideal, but we have to work with what we're given.'

'The Goddess will understand,' Esther said confidently.

Chris nodded and continued, 'I'll text you my address and postcode and you can come round a few weeks before – shall we say, oh I dunno, sometime at the end of June?'

I checked my calendar on my phone. 'That'd be great.'

'We call it Litha, the most powerful day of the year for the Sun God,' said Chris dreamily, moving back to his solstice theme '. . . we shall leap sky-clad through the sacred fires. . .'

I looked dubiously at him and repressed a shudder. The thought of Chris's scrawny limbs leaping naked through anything, much less a sacred bonfire, was frankly off-putting. Esther caught my eye and grinned. I blushed, feeling sure she knew exactly what I had been thinking.

'Well, let's hear some of Charlie's ideas for the catering. . .' Esther said firmly.

'Oh yes,' said Chris, 'I was at the feast of Imbolc that you did here for Esther. I loved the food.'

'Well' – I brought out my tablet – 'the fact that you're celebrating with fire kind of conjures up a barbecue. . .' I showed them photos of mini-burgers, marinated lamb kebabs, teriyaki-style chicken and tofu brochettes. 'I decided to go with the fire theme with the salads, beetroot and lentil, the redness mirroring the fire.'

'Cool,' murmured Chris. He was giving me a rather peculiar look. His eyes, surrounded by the eyeliner, smouldered. OMG I thought, Chris fancies me. I felt slightly nervous. He leaned over the table to get a better look at the image on the screen. He had unbuttoned his shirt and I averted my eyes from his scrawny, hairless chest adorned with a couple of heavy silver necklaces strung with skulls and charms. If they were love charms, they certainly weren't working.

I tried to take my mind off things by looking at my surroundings. I had been in Esther's kitchen before, using it for the aforementioned Feast of Imbolc. It was a massive room, extremely well equipped. The three of us were seated on stools around the centre island with which every large kitchen these days seems to be furnished. I had already made a small stack of plates and now I unzipped the cool-bag I had with me and plated up some of the salads. 'This is a Lebanese dish, *"moussaka batinjan"*; it's a kind of aubergine stew.'

I watched anxiously as she tasted it. I'm a huge fan of the aubergine, but it's a divisive vegetable.

Chris frowned at first. I don't know why you're frowning mate, I thought, you've dyed your hair aubergine, the least you can do is eat one – and then his face brightened. He pushed his bird's nest of hair away from his forehead. Bracelets clanked on his thin wrists.

'I think that's great.'

I felt immensely relieved. The other dishes all went down equally well.

'And how much will all this come to?' he asked. I tapped the tablet, seeking shelter in the white screen with the figures in black. I hate the whole business of asking for money. I find it embarrassing, ridiculously so.

The invoice I was quoting from had actually been prepared by Jess. She had seen my original quote and said, 'Are you crazy? No wonder you can't afford any staff. Give it to me.'

I propped the tablet up between Chris and me, creating a kind of shield while he frowned at the numbers.

'It's not cheap I'm afraid,' I apologised (I could almost hear Jess's exasperated voice: 'FFS, man up, you're not a charity').

'That's not a problem,' said Esther cheerfully. 'Chris's wife's job is as a treasurer – she's got loads of money.'

Chris rolled his eyes, then looked closely at the figures in front of him and nodded in agreement. 'That looks fine,' he said. Good, I thought, that's that.

'We'll talk things over in July at my place. . .' he pushed a hand through his hair and moved imperceptibly closer to me, I moved perceptibly further away.

'Then we'll go down. . . down to the cricket club. . .' Chris smiled at me, and I smiled nervously back. He had managed to imbue the words 'cricket club' with a kind of lascivious air, as if a cricket club were some kind of orgiastic hot-house.

I stood up. 'Well,' I said, 'it's been a pleasure.'

As I walked back to my car, I wondered what kind of woman would be crazy enough to marry Chris. Some, poor, down-trodden timid soul, I thought as I loaded my stuff into the old Volvo. At least she would never run short of eyeliner with him around.

Chapter Fourteen

I had given Francis Friday evening off and £50 spending money as a thank you for rescuing me from Giorgio. He solemnly told me he was going to have a jumbo kebab from Ali's Kebab Van in Frampton End, the village up the road, and then play pool all night in the Three Bells. His face under his thatch of blond hair flushed crimson at the thought of the excitement.

His face beamed. 'Thank you Chef!'

'No, thank you Francis!'

'And I really don't have to wash up tonight?'

'No.'

'Well.' He pulled off his apron and chef's jacket. He was wearing a T-shirt underneath, his biceps I reflected were bigger than Chris's head. He pulled on his jacket

'I'm happier than a Bishop in a boys' school!'

'Francis,' Jess had come in, 'I've told you before that you can't say that. . .'

'Sorry, Jess. I'm very happy though. . .'

'Yes, now off you go. . .' I said. We watched as he

blundered out of the kitchen door into the yard. Jess shook her head wonderingly.

'Cheque on, two spaghetti alle vongole, no starters. . .'

She spiked her copy of the cheque and gave me mine.

I put a couple of handfuls of spaghetti into a pan of boiling water that I had on the go at the back of the stove and made a mental note of the time, adding it to the other timers that were ticking down in my head. It's a knack all good chefs acquire.

I got a frying pan ready for the clams and said to Jess, 'He was amazing with that cricket ball. . .'

She laughed. We both knew Francis was a great bowler and batsman too, but his fielding was truly incredible, he could hit the stumps from way on the outfield; braining Giorgio was child's play.

Jess said, 'Wish I'd been there to see it.'

I smiled at her over the pass and handed over two chicken liver parfaits with sourdough toast and cranberry relish. 'Thanks for looking after me, Jess' I said. It was a measure of how busy we'd been that this was the first time I'd had the chance to thank her for having dispatched Francis to babysit me.

She said, 'De nada. Just don't go hiring any more creeps like Giorgio.' And she disappeared with the starters.

About 9 o'clock I had sent out the last main course. We were fairly quiet for a Friday evening; a large table had cancelled, but the large dual sink was piled high with washing up (in a commercial kitchen you rinse everything to get rid of the worst of the debris before you fill the dishwasher). As I looked at the mound of plates, bowls and of course all the pots and pans I'd used, I felt my heart sink. I was now beginning to regret my noble gesture in giving Francis the night off.

As I started the washing up, hoping there wouldn't be any dessert orders, my phone rang. It was Matteo.

Cursing, I pulled off my gloves and picked up.

'Hi,' I said, tersely, communicating my displeasure down the phone. He, of all people, should have known not to call during service hours.

'Charlie,' he sounded scared and desperate, 'can you come over after service?'

'What, tonight?' I said, staring at the washing up.

'Yeah, it's important, please come. . .'

I wondered what was going on. Something had obviously happened.

'Ok, I'll be over as soon as I can.'

'Thanks, I appreciate it.' He ended the call. I shrugged and pulled my gloves back on. What now?

Later that night, about half ten, I drove over to Matteo's house. Two stone pillars and enormous, ornamental metal gates marked the entrance of the Old Vicarage, and I drove up the long gravel drive between what felt like endless rhododendron bushes. They looked beautiful by day, the blossoms were out and they were a riot of reds and pinks but at night it was just creepy. The headlights washed over a claustrophobic wall of solid foliage. It was easy to imagine monsters lurking in them. Part of me is ridiculously superstitious.

I turned the final corner and the vicarage, like a Hammer House of Horror, was silhouetted against the moonlit sky,

Matteo's Maserati out in front together with Graziana's Range Rover. I parked my old Volvo between them. They reflected our mutual careers: Matteo with his up-market restaurant and TV shows, and me, slaving away in my small café in an out of the way village.

I scrunched across the gravel and rang the doorbell. It triggered not a ring but a snatch of classical music that I'd heard before so it had to be well-known.

The door opened, it was a harassed looking Douglas.

'Hello, Charlie, do come in, he's expecting you. . .'

I walked into the hall of the disgraced businessman's lair. It was huge and had several pairs of mounted antlers on the wall.

'What's with the doorbell?' I asked.

'It's Wagner's "Ride of the Valkyries", we can't change the setting on it,' Douglas said. 'It's driving us mad. . .' he bustled ahead of me. He was wearing blue trousers and rather horrible shoes, the kind that look a bit like Cornish pasties. His white shirt was poorly ironed. On his wrist some kind of smart watch, doubtless monitoring Douglas's number of steps and vital signs. God knows what he was going to do with the information. He needed a bloody good haircut in my view more than health protocols. Propped against a chair I noticed his gun bag.

'You could always put a bullet through the doorbell,' I suggested.

'What!' He looked disconcerted and slightly shocked.

'Your gun. . .' I nodded.

'Oh, yes. . . ha, ha!' Then, 'Do you want to see it?' His face lit up like a child wanting to show off a treasure. I know nothing about guns, they don't interest me remotely, but he looked so excited I didn't have the heart to say no.

'That would be nice.'

He unzipped the bag and slid out his rifle and handed it to me.

'Isn't she a beauty,' he crooned. I took it gingerly. I'm always surprised when I pick up a gun by their weight, this was no exception. Cliff Yeats had taken me shooting a couple of times, as had Andrea. I can't say I warmed to the experience.

'It's a CZ 457, it's a lovely gun,' he enthused, as I cradled it awkwardly, like I was holding a baby for a doting mother. He rattled off some technical details which meant nothing to me. I handed it back to him and he put it back in its case, reverentially.

'Right, I'll take you through. . .' His face lost its animation now he was back to the mundanities of his job. He led me to the study. 'He's in there. . . do go in.'

I looked more closely at him. He looked exhausted, his eyes bloodshot behind the lenses of his glasses.

'You look terrible, Douglas,' I said, and immediately regretted it.

'I'm fine, I had to spend some time being interviewed by the police about Giorgio. They're only doing their job of course, but it made me very behind with my work, I've just got to finalise the costings on the food, no point doing all this catering if we walk away with a loss,' he said. He smiled wanly. 'But thanks for your concern.'

He walked off. Poor sod, I thought. He could do with more time at his gun club.

I knocked on the door.

'Come!' said a disembodied voice. I nearly jumped out of my skin. Douglas heard it too and stopped, turning round. He noticed my confusion.

'It's that intercom thing,' Douglas said, pointing at a speaker on a table by the door. It was large and white and had three lights on top, like a traffic light, red, amber and green. The amber changed to green. I stared at it in fascination, this had been cutting edge in 1973.

'See you later,' he said and went off down the hall back to his Excel spreadsheets.

I opened the panelled door and went in. Matteo was sitting on a sofa next to Charlotte; they both looked up as I came in.

'Hi Matteo,' I said, 'Charlotte. . .'

'Charlie, thanks for coming.' He looked delighted to see me. He stood up and ushered me to one of the chairs opposite the sofa and I sat down. Charlotte regarded me silently; I wondered if I had done something wrong.

'Do you want a drink?' he asked.

'White wine,' I said. He nodded and walked over to the corner of the room where there was a huge globe of the world on a stand. It was made of wood and reached from the floor to about my shoulders. Facing us were the Americas, North and South. He pressed a button on the North Pole. The globe silently unfurled itself into four quadrants, revealing two rows of bottles and a bottom section full of glasses. It was brilliantly lit and it sat there glowing with alcohol and self-importance.

'Good God!' I exclaimed.

'Tasteful,' Matteo said with heavy sarcasm.

It was a masterpiece of kitsch interior design. I guess it was the kind of thing that had been popular back in the 1950s. There was, naturally, a small refrigerated area in the region of the South Pole. Where else? He pressed the button again and it quietly re-configured itself into the shape of our planet.

He brought me over the wine and then handed me a piece of paper that had been lying on the table. I read it and my heart sank.

It was another blackmail letter, more or less identical to the other one I'd seen but with today's date on. And the amount of money demanded had been increased from four to six thousand.

'I found this earlier today, in my locker in the London restaurant.'

'So it wasn't Giorgio after all,' I said.

He sighed. 'He must have been there just to buy porn after all.'

'Or in cahoots with the blackmailer,' Charlotte said, speaking for the first time. 'He wasn't necessarily acting alone.'

'I'm so sorry,' I said. I suddenly felt very wretched, almost as if it were my fault. 'I thought I'd solved it.' I put the blackmail note back on the table.

'We all did,' Matteo said, dejectedly. Charlotte nodded agreement.

'Well,' I said, looking at them, 'what do you want me to do?'

'We'll stick with the original plan,' Charlotte said firmly.

'We want you to work with the team. It has to be one of the chefs, they'll give themselves away, I'm sure of it. Particularly after this. . .'

'Exactly,' Matteo said. 'Only the people in my brigade have access to the room where my locker is. We're back where we were, at square one.'

'The only difference is,' Charlotte said, 'it's very probable that the blackmailer is also a killer.'

I nodded. 'It certainly looks that way.' I thought it would be wise to work out just where we stood at this precise moment. 'So, just to be clear, we think that Giorgio and an accomplice were blackmailing Matteo, Giorgio was at the porn shop to pick up the money then, for unknown reasons the two later had a falling out and the other blackmailer killed him.'

'That's exactly what I think,' Charlotte said. 'Maybe he thought that since Giorgio's identity was known he might reveal their name. . . who knows.'

Then I said, 'Shouldn't you go to the police with this? Giorgio was probably murdered by him after all.'

Charlotte shook her head. 'No. I can't take the risk of them causing trouble for Matteo. If they find the killer, fine, so be it. That's the police's job. They don't need to be informed about the blackmail. Your job, however, is different, to catch the blackmailer.'

'And if they're one and the same as we think?' I asked.

'We'll cross that bridge when and if we come to it,' Charlotte said decisively. She was a very decisive woman. No wonder Matteo had come to rely on her so much, I thought.

'But we don't know anything for sure,' Matteo said. 'We don't know if the blackmailer killed Giorgio in a falling out, or if it was the work of a third party.'

'The important thing is to find the blackmailer,' Charlotte said irritably, tapping the table to drive home the point. 'How many more times!' Then, turning to me, 'Are you with us, Charlie?'

'Ok,' I said. 'I'll do it. . . and you'll get me a replacement chef?'

'I will indeed,' Charlotte said. Now I had agreed to do what she wanted, she smiled at me with genuine warmth.

Matteo stood up. 'I'll see you out. I'm so glad you're with us, we'll crack this together Charlie!'

He led me down the hall to the front door. On the doorstep, he paused. 'So, can you start work in my kitchen next Wednesday? That's when the ten day practice run before the grand opening starts.'

I nodded. 'I'll be there.'

'Ciao, Charlie.' He put his hands on my shoulders and his beautiful, soulful brown eyes looked into mine. 'I really appreciate you helping me, and I know Graziana does too. You take care now.'

He closed the door behind me.

I scrunched across the gravel to my car and got in. I started the engine, put the old car in gear. I had kind of brushed it aside in his living room but now as I drove down the long drive with its ghostly foliage I thought to myself, I'm not just dealing with a blackmailer, I think I'm also dealing with a killer.

Chapter Fifteen

Over the next few days, I kept wondering who had killed Giorgio and why. He was a bully – had he pushed someone too far at work? Someone who had snapped. I had cooked in kitchens with a couple of chefs whose behaviour would not have been tolerated anywhere but a kitchen. There's a tradition, beginning to die out thankfully, of unbelievably bad treatment of junior chefs by more senior chefs, verging on the barbaric.

I wondered which of the junior chefs in Matteo's brigade might have fought back. Octavia? Giorgio had molested Jess; he had form for this kind of thing. Might Octavia have retaliated? Or maybe someone did it on her behalf? A boyfriend? Her father? I reined my imagination in; more likely it was someone closer to home. I could imagine someone already nursing a festering grievance against Giorgio going one step beyond reasonable force. And the fact that he was stabbed seemed quite in keeping with being killed by a chef. Face it, we all have sharp knives, and often equally sharp tempers driven by overwork and often too much alcohol.

The red-hot coals of resentment are fanned by the winds that blow through the commercial kitchen – stress, proximity, lack of sleep, long hours, drink and drugs – to flames of extreme violence.

I tried to put Giorgio out of my mind by concentrating on my own life and my own work.

It was early on a Tuesday morning and tomorrow I would start working with Matteo's chefs, but today I was still my own boss. I looked at my mise en place sheet, my prep list, for that day. Mercifully it wasn't too bad, about an hour's work. I could leave it until later – maybe I would feel better then.

My phone rang. It was Esther Bartlett asking if I could come round and talk some more about the midsummer feast. Chris had been going through my suggestions with his colleagues from NoBWic and they had finalised their choices. Most certainly, I could. I told her that I'd be over in about ten minutes and put the phone down. She would be a welcome distraction from my puzzling over the identity of a murderer.

I drove just out of the village to Esther's house. It always seemed, to my eyes, quite ugly, built I guessed in the Twenties, lots of red brick and narrow, leaded windows. Lutyens style, I think it's called. It was a large place and seemed to serve as a communal meeting place for many of the local pagan groups, including of course, Chris's group, the Milton Keynes branch of the witches. I guess it helped too that it was handy for my restaurant, I seemed to be doing a lot of catering for these occult organisations.

I rang the bell, and the dogs barked before Esther's husband, Roy, a short, slim man with a bushy Amish-style beard, opened the door. His two dogs, a black Lab and a huge Dalmatian, ran out and sniffed me enthusiastically.

Roy and Esther were one of those couples who seem to have zero things in common with each other but who nevertheless have a successful marriage. Roy, who had been in the army in the Royal Engineers, shared none of her beliefs in the occult. At least, he never expressed them if he did. He was a practical man who had a passion, which I didn't share, for cars.

He tended to keep out of the way, I had noticed, when Esther's witch friends were around. When I had done the catering for the Feast of Imbolc and met him several times, he would occasionally look at me and raise his eyes heavenward at some of the more outlandish statements made by Esther and her friends.

'Hello, Charlie, do come in. Esther's in the living room with Chris and Rowan Herne. The High Priest of the Milton Keynes South Coven, no less!'

'Oh,' I said. It was hard to know what to say to that. I had no idea who these people were, presumably affiliates of Chris's NobWic coven; it was all quite confusing. Maybe they weren't Wiccans but some other pagan group.

He ushered me into the house and then closed the door behind him, the two large dogs frolicking adoringly at his heels. 'So, you're involved in the opera thing, eh?' he asked as we walked down the hall, which was decorated with pictures of assorted militaria: tanks, planes, all the panoply of war in the British Army throughout the ages. I'd noticed on my many trips here that there was not a single nod to witchcraft in any shape or form.

'Well, not really,' I said. 'I get to help out with the food. . .'

'I love opera. I've got tickets for all three of them, *Rigoletto*, *Traviata* and *Carmen*. Bloody expensive, mind you, but at least we don't have to schlepp up to Covent Garden. Are you going?'

I just don't really get opera, although I did like Freddie Mercury singing 'Barcelona'.

'It's not really my thing, Roy. . .'

I found Esther in the living room dressed in a stripy caftan, looking like a mobile circus Big Top. Chris stood up as I entered and embraced me, rather more enthusiastically than I felt was called for. Surprise, surprise, he was wearing black, with a rather nifty spiky necklace on. It had a large linked silver chain with the aforementioned spikes like little spearheads hanging from it. I rather liked it, shame about the turkey neck it was hanging round though. He had a silver dagger earring in one ear and a silver bracelet like interleaved snakes on his slender right wrist. To be honest, I rather liked his taste in jewellery, him, not so much.

His bird's nest hair was pinned up today and, as he slipped his jacket off, he revealed an Egyptian soul symbol, an ankh, tattooed on his scrawny upper arm. His trousers were faux black leather. The way he looked at me – a kind of hungry, calculated stare – made me glad I wasn't alone with him.

'You remember Chris, don't you, Charlie?' said Esther cheerfully.

'Of course I do, nice ankh. . .' I said gallantly.

'Thank you,' Chris said. His eyes smouldered at me. 'They were so spiritual, yet so sensual, the ancient Egyptians. . . Karnak, have you been?'

'It's on my to-do list,' I said. I had seen pictures of the ancient temples. I had no intention whatsoever of going.

'And this is Rowan. . .' Esther turned and introduced a silver-haired man, his hair brushed back, with a red face wearing a black leather jacket.

Rowan Herne looked more like a powerfully built bank robber than a Wiccan High Priest. His face was more brutal rather than spiritual. He grunted something in my direction.

'Rowan is co-running the Festival with me, aren't you, Ro?' said Chris, smiling at Rowan.

He nodded. 'Yes.'

I smiled hello at the High Priest who regarded me balefully and I sat down on a chair indicated by Esther. She pointed at Rowan.

'Dr Rowan Herne, to give him his full title,' she said grandly. Like Dr John Dee, I thought, the famous Elizabethan magician, famous for his scrying glass. I wondered if 'Dr' Herne had one.

'I'm a GP,' said Dr Rowan Herne, irritably, by way of explanation.

'Oh,' I said. Of course, a GP wizard.

'Right,' said Esther breezily, 'now we've got the introductions over with, let's finalise the menu. . .'

And so we did. Starters, much as discussed at our last meeting, canapés, which were no problem. The main course would be a lamb tagine and then there was the vexed question of the vegetarian option.

Chris said, 'I loved the lasagne at the feast of Imbolc that you made. . .' he paused and got his phone out, then his thumbs clicked away. 'And it's made a big comeback on the Clean Eating sites.' He showed me several lovingly photographed dishes: lasagne with quinoa and chia salad, lasagne garnished with foraged wild garlic pesto, lasagne with charred beets. He looked me in the eye from under his makeup-enhanced eyebrows and emphatic eyeliner.

'Lasagne it is,' Rowan added, with an air of finality.

'OK then,' I acquiesced. Vegetable lasagne is one of the few dishes I really dislike making, but if that's what he wanted. . .

Half an hour later, bruised of principles and made slightly queasy by Chris's obvious interest in me, I returned to the Old Forge Café.

As I parked my car outside, a Bentley silently pulled up beside me. It had black tinted windows but although I couldn't see in, I knew who was driving. I got out of my car and the window of the luxury car silently lowered.

The cold eyes of the Earl rested on me.

'Good morning, Charlie, please get in.'

Chapter Sixteen

My relationship with the Earl of Hampden (or Earl Hampden, I was never quite sure which was the correct form) was ambivalent. On the one hand I admired him for his tireless eco-work: he was a passionate advocate and a highly efficient fund-raiser for endangered animal species. But there was a negative side. He had a chequered, if not lurid, past involving high living, fast cars and fast women, not to mention a well-publicised dalliance with drugs that he still seemed to be keeping up into his late sixties. The fact that his current girlfriend had been at school with Jess was also disturbing to me. The age difference was crazy, but then again, Bryony was certainly old enough to make informed choices. Anyway, the Earl didn't care what anyone thought, he was monumentally arrogant.

I wondered what he wanted as I opened the passenger door and got in beside him. As usual he was expensively and flawlessly dressed, today in a lightweight linen two piece suit. There was not a grey hair out of place on his distinguished head as we swept out of my car park.

'I can only give you an hour,' I said. 'I've got an agency

chef coming at half eleven.' Charlotte had been as good as her word but for various reasons the guy couldn't start until today.

'That's fine,' he said, 'that's long enough.' Long enough for what, I wondered. Strange as he was, I trusted the Earl, he was a man of a certain integrity.

We drove out of the village and along the road to his house. We passed the field where the opera would take place. I could see workmen making a start on the gigantic marquee together with ancillary ones which would house bars, merchandise franchises and cloakrooms. I could see a couple of flat-bed trucks unloading Portaloos. It was a huge operation. Being so involved with Matteo had made me forget that the catering was only one piece of the enormous jigsaw puzzle that made up this three-week festival.

We pulled into the road that led to his house. This was the drive at the back, not the imposing sweeping tree-lined drive that led to the front of his property. The tradesmen's entrance.

'Anna came over earlier to do a reading for me.'

'Anna? How is she?' Anna was Anna Bruce, a medium/psychic that the Earl used occasionally to advise him on business deals when his own financial acumen did not suffice. When I first heard about it I had been surprised, but I had since come to learn that most of her clients were from the corporate world. I had been deeply sceptical of Anna Bruce but she had helped me once before in a disturbingly inexplicable way. I guess the same was true of many of these hard-headed businessmen and captains of industry.

'She's fine, she wanted to see you.'

He parked the car at the rear of the house and we got out. He led me round to the front and I caught a glimpse of the lovingly tended gardens that stretched out below us as the ground fell away down to a valley below.

He opened the front door and about half a dozen dogs, all of whom had been rescued by the Earl from terrible backgrounds, barked joyously around him. His commandingly austere face relaxed into a genuine smile of delight as he greeted them all by name, then he turned back to me. As a human I was not deemed that worthy of warmth and his face reverted to its habitual expression of chilly command.

'Come through.'

He led me along the hall to the living room. It was sizeable but not crazily so and the furniture that I imagine had been in the Earl's family for years was a mixture of antique – a sideboard and some tables, the odd chair and sofas and bookcases filled with an eclectic mixture of literature: Georges Bataille, Anthony Powell, the Marquis de Sade, Hunter S Thompson, Nietzsche, Evelyn Waugh and Angela Carter. Contemporary and classic Persian rugs covered the parquet floor. On the walls hung art from Stubbs style horses to what looked like a couple of Francis Bacons, although whether they were original or copies I had no idea.

Sitting on one of the two sofas was a slim, middle-aged woman with short white hair. It was a haircut that looked expensive, but then Anna Bruce could afford it.

She stood up as I came in.

'Charlie Hunter!' she exclaimed as I walked in, and

embraced me. I smelt expensive, light floral perfume as she hugged me and my fingers touched the back of the silken fabric of her dark blue tailored jacket. She had blue sapphire earrings and a matching two-tone Prada handbag. I wasn't psychic like Anna, or a style expert, but I knew it was Prada – it said so in gold letters on a little inverted triangular sign equidistant between where the two top straps met the body of the bag.

'I'll leave you two ladies to it,' said the Earl.

'Come back in quarter of an hour, James, and take Charlie home,' Anna said to him, imperiously. Very few people, if any, would be brave enough to boss the Earl around, I thought; Anna was one of them. The Earl nodded, he obviously didn't mind. Anna was one of the few people he respected.

'I'm sure that she's busy.' She added, 'I think there's a new man in her life.'

The Earl's eyebrows rose. 'Professionally,' Anna explained. How did she know, I wondered, that an agency chef was arriving today?

The Earl nodded and left the room.

'Have a seat,' Anna said. I did so and I sat upright, almost to attention, looking at her like a kid at school being told something important by a teacher.

'I was thinking of you the other day,' Anna said. 'Then various other signs, you could call them synchronicities involving you happened. . . so, there's a couple of things I need to tell you.'

'Synchronicities?' I'd heard the word but couldn't remember its exact meaning.

'Meaningful coincidences,' she clarified. 'So, I did a couple of things. . . just to check,' she continued. 'I consulted my usual sources, the I Ching, the Tarot' – she smiled – 'the internet, there's a very good article in *Restaurant* magazine on Matteo McCleish and his work, you get a mention. . . anyway, I have a couple of messages to give to you.'

'Please go on,' I said.

'Firstly,' she said, pleasantly enough, but frowning slightly, 'things are not what they seem. Someone is spreading a web of delusion around you. The second thing is, there is danger involved with a woman. A violent woman possibly, or maybe a deceitful one. Either way, she is malignant, more than that, she poses an existential threat.'

'An existential threat?' I repeated, stupidly.

Anna sighed. 'It's a polite way of saying that she could well kill you. There's danger in your life, Charlie, and it comes from a woman.'

'Thank you,' I said faintly. I knew there was no point in asking her to be more specific.

There was a knock on the door and the Earl opened it.

'Take Charlie back, James, please, we've finished.' That was me dismissed. I thanked her again and got up to leave. As I reached the door she said, 'Oh, one more thing, have you got a valid passport?'

I looked at her, puzzled. 'I think so, why?'

She smiled. 'Just a hunch, that's all. Ciao.'

Chapter Seventeen

Matteo's agency chef, Sam, arrived later in time for lunch. He, thank the Lord, seemed reasonably sane and refreshingly normal. He was in his mid-thirties, calm, stout and balding with an ill-advised combover and an unflappable, confident air.

'I think this one is going to be OK,' said Jess after we'd worked the shift together. I breathed a sigh of relief. I'd had quite enough needless stress and drama over the past few days. The evening shift went well too. It was nothing like the nightmare that Giorgio had been. Well, that was one less thing to worry about; now I could concentrate on finding out who was the viper that Matteo was clutching to his bosom.

And, of course, all the time when I wasn't thinking about who the blackmailer was, I was pondering Anna Bruce's warning about the dangerous woman. I fell asleep that night and suffered confused dreams about being pursued by shadowy female figures.

The following day I showed up for work at Matteo's kitchen.

As I walked up to the front door of the Earl's house, I reflected that it had been quite a journey since I had first noticed the council change of usage notification on my morning run. A lot had happened in the intervening weeks. I had met one of Britain's leading celebrity chefs, become involved in a blackmail investigation and a murder, and now here I was about to spend the morning cooking with a celebrity chef's team. Life certainly wasn't boring – and that was not even factoring in meeting the creepy Goth wizard who fancied me (be still my beating heart!) and the tough looking, Warlock MD.

The house itself was unremarkable. Big yes, imposing, no. From the front it looked like a small, family run hotel. It still looked that way. Comfortable, unpretentious, but now it had an opera festival tacked onto it in a gigantic tent with a pop-up restaurant in one of the ancillary marquees in the garden. The heavy lifting, the bulk of the prep and the cooking would be done here in the house kitchen.

As I approached the front door, the Earl's girlfriend came round the corner. She was talking animatedly to Murdo, the gangly Scots kid I had last seen when I had initially met the brigade. That was only just over a couple of weeks ago, but felt like much longer. A lot of things had happened since then.

'Charlie!' she called out. I smiled warmly at her. I was quite fond of Bryony. I had known her since I first moved to the village and our paths had (in her case woozily) crossed several times. She was part of the village drug scene (Q: What do young people in villages do? A: Drugs) and a contemporary of Jess's although their paths had diverged considerably since leaving school. Jess disapproved strongly of Bryony.

The Earl was far too old to have such a young partner – she was Jess's age – but Bryony had a liking for unsuitable men (her last boyfriend had been a dealer) and drugs, and the Earl ticked both boxes.

Today she was wearing a very tight, scoop-necked white top, white jeans and a stoned expression. She looked very pretty and I wondered if Murdo was hoping for more than the goodwill of the Earl's partner. The scent of weed commingled with some heavy, sultry perfume and hung around her like a halo. Five dogs frolicked around her feet. She smiled welcomingly at me in an unfocused kind of way. Both she and the dogs seemed genuinely pleased to see me. I couldn't speak for Bryony, but I guessed that as far as the dogs were concerned it was the pleasing aroma of food that, as a working chef, clung to me.

'I'm looking for the kitchen,' I said. 'Where is it? I'm supposed to be working with Matteo's team.'

'I'll show you,' Murdo said. 'It's round the back. Let me give you a hand with your stuff.'

I had my chef's whites and shoes for the kitchen in a sports bag and a box with my knives inside in the other. All chefs bring their own knives to where they work, they're very personal things, not to mention expensive.

He picked up my knife box. 'It's good to see you again Charlie, I'm looking forward to working with you.'

'See you later babes,' Bryony said to him. 'You too Charlie.' She wandered off back round the corner. I noticed Murdo's gaze lingering wistfully on her shapely backside.

He led me through a side door by the kitchen and pointed.

'If you go down the corridor there's a changing room at the end.' He handed me back my knife box. 'I'll see you later, Charlie. If there's anything you need, just ask me.'

He grinned and walked away and in through the kitchen door. As it opened I heard the familiar din of a kitchen in full swing: the roar of the extractor fans, the noise of blades chopping on boards, the slamming of oven and fridge doors, the clanging of metal pans on the iron range, loud music from a radio and people shouting to make themselves heard. As I walked down the corridor to change I was pleased that there would be at least one person in there who was my friend. A strange kitchen full of unfamiliar people and a new menu can be a very intimidating place indeed, even for me, a person of considerable experience.

The lockers in the changing room were the kind for which you had to supply your own padlock; everyone else's had one. They were made from a type of metal mesh, rather than solid pieces of steel, so the contents inside were visible. I didn't have anything valuable with me but I made a note to bring a padlock the following day.

I found myself feeling quite nervous as I pulled my clothes off, put them in a locker and slipped into my whites. Lacing up my Caterpillar work boots, I told myself not to be so silly, I was here not to try out for a job but simply to be as unobtrusive as possible and catch a blackmailer.

I walked into the kitchen. The first thing that I noticed about the Earl's kitchen was its unexpected size. That, and its professional layout. It was all brushed steel and laminate, non-slip floor with touches that I would never have expected from the kitchen of what was essentially a private, even if quite large, house. The equipment was brand new. Then I remembered that the house hosted a lot of weddings in the summer. Somewhere in the grounds was a private chapel and the ballroom at the side of the house could seat about a hundred. The Earl made a lot of money from these events and that was why the kitchen was so well-equipped. Everything that the outside caterers needed was here. That included a walk-in fridge and a separate walk-in freezer.

I was jealous of the machinery I spotted as well, including a large Bratt pan, essentially a freestanding rectangular metal dish with a built-in heat source so you could fry or roast or stew about a hundred portions of whatever. Yours for a bargain, at £5,000. There was a Rational oven too – that was to die for.

I've got a bit of a thing about ovens – ovens and shoes.

Tom, the muscular, bearded, development chef, showed me around.

'So how's the book with Matteo going?' he asked, raising his voice over the din around us.

'Great,' I said with a confidence I didn't really feel, 'we're just kicking around ideas at the moment. I'll fine-tune them when I've got a better idea of Matteo's way of doing things from you guys. I hope I won't be in the way. . .'

Tom laughed. 'Don't worry, there's plenty for you to do while you're making notes. I'm glad you're here to help, this Giorgio business keeps getting in the way, I got given a really tough time by some spotty, young cop, Paul someone or other. Really bloody aggy he was. . .' I nodded sympathetically. So it wasn't just me then who he didn't like.

'Now, come over here and I'll show you where you'll be working today.'

The first night of the opera fortnight was in ten days' time, and would be preceded by three days of trial runs at the new menu, where we would cook for invited guests – the media and VIPs – before the first opera was aired. In the interim we would be doing the food for the musicians, stage hands, basically the whole crew needed to put the opera on. As well as that, we would be practising the new dishes so things would be faultless and any mistakes ironed out before the big day started. Nothing was being left to chance. I guessed I was seeing the hand of Charlotte in this meticulous, almost military, planning.

I looked around the kitchen. The chefs from Matteo's team were working purposefully at their respective stations. They glanced at me stonily, with the exception of Murdo who waved enthusiastically. I noticed that the core team had been joined by three Eastern European-looking guys whom I hadn't met.

'Who are they?'

Tom glanced over at where I had indicated. 'Oh those guys, the Poles, they're agency – they've been brought in to help with the staff food and the prep.'

I saw Murdo over in a corner with a pile of chickens, busy jointing them. He grinned and winked conspiratorially at me from across the kitchen. I smiled back.

'I see you've met Murdo,' Tom said with dry amusement. 'He's a good kid.'

I took in the bustling scene in front of me. Soon I would be too busy to think. But not too busy, I hoped, to try to get some sense of who Matteo's blackmailer might be. A kitchen is such a fraught, stressful place to work in that I felt it would be hard to maintain a mask, to keep your guard up, and the perpetrator would give him or herself away in a careless moment. A throwaway remark that wouldn't be noticed by anyone else might be enough to give the game away. The blackmailer had no idea that I was solely there to unmask them. I was also uncomfortably aware that they might be (in my opinion, probably were) a killer.

And they all thought I was an old idiot anyway – at forty-three I was practically clapped out and ready for the scrapheap, so whoever it was would be relaxed in front of me. Too senile to notice anything.

I was put to work with Octavia. I hadn't appreciated how tall she was. I studied her with particular interest. I wondered if she might be the woman that Anna had warned me about. She was Tom's height and that made her a good five centimetres taller than I am. She had large grey eyes that viewed me with cool disdain. I say 'cool disdain' – contempt was maybe nearer to the mark. Well, Anna had said the woman who was a threat was malignant. Was she the one?

'What are you doing here?' Octavia's rather beautiful eyes seemed to be saying to me.

She was busy blanching and skinning a large plastic container of tomatoes, 'over a hundred,' she told me, for making tomato concasse. You quarter the peeled tomatoes, then you get rid of the pulp and cut the flesh up into small dice. It's quite an unpleasant job. The acid in the tomatoes reacts with your skin and your hands feel most unpleasant after a while. So she was glad of the help despite her unwelcoming attitude.

Working with someone in a kitchen is, generally speaking, a good way to get to know them. Prep work is usually simple and monotonous and cutting up tomatoes was certainly that.

In the background we could hear the Poles chatting away while they made chicken Marengo for 150 people. They were making full use of the Bratt pan – oh how I wanted one! The NoBWic party would have been so much simpler. It's hard work making large quantities of food in big pans with high sides: they require continual stirring and there's the constant danger of the food at the bottom burning and ruining the rest of it. With the Bratt pan I could have done it without breaking sweat.

'So,' I asked breaking the ice, 'how come you're working for Matteo?'

'He recognises skill and drive when he sees it,' said Octavia, modestly, 'and I'm going places, Charlie.'

Her eyes flickered contemptuously over me. Unlike you, you old hag, they seemed to say. I smiled pleasantly back. One of the things about being older, you get used to the contempt of youth. Or the patronage, it's hard to know which is worse.

'That's nice. . .' I said, dicing my tomatoes. I was working a lot faster than she was. Octavia had the fatal habit in a kitchen of slowing down when she talked.

It actually wasn't that nice, of course, nor was it meant to be. It was said in a way that implied: '. . . and you're going nowhere.' I wondered if Octavia used this kind of arrogant tone with everyone she judged her inferior. I didn't particularly care. I have a healthy sense of my own worth, but I could imagine there were people who would. And resentments fester in a kitchen. They can fester a lot.

'Malignant', Anna had said. Was Octavia malignant? She certainly wasn't being very nice.

I looked at her haughty profile, long blond hair escaping from under the chef's hat that she wore.

She carried on talking about herself: Cheltenham Ladies' College (where else!), her successful businessman father (putting her knife down, she showed me a photo of him, hand resting proudly on an Aston Martin, 'Daddy loves his cars!'), her first from Oxford in English.

'What does your dad do?' I asked politely.

'Oh, he's a banker.'

'My last but one boyfriend was a banker,' I said, skipping over the boyfriend who'd turned out to be a murderer – we all make mistakes. Octavia wasn't interested.

'Really?' she said in a tone of disbelief tinged with indifference. I was another generation and any opinions or experiences I may have had to offer were utterly redundant. I was getting a bit tired of Octavia's company. But was she the kind of girl who would blackmail someone? It was interesting that she obviously came from a privileged background. It made her an unlikely candidate for criminality. I couldn't see her needing the money.

She carried on speaking about herself. It was a mix of

boasting tinged with malicious comments about the other chefs. Not a pretty combination.

Behind me I sensed a change in atmosphere – something was happening. I saw Octavia's eyes narrow in dislike. I turned around.

It was Graziana.

Chapter Eighteen

Graziana noticed me and came over. 'Ciao, Charlie.' Her brown eyes were mischievous, fun-filled. She was wearing Daisy Duke shorts and a tight T-shirt with an unbuttoned plaid shirt over it and gladiator sandals. It was an outfit that looked like it had been put together for a sexy photo shoot, not for visiting a workplace.

'Oh, did you do all these tomatoes. . .' she asked me, ignoring Octavia. 'Let me take a picture. . .' She shooed us away, we weren't going to be in her photo – Octavia in case she upstaged her, me because I was too dowdy and would have let the side down. Octavia and I exchanged glances. Graziana struck a practised, pouty pose (enough of the social media pouting!) in front of the chopped tomatoes, picked up my knife, stuck out her chest some and then clicked away with her phone.

So far, so innocuous. But in the context of knowing that someone was a blackmailer and someone was probably a murderer in this kitchen, it raised disturbing questions and possibilities.

'*Grazie*,' she said. It was painfully obvious to both Octavia and me that the photo would end up on Instagram with her taking the credit and a line of text saying something like, 'Working in Matteo's kitchen, mamma mia!!!' followed by a line of emojis.

Sure enough, she selected a large, ripe tomato, tilted her head back, bit into it showing suspiciously dazzling white teeth. More clicking of phone with her free hand as the juice ran out of her mouth, down her chin onto her T-shirt in a master-class study of suggestive behaviour.

Oh well, I reflected, you can take the girl out of OnlyFans.

She binned the tomato – its use as a prop was over, it felt like a telling metaphor – and turned to me.

'. . . And it's so nice to see a fresh face in the kitchen, Charlie.' She smiled sweetly at Octavia.

'I know that Matteo is really looking forward to starting work with you on the book, as soon as he gets a free moment. He admires you so much.'

'That's great, Graziana,' I said, flushing a little. Despite knowing I wasn't working on a book with Matteo McCleish, it still felt flattering to have Graziana single me out in the kitchen. The fact it was annoying Octavia was a bit of an added bonus.

She chatted to me for a couple of minutes, resting her hand lightly on my shoulder occasionally, and laughing a lot. Her face was very mobile, quintessentially Italian, lots of gestures.

'He's really hoping that working here with his chefs will give you an idea of his. . . *come si dice* ethos, which you can put into the recipes.'

'The best of both worlds,' I said, helpfully.

'*Esatto*, Charlie.'

She pointedly ignored Octavia who, tight-lipped with irritation, concassed away with her knife – a knife which, judging by the look in her eyes, she would have been more than happy to bury in Graziana's back.

I reflected that maybe dislike of someone could be motive for blackmail, make them squirm while they prayed their secret would never come out. Octavia obviously disliked Graziana, it was a plausible motive.

Or had she maybe literally stuck a knife in Giorgio's back? He had assaulted Jess, had he tried to do the same with her? Invited her round to his flat, then pounced and she'd fought back? Or gone round there armed with revenge on her mind? That was more likely; no woman in their right mind would have willingly gone round to Giorgio's flat. With its enormous collection of porn.

Graziana said a breathy 'goodbye' to me, smiled at Octavia and moved away.

I turned back to the job in hand and allowed my mind to wander. I suddenly wondered if maybe she had a thing going with Matteo. I glanced up and Octavia glared at me. I realised that I was now labelled as a friend of Graziana, and therefore was a total bitch. A has-been old hag, and a bitch.

Furthermore, I was doing a book with Matteo. Well, not really, but Octavia didn't know that and her looks suggested that she was thinking, 'It should have been me.'

We worked away in an unpleasant silence and finished the tomatoes. We were now on to broccoli prep, three boxes of it, trimming the florets down so they had only a very small piece of stalk left. Octavia had banged the plastic tub down on the table with a crash. I made some vague remarks about cooking, trying to draw her into conversation. Stony silence.

She didn't want to talk about cooking, so I turned the conversation back to her and her university career. I wasn't interested per se, I just wanted to check that she actually had been to uni and wasn't just making it up. I was on the lookout now for deceitful women and things that were not as they seemed.

'What was your thesis on?' I asked, feigning an interest I didn't have. I felt quite proud of the question, it would put someone on the spot if they had never written one.

She didn't miss a beat. 'Mine was on the role and influence of witches in Elizabethan drama,' she said. Then she added, unpleasantly, 'I don't suppose you know much about that.'

'Maybe not,' I said, thinking of Dr John Dee and his latest iteration, the current Dr Wizard, 'but I know a lot of witches.'

Octavia looked at me like I had gone crazy. I carried on: 'If you have any queries or need any assistance, just let me know.' I smiled politely, 'I'll put in a good word for you. I'm very big in the warlock community.'

I could introduce her to Chris, they'd get on like a house on fire.

Chapter Nineteen

I finished at five, changed out of my work clothes, locked my knives away in my knife box and walked back across the fields to my restaurant, the Old Forge Café. There was a shout from behind me. I looked round, it was Murdo.

'You going to the village?' he asked.

'Yes, I'm finished for the day,' I said, 'and you?'

'Aye, I'm meeting some of they Polish boys at the pub,' he said. 'Chum you to the Green?'

'That would be nice, Murdo,' I said.

We spent the next twenty minutes chatting as we walked across the fields to where I lived. I had hoped to get Murdo's take on things but he just wanted to talk about food with Tiggerish enthusiasm and I hadn't the heart to introduce the gloomy topic of Giorgio's death.

We crossed the stile by the Green and I pointed to the Three Bells.

'The pub's over there Murdo,' I said.

'Are ye joining us Charlie?' he asked. 'A wee half and half?'

'No thanks, Murdo,' I said. I pointed to the Old Forge

Café. 'That's my place over there, I'd better check it's all OK.'

'Cool,' he remarked, looking across the Green at my restaurant. It did look pretty cool, I thought. I reflected on how much I actually liked the Old Forge Café and how proud I was of it. 'I'll have to come and eat there one day,' he said.

I smiled. I liked him. 'It'll be on the house, Murdo. . . see you tomorrow.'

'See yez,' he replied and bounded off, his long legs carrying him swiftly towards the pub.

I walked back over the manicured grass of the Green towards my restaurant considering my day and what I had achieved. I had found out Octavia disliked Graziana, and vice versa – and that on balance she probably had been to Oxford as she claimed. She was also, courtesy of her father and the bank of Mum and Dad, independently wealthy. I felt pleased with myself. It was a reasonable start to my investigation.

I got home at half past five. Sam was sitting in the afternoon sun in the little yard outside the kitchen back door.

'Hi, Charlie, how was your day?' he asked.

'It was fun, nice to be doing incredibly simple work for a change,' I laughed. 'I was on veg mostly, how was it today here?'

'It was good.' He yawned and stretched. 'We did about thirty at lunch. I think there's twenty-odd booked in for tonight.'

'Do you need a hand?' I asked.

'No, I'll be fine.' Then he said, changing the subject slightly, 'Your kp is a strong bastard isn't he?'

I nodded. 'He certainly is. What did he do to impress you?'

'We had a veg delivery and I sent him out to help. He came into the kitchen carrying two sacks of spuds, one in each hand' – he shook his head admiringly – 'like they were two little bags of flour. . . incredible!' They were 25-kilo bags.

I thought of Francis with affection tinged with pride. His weight-lifting abilities had literally saved my life in the past and they had certainly come in handy when dealing with Giorgio. As had his ability to throw a cricket ball. We chatted a bit more and then I left him to catch up on the evening prep.

I went upstairs and showered. I lay down on my bed. The sounds from the kitchen drifted up through the floor. It was nice having a break from my own menu for a bit.

I thought some more about the differences between Matteo's catering world and my own. Would I really enjoy having so many people working for me, being so reliant on others to execute my ideas?

I shut down this pointless thread of speculation. It was never going to happen anyway. I thought instead about Graziana's behaviour, the way she was kind of taunting Octavia. I wondered about that. I also wondered if Matteo made passes at his employees, or indeed vice versa. Had he had a fling with her and that's why Graziana was so nasty?

I got my phone out and went to Instagram and searched for Graziana McCleish. There she was today, she'd already posted the tomato pic to her three quarters of a million followers. How many of them would care if she'd gone nuclear naked on Per I Tifosi – the OnlyFans Italian version? I scrolled through thirty or so posts: Graziana in a bikini, Graziana naked – screening her groin with a cauliflower and her boobs with a loaf of bread, Graziana in a shower, all misted up through the glass except for her head thrown back in orgasmic ecstasy – it was all pretty much soft-core porn anyway.

Something didn't quite add up, but I wasn't sure what. A sudden thought crossed my mind, was it true? I scratched my head, but why would Matteo lie to me? Once again I remembered what Anna Bruce had said to me about deception. Was this 'Per I Tifosi' really a thing?

On a whim I texted Andrea, my ex.

'Do you happen to know anyone who works for Per I Tifosi?? xCharlie.'

'Why? Are you signing up for it?' came the reply. I blinked in surprise, he'd answered virtually immediately. And Andrea was not the kind of man who had time on his hands.

'No.' Frowny face. 'I want information from someone who works there.'

Andrea was the banker I had mentioned to Octavia, but he came from a business background in Italy. He was kind of restless by nature and had worked for quite a few companies and knew an unbelievable number of people. Not just businessmen or bankers. If you wanted to know a good restaurant in Ulaanbaatar, Andrea probably knew the sommelier. If you went to Riyadh, he'd know which Al Saud you should be talking to. You want to know the world's foremost guano expert? He'd be worth asking. Let's see how he was on porn sites.

'I'll see what I can do.' I stared at his message for a while, but that was it. So I put my phone away.

I stared at the ceiling. I didn't know what to do now. I'd forgotten how to enjoy myself when I wasn't working. Sod it, I thought, I can't stay here puzzling over Graziana. That got me thinking about Italy which made me remember my passport. Was it in date? I hadn't been abroad for several years. I got up and went to the drawer in which I kept important papers. I breathed a sigh of relief, it was there. I opened it. The terrible thumbnail photo of me looking like a mad hag stared back at me. It was still in date. I wondered why she'd told me to check. It wasn't like I'd be going to Italy to check up on the McCleishes in the near future.

I sighed. All this speculation was futile; there was only one way to drive this out of my mind. When in doubt, cook something. It had always worked for me anyway.

I pulled on a fresh pair of chef's whites and went downstairs to help Sam.

Chapter Twenty

Octavia surprised me thirty minutes into prep time. It was the following day and we were working together again when, out of nowhere:

'Who do you think killed Giorgio?' she suddenly asked. 'The police obviously interviewed us all,' she said, 'that young looking detective seems very nice. . . he tried to get my phone number, but I don't think that was in connection with Giorgio. . .' She laughed, supremely (and justifiably,) confident of her good looks and their effect on men.

The murder was the subject I had been wondering how to introduce into the conversation myself.

'Umm. . .' I said – I didn't really know what to say.

'I think it was Tom,' she said with certainty.

'Why's that then?' I asked.

'Tom's in love with Graziana,' said Octavia. 'That bitch. . .' She leaned against a fridge and pulled the cap off her head and started playing with her hair, thrusting her hips out in a parody of sexuality.

'Oooh, look at me with my two million Instagram followers. . .' 748,000, I think you'll find, I thought to myself; I had checked. But I said nothing. 'I'm Graziana McCleish and I'm going to wear a tight T-shirt with nothing on underneath. I'm freeing the capezzolo.'

'The what?' I asked.

'Capezzolo – it means "nipple",' she explained. 'Anyway,' she said, 'they spent a lot of time interviewing Tom, they obviously suspect him.'

Over her shoulder, I could see Tom advancing across the kitchen towards us.

He did not look very happy. I noticed again, as he strode towards us, that he was built like a bullock. Under that chef's jacket was a lot of muscle. His sleeves were short and his heavily tattooed arms were corded, powerful.

'Errr, Octavia. . .' I said in a warning voice accompanied by agonised face. Octavia had been in no mood to pay me any attention earlier; she was in no mood to do it now. She changed the subject anyway, unfortunately to one guaranteed to provoke a reaction in the sous.

'Graziana McCleish, what a bitch. . .'

Tom certainly overheard that. His bearded face darkened. He was obviously very cross indeed.

'That's enough from you.' The words were rapped out, staccato style. It was more than someone just annoyed that loyalty to an employer had been breached, I thought. Octavia was right; he was in love with Graziana. Octavia spun round, her face blanching. It's always terrible when someone overhears what you're saying and takes offence. It's certainly happened to me on more than one occasion and it's never good. Things cannot be unsaid. There's never a way back from something like that.

'I. . .'

I wondered what she was going to say. Tom stood there in front of her, radiating anger. He glanced down at the broccoli and picked a handful up. I thought for a moment he was going to scream at us for having done it badly, which we hadn't, but that wouldn't necessarily stop anyone who was on the warpath. The chef who is senior to you is always right – that's the way it is in a kitchen. But he just frowned, stared at the broccoli intently as if it were evidence of some crime, then shoved it under her nose menacingly. 'So, with Charlie's help you've managed to finish this then?'

Through gritted teeth, Octavia said, sullenly, 'Yes.' Her eyes were downcast. Her cheeks were burning. Waves of rage almost crackled around Tom. I stood there, embarrassed.

'Yes, what?' he demanded.

'Yes, Chef,' she said. Tom, his superior rank verified, nodded, satisfied.

'Good. Now since you're an hour ahead of yourself, you can go and clean the fridge.'

Octavia's cheeks burned a deeper red, anger taking the place of embarrassment.

'Yes, Chef,' he muttered.

'And do it properly!'

Tom glared at us both and stalked back across the kitchen, pausing only to inspect the contents of the Bratt pan, glare at the chef who was stirring it, give him a bollocking too for good measure, and then he left the kitchen, slamming the door behind him for effect.

'I'm sorry, Octavia,' I said, exhaling. I think I'd been holding my breath all this time. 'Life sucks sometimes.'

Octavia looked as if Tom had slapped her across the face. But credit where credit's due, she took it on the chin. She flashed a genuine smile at me, and her face was transformed. 'Oh well. Better get on with it I suppose.'

Octavia went off to clean the walk-in fridge, a tedious and chilly job and I was left to finish what we had been doing. It was a good time to assess Tom's role as his suitability for the role of blackmailer. I could well believe that Octavia was right and Tom was in love with Graziana. That obsession could have led him to track her down to an Italian porn site. And a lover spurned can sometimes want to inflict harm on the person who has rejected them. Or maybe he had felt if he couldn't have her, nobody should and so he would destroy Matteo. All these were possible reasons for blackmail.

Killing Giorgio though. Could that love for her have led him to kill for her, in a kind of knight in shining armour way? I thought of Giorgio's taste for hard core porn, he was obviously someone who enjoyed objectifying women. If Giorgio had hurt Graziana, and I had no doubt at all that Giorgio was a misogynist, maybe Tom had reacted against this? His powerful physique would have helped. Giorgio would have been no match for him in a fight.

I sighed. If only I had something to go on beside speculation.

The following morning, I got the opportunity to size up another member of the team. I was put on duty by Matteo, helping Attila in the dessert section.

Attila's jowly, heavily stubbled face surveyed me

mournfully. His ample frame – as befits a pastry chef he was very overweight – padded out his chef's jacket. I'd worked with another Attila before, ages ago. I believe it's quite a common name in Hungary but it inevitably made me think of Attila the Hun. Attila the Pastry Chef was not cut from the same cloth as the savage warlord who had terrorised Europe, that was for sure.

'Have you ever made tiramisu?' asked Attila, in a dejected kind of way. Across the kitchen I could see a tight-lipped Octavia surrounded by boxes of vegetables. She caught my eye and gestured with her knife at five trays of carrots and gave an eloquent shrug.

Oh, the glamour of working in a kitchen, I thought. Bet you never imagined it would be like this when you were at Oxford fantasising about fame in a kitchen in the city of the dreaming spires. And as an intern, 'working a stage' as it's called, from the French 'stagiaire', she wasn't even getting paid. I'd grown fond of Octavia in the last twenty-four hours, despite the unfortunate start, but she was still there as a potential suspect.

'No,' I said, pulling my thoughts back to Italian desserts, 'I've never made it.'

'No,' he said, gloomily, 'I guessed that. . . Is the tiramisu going in the book that you're helping Matteo with? It doesn't seem very English.'

'Ah, but it's going in the dessert section next to trifle,' I said, feeling inspired to concoct yet another plausible lie. 'They both use liquor-soaked biscuits as a base layer and build up from there – that'll be the link. You have to think laterally in this game, Attila.'

He nodded doubtfully. I was delighted with my answer, brilliant improvisation I told myself, and it struck me as a very one-size-fits-all response to what I was doing here, marrying Italian food and techniques with English ones.

We started making tiramisu. It's quite straightforward, beaten egg-whites, whipped cream, folded into mascarpone cheese and spread over a double layer of sponge fingers soaked in coffee and alcohol. Not hard.

A little while later I was tipping five litres of double cream into two and a half kilos of mascarpone (we were making a lot) in a large Hobart mixer and watching it whirl round, emulsifying.

'The cream is not traditional. . .' Attila said, mournfully, 'but Matteo says it enhances it.' He shook his head. 'I don't know. . .' He relapsed into silence.

'Where's Matteo from?' I asked Attila to tempt him into speech.

'Originally from the UK, but he grew up in a village called Monte Salvia, that's in an area called Le Marche in Italy. . . have you ever been there?'

'No,' I said. 'Have you?'

'Yes. They have a terrible bread, pane sciapo, it has no salt. . . it's awful.' He looked as if he were going to burst into tears over this.

I was wondering how best to bring up the subject of Giorgio when, like Octavia, Attila did it for me. I suppose it should have come as no surprise that the topic should be occupying their minds so much. Or maybe it was to jolt his mind off the terrible unsalted bread.

'So, which one of us do you reckon killed Giorgio?' he

said, as he separated twenty-four eggs into two enormous steel bowls.

'I don't know,' I replied. 'Who do you think did it?'

'I think the police think it was Tom, so does Octavia. . . I do not like the police,' he said, 'In Hungary, I have had experiences. . .'

I never got to hear what those experiences were. He looked over my shoulder.

'Sssh!' Attila said, 'Chef's coming over.' Like children at school we bent diligently over our tasks.

Matteo, looking implausibly handsome in his chef's whites, crossed over to us and Attila's face lapsed into its habitual melancholy state. He'd looked almost animated when talking about Giorgio.

'Hi, you two, how's it going? Mmm, tiramisu!' Then abruptly switching from Mr Genial to head chef mode, his eyes narrow and his voice staccato, he asked, 'How much are you making?'

Attila stiffened like a soldier on parade. 'Sixty to seventy portions, Chef.'

'And you're using the *savoiardi* biscuits?'

'Yes, and good espresso.'

'Layers?'

'Three, Chef.'

'Grated chocolate or cocoa powder?'

'Powder, Chef.'

Matteo nodded, satisfied, catechism over. 'Good.' He turned to me, his voice modulating to a more normal, conversational tone, 'How are you finding working with my team, Charlie?'

'Very instructive, Chef,' I said, 'I think I'm learning a lot.'

'Good,' he said, 'well, crack on.'

He turned on his heel and left us.

Attila pondered my earlier question while fitting a whisk attachment to a hand mixer.

'I don't know either,' he said thoughtfully. 'We've all talked about it. It might not even be one of us, although we all hated that bastard's guts.'

'Why did you hate him so much?' I asked. I thought, now we're getting somewhere. Attila pondered the question.

'He was a bully and that's why I couldn't stand him,' Attila said. 'He always had a go at me about being Hungarian, and my name and what shit food Hungary has. . . but it was Douglas who got the most of it.'

'Douglas?' So I had been right when I'd seen that look of scorn way back now when I had first met them.

'Yeah. One day, I'd had enough. I hit Giorgio with a ladle.' He picked up a heavy metal 250ml ladle. I've got one similar – mine's Vogue and stainless steel. His was much older. It looked like it was made of pewter or some-thing, the metal was thick, a dull silver and pitted. It was much heavier than mine. 'Then he stopped. But Douglas. . . well, he tried to. . . I don't know the word in English, he tried to make Giorgio like him, like he was his bitch.'

'Ingratiate?' I suggested.

He nodded. 'That's it. He kissed arse big time, to keep Giorgio sweet. It was horrible. Douglas must be so pleased he's dead.'

I thought about that, slowed my mixer and added sugar and nearly a litre of Marsala wine.

'Why did Matteo employ him anyway?' I asked.

Attila looked at me. 'Matteo doesn't like telling people off and I get the impression that his old brigade, this is before he got famous, were taking the piss. So he brought Giorgio in as a kind of taskmaster to frighten them, to discipline them.'

I seem to remember that was more or less my thoughts on the matter.

He started the mixer. 'Trouble is, like Frankenstein's monster, he got out of control.'

Chapter Twenty-One

As I walked across the fields to work on Saturday, I thought again about the day before with Attila and what he'd told me. That Giorgio had been a bully was unsurprising. Attila claimed that he had dealt with the problem but I only had his word for it. His namesake had conquered most of Europe, slaughtering a huge amount of people – I wondered if Attila the Pastry Chef had taken a leaf out of his book and been a bit more proactive with something a little more lethal than a ladle.

I was hoping I would be working with him again but as I walked into the kitchen Matteo came up to me.

'Good morning, Charlie. You can work with Octavia.' He paused and smiled, 'here's a bonus, I'll show you how to make a perfect *soffritto*.' He led me over to where she was preparing vegetables. Octavia put her knife down. 'Good morning, Chef,' she said to Matteo. She looked flustered at his arrival and gave him a kind of nervous smile.

He smiled warmly at her. 'I'm just going to give you a brief cookery lesson, Charlie, not that you need it,' he added hastily. 'I meant we can work it into the book, maybe a short section on cutting and dicing? Now, the *soffritto*, the holy trinity: carrots, celery and onions. In France they call it a *mirepoix*, but we're not in France and besides they nicked a lot of their cooking from us, the Italians, and claimed it as theirs. Typical French. Anyway, this is how I want it to look. . .' In a few seconds, Matteo had reduced a carrot to tiny cubes. I was very impressed. Celery and onions followed.

'That kind of size,' he instructed.

'Yes, Chef,' I said. 'How much do you want doing?'

Octavia hid a smile. She looked at Matteo adoringly. If Tom was in love with Graziana, I thought, Octavia was in love with Matteo. Matteo, oblivious – he was probably used to that kind of thing – pointed to a tower of vegetable boxes.

'That much.' My heart sank. 'Anyway, I'll be back this evening for service. I have to be in London this lunchtime. See you later.'

'OK,' I said, looking at the stack of vegetables. There was an awful lot of carrots, bushels of celery and a sack of onions.

I looked at my co-worker and pulled a face.

'Welcome to my world.' She grinned. When Octavia did that she suddenly looked about twelve, a mischievous child. It was quite a magical transformation. I wondered if this was the real her, rather than the glacial, upper-class persona that she usually put forward. Like strapping on armour to meet the world. I took a handful of carrots. 'You peel, I'll dice,' she said. I shrugged, filled a steel bowl with water, dropped the carrots into it and started work. I had seen her working the day before, and I was better with a knife than she was, but I didn't want to offend her.

Octavia raised a perfect dark-blond eyebrow, as if reading my mind. She took a carrot that I gave her.

The day before Octavia was obviously in second gear. Not so today. I had thought she wasn't very good in the kitchen, but now I was about to change my mind. She pressed her pedal to the metal. The large knife was a blur of action. VRRRRROOOOM! The carrot lay in tiny little chunks. She took a handful of the ones that Matteo had done and showed me. An exact match. She was awesomely good.

'You're much better than me,' I said, humbly. 'I'll peel faster.'

'Thank you, Charlie.'

She smiled and bent over her chopping board. Idly, I watched the polished steel of her large, very sharp chef's knife go to work.

I spent the rest of the day working with Octavia and found that, once I got to know her, she was extremely pleasant. It just went to show how prone I was to misjudging people. I guess that in the competitive, brutal work environment of the kitchen, she had evolved a protective carapace. And who could blame her? I casually introduced the topic of Giorgio into the conversation.

Octavia pulled a face at the mention of Giorgio's name.

'He tried it on with me, yeuch! And I'll tell you what's even creepier. . .' She shuddered. 'He had a partner too, that creepy Frenchman they sacked.'

'Jean-Claude!'

'Yeah, how revolting would that be, the two of them and some girl.' Octavia pulled a horrified face at the thought. 'They tried it on with every woman they could. They could exert a lot of pressure on waitresses, between the two of them.'

'Why did Matteo not get rid of Giorgio like he did Jean-Claude?' I asked, thinking of Frankenstein's monster.

'Two reasons,' said Octavia. 'Come and give me a hand with this pasta, and I'll tell you.'

We were feeding homemade pasta dough through the rollers of a pasta machine to make ravioli. Octavia fed the dough in and cranked the handle while I gathered up the long, broad ribbon of dough as the machine extruded it, about a metre in length.

'Number one,' she said as she worked the machine, 'I think Matteo was scared of him.'

'Scared of him?' I repeated. 'Why?'

'I don't know,' she said, 'but it was like he had some kind of secret or hold over him, I don't know what. Like once or twice when he'd overstepped the mark and I knew Charlotte was furious with him, he'd say something to Matteo in Italian and Matteo would take his side.'

'But you don't know what this secret was?' I said.

She shook her head. 'No. No I don't.'

Well, I thought, I do. So that brought us back to Giorgio as the blackmailer. But he was dead and the blackmail was ongoing. So he must have had an accomplice.

'And the second reason?' I asked.

'Graziana was sleeping with Giorgio.' She spoke matter of factly, just trotted this bombshell out as if commenting

133

on the quality of the pasta going through the machine for the third time as we adjusted the rollers.

'What!' I was shocked.

'She was knocking him off, the slut,' she repeated. I digested this news. Surely not! Graziana with Giorgio? He was horrible.

'Are you sure about that?' I said.

She nodded. 'Totally. I had it on very good authority. You'll never guess who it was who told me.'

She went over to the hand-wash sink and scrubbed her fingers clean.

'You're right,' I said, faintly. Talk about Beauty and the Beast. 'I'll never guess. Why don't you tell me?'

She looked at me in a kind of mocking way. 'Ok then, it was Giorgio himself. I said I didn't believe him, he said that Graziana had an intimate tattoo,' she indicated an area at the top of her groin, 'just here, of a devil with a pitch-fork, pointing, well, you know where. . .'

'Perhaps he made it up,' I said. I still couldn't believe this. How could she?

'He didn't,' she said, shaking her head. 'I've actually seen it. When Matteo won his Michelin star we went on a celebratory midweek break to a hotel that had a spa and I was with Graziana in a women only sauna. I've seen her naked. I saw the tattoo, believe me, it's real and it's not in a place that *Heat* magazine or *Grazia* would show. There's only one way he could have seen that.'

'I see,' I said. Well, there was another way it had been seen and that was on the porn website Per I Tifosi that the blackmail was about, but I couldn't say that. I fell silent while I tried to process this shocking development. What should I say to Matteo when he asked me what I had found out? I could hardly report this. We finished rolling out the pasta and put little scoops of the filling, a crab mix that Tom had made, in dollops along one ribbon, dropped the other ribbon on top, pushed them together and then cut out the ravioli with a pastry cutter.

'Did you tell the police this, when they questioned you about Giorgio?' I asked.

She shook her head. 'I don't want to get involved.'

'Someone has been murdered,' I pointed out. 'It doesn't matter how nasty they were, whether they deserved it or not. There's a killer somewhere out there, probably wandering around that kitchen. You're not safe, Octavia, if you keep secrets, none of us are.'

'It's all right for you,' she countered, 'you don't work here. I don't give a rat's arse who killed Giorgio, but I do care about my career. . .' But I could see my words were having an effect, she looked agonised, obviously in a difficult place. 'Shit, Charlie, I take your point. . . I tell you what. . .' She took a deep breath and then sighed. 'I've got some more cleaning to do now.'

'More cleaning?' I marvelled. Tom really had it in for her.

'Bloody Tom. Look, Giorgio told me some more stuff involving someone else who works here. I'll think about it while I'm cleaning and maybe I'll tell you all about it. What they were doing was illegal, and you can go to the police. But you need to promise to keep my name out of it.'

'OK, I promise.'

'Deal. I'll tell you after I've cleaned the freezer – you're back this afternoon, aren't you?'

'Yes.'

She reached under the steel prep table to the shelf below and took out a big blue hoodie.

'Isn't Tom kind,' she said, 'he lent me his hoodie so I wouldn't get too cold.'

Octavia pulled on the hoodie. It fitted lengthwise – she was as tall as he was – but it hung baggily around her. She turned around. On the back in big letters it said, 'Tom McGregor, Wessex Iron Man 2021'.

She pulled the hood over her head. 'Do I look sexy, Charlie?' she asked, grinning from under the folds of the hood. All I could see was her nose.

'You look great Octavia, ready for the ice.'

'Brrrr.' She shivered dramatically.

'At least it's not cleaning out the deep-fat fryer,' I said. That was a horrible job.

'Or degreasing the extractor filters,' she said, smiling at me.

I smiled back and nodded. That was probably worse than the deep-fat fryer. Any form of kitchen cleaning involving the stove, the oven, or the fans was pretty grim. It made washing dishes or pots and pans look like a truly pleasant chore. I felt we were bonding over the horrors of kitchen cleaning. The freezer was grim mainly because it was so bitterly cold.

'Well, better get on with it. Tom's gone out, got to meet a supplier he said. Bet I know what kind of supplier it is too.' She sniffed loudly, tapped her nose and winked. 'I'll talk to you later. Ciao, Charlie.' She disappeared inside the freezer. At least it was much smaller than the walk-in fridge, it wouldn't take too long to clean. There was enough room inside for two people standing side by side, and three of its walls were covered with steel shelving. It was going to be cold in there, about minus eighteen degrees.

She was going to need that hoodie.

Chapter Twenty-Two

At the far side of the kitchen I caught sight of Charlotte and Douglas. Douglas had his clipboard and the inevitable lap-top and looked harassed as ever. Charlotte had a steely air about her as she marched around, peering into pans and questioning people. I waved a hello and walked away to get changed.

There was only one shared changing room for men and women. This had been created for the catering staff who worked in the kitchen when the house hosted a wedding. Out of curiosity I had looked up the cost of a wedding at the Earl's house. The basic package started at about ten thousand. I thought of my own situation, I seemed unlikely to be walking down the aisle any time soon, if ever. On the plus side, think of all that money I was saving.

I wasn't keen on the idea of some chef wandering in when I was in my underwear so I'd spoken to Bryony and she had provided a kind of folding screen from a bedroom in the house to preserve my modesty. It was Victorian and looked somewhat out of place in this small room which was like a gym changing room with wire lockers for clothes and bench seating. The screen was an antique and I hoped that someone wasn't going to nick it. There's a lot of thefts in a kitchen, it's why fridges and freezers often have locks (mind you, blackmail was a first for me). There was a shower in one corner and a couple of toilet cubicles. Again, provided for the caterers to avoid having them wandering around the main part of the house.

I disappeared behind the screen with its William Morris floral design. As I did so, kicking off my boots and pulling off my whites in the cramped space, I heard the door to the changing room open. Wondering who it was, I put my eye to the crack where two panels met and gazed out.

It was Murdo.

He looked around him in a kind of furtive way, obviously checking he was alone. Then he walked over to one of the metal mesh lockers. They were made of criss-crossed strands of steel so you could see the contents inside. Every locker had a hasp for a padlock, everyone had padlocked theirs, myself included. Most chefs have a padlock with them to secure their knife boxes. I could see a collection of these secured inside the lockers. Murdo glanced around again to make sure he was alone, put his hand in his pocket, crouched and produced a sliver of metal which he slipped into the padlock of the locker that belonged to Attila. I knew it was Attila's, I could see the Panama hat that he habitually wore to protect his bald spot when he wandered around the garden during the break on his split.

I shook my head sadly, I would never have put Murdo down as a thief.

The kid worked the pick, frowning in concentration and

then nodded to himself satisfied as he felt the lock give way beneath his questing probe. His back was to me, and I saw him reach his hand inside the locker. I walked out from behind the screen and stood behind him making no sound on my bare feet.

'What do you think you're doing!' I said, quietly with an air of menace. I was angry and disappointed in equal measure. I also felt betrayed. I'd liked him!

Murdo jumped out of his skin, turned round, saw me in my underwear standing behind him, arms folded, did a double take and blushed a fiery red, one hand still in the locker in Attila's jacket pocket.

'I'm. . . just. . .' he mumbled.

'I can see what you're doing,' I said, coldly. 'Replace that lock and wait outside. I'll be out after I've changed.' I shook my head sadly. ' You've got some explaining to do, young man.'

'I owe money,' he said, miserably. We were standing on an ornamental Japanese style bridge in the Earl's garden over a pond stocked with koi. Murdo was leaning over the balustrade, hands clasped together, head hung low, staring at the water. Gigantic orange and red fish moved beneath the surface.

'For drugs?' I asked. It seemed kind of obvious. A nod of the head.

'Some dealer guy from London, not my usual supplier.' As if that made any difference. 'I owed him for some coke and then he disappeared. I found out later that he'd been out on licence but broke the conditions of his release and got sent down again.' He smiled ruefully. 'So I thought, well, that's that, I won't need to repay him.'

'How'd he find you, from inside?' I asked.

'He got some bikers to threaten me, some woman Hells Angel.' He turned and pulled his T-shirt up, his chest was a riot of blue, purple and yellow bruising.

'A woman did that!' I marvelled. Not that Murdo would have put up much of a fight, he was a sort of lanky beanpole. I should have been pleased that the Angels had become equal opportunity, but I wasn't sure that women enforcers were a step forward in the battle for equal rights.

'Aye, I've got to pay her the day after tomorrow, ken. . . in full. Or else.'

'So you thought you'd nick it from your co-workers?'

'I was desperate, I know how to pick a lock. . .' he gave a quick grin, a flash of his former self, 'lot of that where I grew up, ken. . . so. . .'

I shook my head sadly. Then I did something I suspected I would regret.

'How much do you owe, Murdo?'

'A grand.'

'Ok, I'll lend you the money, interest free. You can pay me off in stages.'

He looked at me in awe.

'You'd do that for me!'

I nodded. I cursed my overly soft heart. I very much doubted I would see that money again. Lending money to a drug addict is hardly a wise investment. But Murdo had stirred up weirdly protective feelings in me. Sod it, I thought, Matteo's paying me well. Let's share the joy.

'Thank you so much!' His face was radiant. 'You're awesome.'

'I know,' I said. Stupid, more like. No point telling him to give up drugs. 'Just promise me you won't go stealing again.'

'I promise.'

'Right, I'll see you later,' I said.

'Are you finished for the day?' he asked.

'No, I'm going to go back to my own restaurant, I'll be back here this afternoon. You can get in touch with the dealer and tell him you've got the money. Meanwhile, try and stay out of trouble, Murdo.'

'I will, promise.'

Hmmm, I thought.

I walked away leaving him on the bridge contemplating the carp.

Chapter Twenty-Three

As I walked back across the fields to Hampden Green, I reflected it had been quite a day so far. As well as the Murdo drama, I'd certainly been given a lot to think about.

Were Giorgio and Graziana really having an affair? I found that incredibly hard to believe. But just because I found someone repellent, didn't mean everyone would feel the same way. Look at Chris, some poor woman had married him, and one with a responsible and well-paid office job. People make mystifying choices. Or had Giorgio some hold over her that only his death could break?

Of course, I knew, but Octavia didn't, that Graziana's antics doing whatever she had done on Per I Tifosi would have led to this tattoo in the most intimate of places being fully visible.

Had Matteo been afraid of Giorgio? Was he a monster whom he had employed, allowed to flourish, who had subsequently got out of control, as Attila had suggested, and needed to be destroyed? Had jealousy led Matteo to kill him?

Had Jean-Claude's involvement with Giorgio's sex life

spilled over into violence, jealousy? What they were up to was very twisted – it could easily have mutated into something even darker and more uncontrollable.

I was also mindful of Anna Bruce's statement that someone was spreading, how had she put it, 'a web of delusion'. I only had Matteo's word for it that he was being blackmailed over Graziana's past. What if there was something else on the menu that he hadn't told me about?

Another man maybe? That wouldn't go down too well with the fans of *Nonna's Kitchen*. Was that what had brought him to England in the first place, a failed gay relationship? Or maybe because he had (shades of Bronski Beat's 'Smalltown Boy') run away from the village in Italy because of his sexuality?

Stop it, I told myself sternly as I wandered into this psychodrama of entirely my own imagination, stick to known facts.

Matteo was being blackmailed – this was for sure.

Someone had murdered Giorgio. This was for sure.

Giorgio somehow had intimate knowledge of Graziana's body. This was for sure. Either through an affair (according to Octavia) or via images of Per I Tifosi, the porn website, making him the likely blackmailer.

Whether or not Giorgio had been involved, the blackmailer was still out there, and a member of Matteo's team.

As I climbed over a stile and crossed another field I remembered that I had asked Andrea if he knew anyone connected to Per I Tifosi. I took my phone out and realised immediately that out here in the fields there was no network coverage. I put the phone back in my pocket.

I shrugged to myself. Well, at least I would have something to give to Slattery if it was needed, even if it was hearsay.

Just a couple of weeks ago I'd thought that Matteo's life must have been perfect and that working in a celebrity chef's kitchen would be a pleasant little holiday.

How wrong could you get.

Chapter Twenty-Four

As I approached the village, coverage restored, the phone in my pocket vibrated and I pulled it out. I smiled. Talk of the devil. It was a message from my ex. Andrea did know someone who worked for Per I Tifosi. They had recently been bought by a venture capital company, the finance director was a friend of his. What did I want to know?

I leaned against a three-barred wooden fence by a horse field and texted that I wanted to know about Graziana McCleish. He replied, The Graziana McCleish? Yes, I wrote, she did a stint 'modelling' for them. She might be listed under her own name or her work name which was Gemma Moravia. Could he find out more about her work for them. I'll look into it he replied. Thanks.

I put my phone away and carried on home. I loved walking this way to Hampden Green. There was a slight ridge to one of the fields, like an escarpment, and you could look down on the village from above, with its roofs and red-brick houses all centred around the village green, like wagons drawn up around a campfire. It looked like an illustration from a Ladybird Book, like *Life in the*

Countryside. You would never know that it contained things like murder, sexual jealousy, violence and drugs. It looked too peaceful and idyllic.

I walked across the common, past the playground where several young mums were with their toddlers. A couple of them waved at me. I was well known in the village.

I walked through the gate into the kitchen yard past the bins and opened the kitchen door. It was half past one. The height of service. I automatically looked at the row of cheques lined up above the pass.

I guessed that Sam, the agency chef, was cooking for about twenty-five. I could see the signs of a well-run kitchen. It was tidy, there was no trace of panic, even Francis looked alert and in control. I watched as he put out some pâté without burning the toasted brioche, which for him was quite the achievement, and a bisque without sloshing it everywhere.

I was impressed.

I walked in and chatted to the two of them, watching as Sam sent out a duck breast with cherry sauce, wilted spinach and Hasselback potatoes, and a hake with red pepper relish. Both were exemplary.

I thanked them both and went upstairs. Ten minutes later, Jess joined me.

She looked calm and collected in the restaurant uniform of white blouse, black trousers, white apron. Everything was going smoothly without me. I felt a twinge of disappointment; everyone likes to feel that work would collapse without them being around, this was evidently not the case.

'It's all fine here,' she said. 'Oh, by the way, your friend

Cliff said he'd pop in to see you later if you were around.'
I smiled at the thought. Cliff had been my father's best
friend. He was actually my godfather, and like the fictional
Godfather, was, or rather had been, involved in organised
crime. Now he was legally engaged in the 'security' trade,
that is, bouncing.

Jess carried on. 'He said he'd text. I wasn't sure when
you'd be finished. How's life in the celebrity fast lane?'

'Oh, fine,' I said, noncommittally. 'Good old Uncle Cliff's
coming, better get in some lager then.'

She listened while I told her of my day, laughed at the
thought of my endless veg prep.

'Octavia sounds quite a character,' she said.

'She is, Jess,' I said, 'you should meet her.' I was sure
that they would get on. 'I think she must be terribly lonely
in that kitchen, even though it's so full of people. She's
very bright' – I'd forgiven her the looking down her nose
at me thing, it wasn't her fault I was a hundred years old
and ill-educated – 'and quite a good chef.'

'Well, invite her over here on her day off, give her lunch.
Perhaps you should offer her a job?' suggested Jess.

I smiled at the idea.

'Anyway,' I said, 'enough of me, what have you been
up to?'

'I'll give you the potted version. Katie downstairs is OK
for five minutes,' she was the other waitress, good, but nowhere in Jess's league, 'but she'll need a hand after that. . .'

Jess filled me in then went back to work and I dozed on
my bed for half an hour, before I got up, showered and
went downstairs.

148

Service was over for lunch and everyone had disappeared for the afternoon until they were due back at half five. I wandered around the empty dining room and checked the kitchen. Sam had left it spotless. The oven was still on at its lowest setting, door fractionally ajar. I looked in. He'd been making meringues, and they were drying out on baking trays, twenty neatly piped shapes nestling on their silicone mats.

They looked good.

I let myself out, locking the door behind me, and made my way across the road.

I reached the end of the common and opened the small gate that led into the grass field that was the first of two that lay between the house and the village.

Jess's idea had planted a seed.

I could actually offer Octavia a job. I liked her; she had the potential to be a really good chef. Right now, she was doing all the lowly stuff, but at the Old Forge Café she'd be cooking mains, she could put her own dishes on the menu.

Yes, I thought, it would be good to have someone young with young ideas to balance things out. I'd ask her when all this was over.

As I walked back across the field that had horses in, I heard a massive roaring noise from above. It was deafeningly loud and for a moment I didn't realise what was happening. Then like a gigantic wasp, a helicopter rose from above the row of trees that screened my view of the Earl's property.

It was something from *Apocalypse Now*. The helicopter

was enormous and seemed to fill the sky, as its rotor blades whumpfed around and the engine noise shattered the peaceful Bucks summer air. The machine was huge and yellow, hanging there like a portent of doom. At first I thought it must belong to some famous person visiting the opera site, helicoptered in rather than being driven, but at that moment I heard sirens and saw the flash of blue lights on the road near the house.

It was then that I realised I was looking at the air ambulance. I knew that there was such a thing, but I'd never seen it. Well, I had now, and it was disappearing fast northwest in the direction, I assumed, of the hospital at Stoke Mandeville.

I wondered what had happened.

I didn't have to wait long before I found out.

Chapter Twenty-Five

I walked up the driveway to the gates of the house. It was long and tarmacked and lined with majestic horse chestnut trees.. There were now two uniformed police standing in the drive by the pillars of the gates to block any entrance.

'I'm sorry, Madam, you can't go in right now,' one of them said.

'I work here,' I said. 'What's happening?'

Behind them I could see the signs of frantic activity. Policemen moved purposefully around, and I could see the white-jacketed kitchen staff in a small huddle. Occasionally someone would break into a run or another vehicle would arrive at the other entrance to the house, from the back road that ran from Hampden Green to the next village, Frampton End.

'There's been an incident, Madam.'

'You don't say!' was what I felt like saying, but sensibly I didn't.

'OK,' was what I did say, then I saw DI Slattery walking from a car towards the house, his face set in its habitual slightly angry look.

'DI Slattery,' I shouted.

He stopped in his tracks, looked in my direction and walked over to where I was standing. As he came purposefully towards me I was struck again by how intimidating Slattery could be. He was a very powerfully built man – right now he looked like he could burst through a wall should he so desire. The uniforms, quite literally, took a backwards step out of respect for the alpha male that was the DI.

'Let her through,' he ordered. They nodded, and I walked in and up to Slattery. You could almost feel the aura of strength and force that surrounded him. It was quite comforting. I looked around. The peaceful forecourt of the house was peaceful no longer. There were three police cars parked in the drive and an unmarked transit van with wide-open back doors and shelving inside. Next to this were a couple of white-suited individuals. 'Forensics and Scene of Crime,' said Slattery, jerking his head in their general direction.

That much I could work out for myself. What crime? was the thing I was wondering.

'So, what on earth is going on, DI Slattery?' I asked.

He looked at me. 'Someone locked Octavia Masters in the freezer.' So that explained the air ambulance.

'Oh my God, is she OK?' I said, in alarm.

Slattery shook his head. 'She's far from OK, that's why the air ambulance was here. We're treating it as attempted murder.' He looked at me somewhat angrily. 'Do you have anything remotely helpful to tell me about it, Ms Hunter?'

I could see that my earlier rebuff to him still rankled. I

suspected he knew that I was withholding something from him and he resented it. I couldn't tell him about the black-mail on Matteo but I felt that the least I could do was to assist him with his investigation into Octavia's attacker.

'I was working with her this morning.' I felt quite shocked, but tried to pull myself together and filled Slattery in with the times and details. I also told him of Octavia's theory that Graziana and Giorgio were having an affair. His scowl softened – I was being useful for once. He nodded as he wrote down what I had to say, including my theory that Octavia was in love with Matteo and that Tom was in love with Graziana.

'Thank you, Charlie,' said Slattery, using my first name to signify he was satisfied that I appeared to be cooperating at last.

'So what exactly happened with Octavia?' I asked.

Slattery gave me a measured look. In the background I could see a general diminution of activity. Two of the police cars drove slowly past, their occupants acknowledging Slattery as they went by. The forensics team were starting to pack up.

'She was found by that kid, Murdo,' he said. 'I don't know if you noticed but the freezer door has a hasp on it for a padlock. She must have been in there cleaning and someone clamped a lock on it. There was no way she could get out.'

I think it was only then that the enormity of what had happened to her began to sink in.

I shook my head slowly at Octavia's grim fate. I have spent a considerable amount of time cleaning freezers, and working at minus eighteen degrees centigrade is pretty hellish at the best of times, and when the door was pushed shut, the light would go out and you'd be alone in the freezing darkness. That would be bad enough. But to feel yourself getting colder and colder, hope slowly dying that someone would come. . . I could easily imagine how terrifying that must have been.

At first, you'd think it was an unpleasant practical joke of the sort that I've seen played in kitchens. You'd bang on the door, assuming that whoever it was on the other side leaning with their weight against it, would relent. But then it would begin to dawn on you that no, it wasn't a joke, and anger would turn to panic.

The growing cold, the uncontrollable shivering. The terrible realisation that you were in very serious trouble. And the other dreadful thing was the freezer was virtually soundproof, a double metal skin filled with insulation. Nobody would hear your frantic banging.

'At first Murdo didn't realise that she was in there. He'd gone to the freezer to get some coley that was to be defrosted for the musicians' dinner. There was an afternoon rehearsal. . . Anyway, when he found it was locked he went to find Tom to get the key and that's when alarm bells rang.'

'My God,' I said, 'how long was she in there?'

'Long enough to put her in a coma.'

A coma! I had really misjudged this. I'd been thinking she was just very cold and very shaken, not that she was in any mortal danger. I suppose the fact that the air ambulance had been called out should have alerted me.

'How is she. . . she will survive, won't she?' I asked.

Slattery shrugged. 'I honestly don't know.'

'What happens now?'

'Well,' Slattery said, 'currently the kitchen is still a crime scene, but tomorrow it can probably reopen. There's not a great deal forensics can do. Realistically we're not going to get anything useful. I'm the investigating officer and I think it's pretty obvious it was someone she worked with – I can't believe a total stranger walked in and did it – so just about everyone could have left prints or hairs or DNA and have a good explanation. We'll see.'

'Well, thank you,' I said. I felt slightly shell-shocked.

Giorgio's death was one thing. Aside from the fact I couldn't stand him, he was the kind of person you could imagine something bad happening to. That he had come to an unfortunately early end would come as no huge surprise to anyone who had met him. But Octavia was a young woman who just five or six years earlier would have been going to her first school prom. Giorgio may not have deserved to die, but Octavia certainly didn't. This was now beginning to feel personal. I liked Octavia.

Slattery pointed to the chefs who were standing in a group in their white jackets, like a gaggle of slightly lost geese. 'You be careful. One of them is an attempted murderer,' his eyes narrowed, 'let's pray it doesn't become a murder.'

He turned on his heel and walked back towards the house.

Chapter Twenty-Six

'Octavia!' Matteo exclaimed, shocked. 'I still simply can't believe it – I mean, why? What had she done to anyone?'

We were in the Old Vicarage. Graziana was sitting on the sofa, her long legs in ripped jeans tucked underneath her. She was wearing a multi-coloured silk shirt and a worried expression. She said something to Matteo in Italian and pushed her raven-black hair away from her face.

'I can't help it,' he said. 'I am upset.' I guess he was feeling responsible. Someone in his team had tried to kill Octavia. It was a fair bet to assume that they had also killed Giorgio. It was a highly worrying development. Any doubts that the blackmailer might have been the killer had now vanished. And, of course, if two members of a team are killed, aside from who did it, the inevitable question is: Who's next? Matteo sat down on the sofa next to Graziana and ran a hand through his long hair. He looked stricken. Graziana patted his hand. 'Perhaps he didn't try to kill her, maybe it was a . . . *birichinata come si dice*. . .' she said.

'A prank!' Matteo snorted. 'I really don't think so. I don't know how much more of this I can take,' he said. 'One of the brigade is a murderer. I just can't believe it. Who the hell can it be?'

The large room with its enormous desk, with its chrome toy and the old-fashioned intercom with its switches and glowing buttons, and the deep shag-pile carpet and black-and-gold wallpaper was maybe the ideal setting in which to emote about a murdered colleague and friend. Redolent of shady goings-on, its four walls and attendant nude portraits must have heard a lot of bad news over the years.

Matteo, in his grief, was even better-looking than usual. Sadness suited him. He had soulful eyes. I wondered again if Octavia had been having an affair with him. And if she had. . . Could she have been blackmailing him? Trying to drive a wedge between husband and wife? Maybe she was going to tell Graziana? Had she declared her intention to do so? Could it have been Matteo himself who had casually slipped that padlock onto the freezer door? I found myself looking at Matteo with suspicion. Giorgio's death, motive: sexual jealousy and dented pride. The attempt on Octavia's life could have been the result of a threat to reveal all. Blackmail? A lovers' row that escalated? Working for Matteo was not the easy stroll in the park it had initially promised to be. The trouble was, I had started to care. It wasn't just a money-making exercise anymore.

I looked again at Graziana. Once again the thought came to me. She couldn't have been having an affair with Giorgio. . . could she? I could, of course, well believe it of Giorgio, even though the sack would have been the inevitable result of discovery. The thing was, kitchens, as I well knew, were hot-beds of sexual activity. But she wouldn't have chosen Giorgio, surely to God.

'I don't know if I want to do this opera thing anymore,' he said miserably. 'It's like this village is cursed.'

Charlotte, the fourth person in the room, stood up and perched on the arm of the sofa, ruffling his hair affectionately. 'We can't pull out now, darling,' she said. It was obvious from her tone she was having none of this. There was steel in her voice.

'I've been speaking to Earl Hampden,' she added. 'He says that while he can sympathise with how upset we are, it's too late now to get new caterers in. If we cancel we're in breach of contract and I'm afraid that will cost us a huge amount of money.'

'Surely he wouldn't be so hard-hearted, would he?' Matteo looked at me beseechingly. 'What do you think, Charlie? You know him.'

I hated being the bearer of bad news but I had no choice.

'I'm afraid the Earl is not full of the milk of human kindness, Matteo. He'll take you to the cleaners if he can. He needs the money the opera will bring in.'

'But he doesn't need the money,' Matteo said angrily.

'He doesn't,' I explained, 'but the orangutans of Sumatra do.'

'What!' Matteo looked confused. 'What have monkeys got to do with it?'

'Orangutans aren't monkeys, they're apes,' I said, a trifle smugly. Bryony had explained the difference to me one evening when I'd bumped into her in the pub. She had snapped out of her cannabis stupor long enough to give a remarkable precis of the orangutan situation, complete with photos on her phone. It had made me rethink her relationship to the Earl. I had put her down purely and simply as a gold-digger but Bryony seemed weirdly clued up on ecological facts and figures. I now believed that she genuinely shared the Earl's eco-passions. Whichever way you looked at it, the future was bleak for these lovely creatures.

'Whatever,' said Matteo.

'He's funding a rescue centre out there for orphan orangutans,' I explained. 'That's where his sympathies lie. There are only about fifty-five thousand of them left in the world, they're on the brink of extinction, or at least on the threatened species list.'

Bryony had further told me that the opera's profits were headed that way. Hard-hearted as the Earl was where people were concerned – he simply didn't, on the whole, like them – he was passionate about animal welfare.

'We chefs aren't endangered,' I added helpfully, if not tactfully.

Well, I thought, in general that was true, but Matteo's kitchen team was looking pretty fragile right now. One down, one injured in hospital.

'There's a lot riding on this, Matteo,' said Charlotte in a warning tone. 'And what with the ongoing problems with the blackmail – we need all the money we can get.'

'Maybe the blackmail demands will stop with these deaths?' Graziana said hopefully. 'It can't go on indefinitely. I mean, for their sake as much as anything, they could get caught!'

'I was hoping to get a better handle on the blackmailer from Octavia,' I said. 'I guess it will have to wait.'

'Sod it,' said Matteo. 'So I suppose I'll just have to turn up tomorrow, cook and get on with it.'

'Not tomorrow morning,' said Charlotte. 'The police have said they're not going to release the kitchen until lunchtime and there are a few more statements that they need to take.'

Silence fell.

'The killer is a matter for the police, Matteo,' she said, 'pure and simple. I don't believe it has anything to do with the blackmail. Giorgio was probably killed by a jealous lover. You are not in any way responsible, and until we know otherwise, none of the team are murderers. Let's just concentrate on what concerns us, blackmail.'

'I think you'd better go,' Matteo finally said, 'both of you. I'm sorry, we're all over-stressed, first the blackmail and now this. . . I think if I'd known this was going to be the price of success I'd never have bothered. I feel like jacking it all in, and so does Graziana.'

Charlotte nodded sympathetically. 'Chin up, Matteo – things will improve. You'll see. I'll be round tomorrow.' She stood up briskly. Once she had made up her mind she acted on it.

'These things have a habit of sorting themselves out. Things will look better in the morning.' She turned to me. 'Come on, I'll give you a lift.'

It wasn't an offer. And Charlotte was not the kind of woman you said no to.

Ten minutes later we were sitting in the Three Bells.

Malcolm, the landlord, didn't seem to have moved from the spot where he had been standing the last time that I had seen him.

'Good evening, Charlie,' whispered Malcolm in his voice from beyond the grave, 'usual?'

I carried my Coke and Charlotte's white wine over to her table. She was looking around her with barely concealed horror. Pubs like this were not, I guessed, her natural habitat. I'd never set foot inside the Groucho but I doubted it looked anything like the Three Bells.

I imagine the stained and scuffed carpet, the threadbare flock wallpaper, the dartboard set in its pock-marked wooden frame and the scratched pool table were not to her taste. Perhaps she was more of a snooker woman. She took a sip of her white wine and shuddered.

'God, that's awful.' She ran her eyes once more in disbelief over the bar. 'And this is your local? You actually choose to come here!' she said incredulously.

I found myself getting a bit nettled by Charlotte's dissing of the Three Bells. I discovered myself in the unlikely role of apologist for the place.

'Oh, it's not that bad. . .' I said. Basically, I was adopting the Village Position on things. Yes, it was a dump, but it was our dump, and it wasn't the place of outsiders to criticise.

'Where do you live?' I asked, changing the subject.

'Hampstead,' she replied.

'Oh well, then. . .' Hampstead, enough said.

Perhaps I could offer her some pork scratchings? Did they have those in Hampstead? Probably not, or if they did it would be Iberico something or other. Or Guanciale.

'Matteo seemed very down,' I said. 'Was he being serious about giving up?'

Charlotte rolled her eyes. 'It's not just the opera. Graziana's been on at Matteo for a while to give it all up. Go back to Italy, turn his back on success, blah blah.' She drank some more wine and pulled a face.

'Really?' I was amazed. 'But he's worked so hard. . .'

'*He's* worked so hard!' Charlotte's face was transformed. Usually she looked icily in control, but in that moment she looked ferociously angry. Her eyes blazed behind her thick glasses. 'Less of the "he"! If you knew the amount of work I've sunk into getting him where he is. . .'

She really was livid. I knew she had a temper, but this was volcanic. For a moment I actually felt scared.

'Do I get any appreciation? No, I sodding well don't. . .'

'OK, I'm sorry,' I said. She took a deep breath, smiled wanly, took a sip of her wine and pulled a face again.

'So. . .' Charlotte settled down to business, 'Matteo's not the only one feeling the strain, most of it devolves on me.' She looked around the pub contemptuously. 'At least it's quiet in here. Now,' that brisk tone again, 'do you have any ideas yet about who our blackmailer might be?'

I frowned. 'Surely that's the least of everyone's worries?'

'How do you mean?' said Charlotte.

'I mean there's been one murder and one attempted murder connected with the blackmail – isn't that far worse than Matteo standing to be revealed as someone whose wife appeared in the altogether on some website way back when. . .?'

162

She looked genuinely puzzled. 'To be honest, I don't give a monkey's if the entire brigade dies. Besides,' she said briskly, 'I'm far from convinced that the blackmail and the murder of Giorgio are necessarily linked. It could easily be an enraged husband or boyfriend. Giorgio had a lot of enemies. To know him was to hate him.'

Well, I could hardly disagree with the last sentence. I didn't want to argue with her in case she lost her temper again. She carried on: 'None of that is any concern of mine. They're replaceable. Matteo isn't.' She took another sip of wine. She must have still been angry, she forgot to wince. She looked me in the eye. 'Look, Charlie, I was in the Army Legal Service for five years after uni, and then the CPS for a bit before I got involved in show biz as an agent's lawyer then I became an agent. I learned there how to make hard decisions. I didn't shy away from them then, I don't shy away from them now. Let me repeat my point from a moment ago. I don't think you quite realise the amount of effort that I've put in to make Matteo what he is today,' she said.

I had forgotten that she'd been in the army. It explained a lot really. Charlotte was quite a hard-ass.

'Did you "make him"?' I asked. I was a trifle surprised. I was under the impression that Matteo had got where he was by virtue of being a very good chef.

'God, yes, of course I did,' she said impatiently. 'How many chefs are there in this country and how many are famous? Lots of chefs, lots of very good chefs too – but face it, just a handful are household names.' She pushed some of her long brown hair out of her face.

'I took a scruffy non-entity chef – cooking so-so Italian food in a dump in Kings Cross, which was a real dump at the time, and made him a star.' She pointed an accusing forefinger at me as if I were doubting her transformative ability.

'Where would he be without me? Nowhere. That's where. Working sixty-hour weeks for forty thousand max, with a fortnight's holiday per annum.'

'Oh,' I said. Well, that was the cream of the catering profession put firmly in their place. Charlotte continued animatedly.

'I'm an agent and a manager. I spot talent and I nurture it.' Her anger had returned. Her cheeks had reddened, two crimson spots of rage, and she took a big swig of wine, her knuckles white on the stem of the glass, and grimaced. 'Matteo McCleish represents five years of my life, five years of hard work, and I am not going to have someone destroy it – is that clear?'

'Absolutely,' I said, in a placatory kind of way.

'Now, think, Charlie.' She sat back in her chair. 'You've met his team. Who is the blackmailer?' She tapped the table sharply with the fingernails of her right hand to emphasise the three syllables of blackmailer.

I asked by way of reply, 'Jean-Claude, I'm assuming you got rid of him?'

She nodded and went on to confirm what I had suspected. Fed up of his continual harassment of the female staff, Jean-Claude and Giorgio egging each other on, she had made him leave, sweetening the pill with a pay-off and a glowing reference. She carried on: 'I didn't know he was down here though. It came as quite a surprise when he turned up that day at Matteo's.'

'And when did the first blackmail demand come?' I asked.

She nodded, beginning to see what I was getting at. 'It was round about the time that we got rid of him. . . That will be a useful angle for you to look into.'

'Any other comments on Matteo's team?' I asked.

'There's a great deal wrong with that brigade,' said Charlotte decisively. 'They're very anti-women. I mean, there was Giorgio who made a point of chasing married women or ones with partners. I don't think it was just sex; I think he liked the idea of their husbands or boyfriends suffering. We had one occasion when a waiter tried to attack him because Giorgio had slept with his girlfriend. The waiter would never have known except for Giorgio bragging about it in the middle of service one night, making sure he was overheard. There was a dreadful scene.'

I said carefully, watching her face to see how she would react, 'Octavia said he was having an affair with Graziana.'

'That's utter bollocks,' she said definitively. 'I don't believe a word of that.' Charlotte's rebuttal was very quick. Maybe suspiciously so. She'd say anything to protect her precious asset, Matteo. But God, I hoped she was right.

'Now someone in that kitchen team has obviously got it in for Matteo,' she said. 'It wasn't Giorgio, it probably wasn't Octavia, and that leaves Murdo, Tom or Jean-Claude.' She frowned. 'I need to know who the snake in the grass is.'

'What about Attila or Douglas?'

'Don't be ridiculous. . .' She dismissed the Hungarian and her assistant out of hand. 'Douglas wouldn't say boo to a goose, he's got no balls, and Attila's got as much backbone as a panna cotta.'

I wasn't so sure about that, he had attacked Giorgio after all. But I held my tongue.

'But what would you do even if you found out who the blackmailer was?' I wondered out loud. 'If what you say is true, and the British public would fall out of love with Matteo if they knew there was some sort of sex scandal surrounding Graziana and she lost all her followers, how are you going to stop them going public?'

She pushed her glasses up onto the bridge of her nose. 'You can go to prison for several years for blackmail – that's my trump card. People who blackmail are cowards. They wouldn't want that. I would get them to sign a notarised, witnessed confession and hold off on pressing charges, so in the event they were prosecuted they would go to jail.'

'I see,' I said.

She stood up. Despite her lack of stature, she was a commanding presence. And she obviously was extremely good at her job. Perhaps I should ask her to run my business affairs, I thought.

'Let's hope you find out who did it soon, Charlie.' She made it sound like a threat. She didn't say 'or else' but it was implied.

She turned and left the pub.

Chapter Twenty-Seven

I watched Charlotte leave and thoughtfully drank some Coke. I was acutely conscious that I had failed completely in my job to track down the rotten apple in Matteo's kitchen. With Octavia I felt somehow had come tantalisingly close, but no cigar.

The door of the pub opened and I looked up. A big, fat powerfully-built man in his sixties with a bad comb-over was now walking across the pub towards me.

'Charlie!'

'Cliff!'

We embraced and I was crushed into his huge chest by his massive power-lifter's arms.

'You're looking good,' said Cliff. He pulled out a chair and sat down, the chair groaning under his ample form. 'Mine's a pint of lager, since you ask – no, make that two.'

I fetched him his drinks. He put one of the pints to his mouth, his meaty, tattooed fingers obscuring most of the glass, and tipped it back, before he put it down empty. He was wearing his bouncer clothes: tight, black, satin bomber jacket, his huge arms straining the fabric, cheap white shirt

167

and a clip-on black tie. His gut swelled proudly, heraldically over his black trousers. His eyes were good-natured slits in his jowly features.

'What brings you over here, Cliff?'

'Had a row with the missus, she flung me out.'

I nodded my head sympathetically. Cliff's relationship with Mrs Cliff could best be described as stormy.

'Can I stay at your gaff tonight?'

I could sympathise with Cliff's wife. He could be hard work at times. But I had known Cliff all my life and he had ridden to my rescue on numerous occasions, my very own Sir Galahad. Maybe a Sir Galahad who'd let himself go a bit; he'd no longer fit the armour. I didn't care, I was very fond of him.

'Of course you can!'

'Top man.' Really? I thought. Surely not. He drained half of his second pint. 'I'll get them in. What are you having?'

'Diet Coke. I hope you're not driving Cliff?'

Cliff shook his head. 'Nah, got my trainee in the car.'

I watched him walk to the bar, his pink scalp shining under the few hairs that he had lovingly combed over his head. He returned with our drinks.

'So, wot you bin up to?' I told him about the Matteo business, leaving out the blackmail. He clucked sympathetically as I told him about Octavia (he'd had no compassion for Giorgio) and then I mentioned the encounter with Murdo and his being beaten up by a woman biker. He nodded.

'Sounds like one of Satan's Sluts.'

'It does indeed,' I said, 'she's probably not a churchgoer, that's for sure.'

'No, Charlie,' he shook his head, 'Satan's Sluts were a thing. There was this woman biker group from North London called that, then they got into some kind of political argy bargy with the Hells Angels – you know how cliquey that lot are – and the group split up and I know that half of them joined the North Bucks Angels. They do quite a bit of dealing round here, we have problems with them sometimes in Wycombe and Slough, as well as Aylesbury so, yeah. I've met a couple of them. . .' he pulled a face. 'They won't be featuring on Love Island, I can tell you.'

I looked Cliff up and down. 'In fairness, neither will you, Cliff.'

He laughed. 'Ain't that the truth.' He returned to his theme of women bikers.

'If you ask me, your mate got off lightly if they just stomped his ribs, they can be really vicious. Y'know, wanting to show they can be better than the men.'

'Well, they won't be a problem anymore,' I said, 'so we can be thankful for something.'

'You wouldn't want to meet them.'

'Well, and I never will,' I said. 'Cheers!'

'Bloody feminists,' Cliff said, gloomily.

Chapter Twenty-Eight

The following morning, I got up early and cooked Cliff an enormous breakfast, the full English and then some, wincing at the thought of all those calories. At least, I thought to myself, as I carried the heaped plate over to my honoured guest, it was top quality ingredients, unlike whatever ghastly cheap stuff they would serve him in his local greasy spoon.

He was looking at his phone. 'The missus says I can come home tonight,' he said.

'That's good,' I handed him his breakfast. 'She's forgiven you then?'

'Nah,' he shook his head, 'but on account of I'm such a babe magnet she wants me tucked up in bed safe at home. . .' His huge stomach shook with laughter.

'Cheers Charlie, this looks blinding. . .' He devoured his breakfast, kissed me on the cheek and was picked up by one of his many employees.

Later in the afternoon, at the Earl's house, the kitchen – now reopened – was silent and depressed as we went about our respective jobs. We all studiously avoided conversation; eye contact was minimal.

I was in the middle of showing the agency chef who was Octavia's replacement – the show must go on – how to make a *soffritto*, according to Matteo's specifications – it seemed especially poignant with Octavia in intensive care. Her condition was described as serious. I got a message from Bryony to meet her in the Three Bells when it opened if I was free.

I checked with Tom to see if it was OK to leave early. I found him in an office off the kitchen surrounded by paperwork, invoices and scribbled notes as well as a laptop and tablet.

'I can't believe what happened. . .' he said, shaking his head. 'I'm sure it was just a prank, or a genuine accident, maybe one of the agency guys trying to be helpful. . .' He looked genuinely distraught, as well he might, since it was he who had unwittingly sent her to her death. 'It was Octavia, for God's sake. Who would want to hurt her?'

'I'm sure you're right,' I lied.

Anyway, he gave me the rest of the day off. My job in the kitchen was ill-defined; I didn't have an official role really, other than general helper. Matteo came and went, overseeing things and dividing his time between here, the restaurant in London and whatever else Charlotte had found him to do. The reality of his life compared to how I had imagined it was very different. He was a hamster scurrying around on the wheel of success. I assumed he would be oblivious to Charlotte's claim that he owed all this worldly acclaim entirely to her. I'd been brooding on what his agent had said. Had she really made him? Could she for example take me and turn me into a multi-million pound brand, for that is what essentially he had become? Would I want that, even if it should be offered to me?

I pulled myself back down to earth and texted Bryony to say that I would be delighted.

At 4 o'clock I was buying drinks for me and Bryony in the bar of the Three Bells.

'Busy day, Charlie?' asked Malcolm in his hoarse whisper.

'So, so,' I said. Malcolm looked at me blankly. The opera fortnight, the arrival of a celebrity chef, the air ambulance and Octavia's 'accident' as it was officially known now – all of these things he regarded with a complete lack of curiosity. His detachment from life was almost admirable.

I handed Bryony a dry white wine (the same brand that had been excoriated by Charlotte, it had big purple grapes on the bottle label – definitely one to avoid for my restaurant), and sipped my Diet Coke. I checked the clock on the wall. I was due back at my own restaurant later for a meeting with Jess.

'So, Bryony,' I said, as I leaned back in my chair and surveyed the pub, 'how can I help you?'

We were the only customers. Malcolm, wearing a threadbare grey cardigan and his habitual blank-faced stare, stood behind the bar, looking into the middle distance. Bryony looked at me. 'I don't know if you can,' she said. She sighed and fidgeted. I waited patiently, then she leaned over to me, confidingly. 'Well, maybe you can, I'm being harassed by a man, and I heard what you did to that chef who gave Jess some grief, so I wondered. . .'

She looked at me blearily. As usual she was having trouble

focusing on anything. There was a strong smell of weed. She waved her hand to indicate confusion. 'Maybe you could have a word with him. Or something.'

'OK.' I thought I may as well live up to my reputation. I liked Bryony. 'What's he been doing?'

By way of reply, Bryony took out her phone and showed me a text with an accompanying photo. 'You know you want it,' said the text. That's original, I thought. The photo was as bad as I feared.

'Oh, yuck,' I said, handing the phone back.

'Exactly.' Bryony nodded. 'I think because James is a bit older than me. . .'

I had to keep reminding myself that the Earl was called James. Bryony could hardly refer to him as 'Earl Hampden' all the time. She carried on: '. . . this guy thought I was easy. I haven't told James. I want it dealt with, discreetly. I don't want James upset.'

I raised my eyebrows at that. I couldn't imagine the Earl being upset by something involving a non-animal. He didn't like people. Evidently Bryony was an exception. She may have been high on weed but she noticed my reaction.

'I mean, it might make him angry and he would do something he would regret. James does have a temper.'

'Oh, I see,' I replied. I could imagine. The Earl angry would be a terrifying prospect. I turned back to the image on her phone. 'Who does that thing belong to?' I asked.

'Jean-Claude, the maître d' at the Kings Head.'

So that was who Strickland's sex pest manager was, I thought. I suppose I should have guessed, but I hadn't. 'How did he get your number?' I asked.

'Oh, James and I eat there quite a lot,' she said. 'He must have noted it down when I made a booking.'

'Can I see that text again?' I asked. I looked more closely. I tried to blank Jean-Claude's tumescent manhood from my mind. The date and time were logged. It was the Monday when Giorgio was killed, in the afternoon. Either Jean-Claude was capable of killing someone in a frenzy, getting an erection from it and then sending a dick pic or he wasn't responsible for Giorgio's death. I knew which I found more likely.

'He started off sending me a text every now and then, but they started getting more and more frequent, more suggestive and more demanding. I tried to get him to chill but that didn't work, and now this.'

I thought back to what Strickland had said about Jean-Claude's behaviour getting more extreme. I guess like most addicts, the abnormal becomes the new normal. He didn't know where to stop.

'Can you forward that to me? I'll deal with it,' I said. At last, I thought, Strickland would have the evidence he had lacked until now. And I'd back it up with some threats of my own, the kind that you wouldn't be able to take to an industrial tribunal. I'd bring Cliff along to underscore my point. I doubted Jean-Claude's wiener would be looking so chipper after Cliff had had a word in his shell-like. Bryony nodded.

'Thanks, Charlie. Let's change the topic of conversation,' she said, then she added, as if it had just occurred to her, 'If I had one that looked like that I wouldn't be boasting about it.' She had a definite point. It would not win best in show. Far from it.

'How's Jess?' she asked.

Jess had been at school with Bryony until Bryony had dropped out to devote herself full-time to drugs without the faff of education.

'Jess is fine,' I said. Jess disapproved strongly of the Earl, and Bryony, come to that.

'We used to be bezzies,' said Bryony sadly, 'back in year 10.'

That was about five years ago, I guessed, a long time in twenty-year-old girl terms. They weren't bezzies now. Jess didn't like stoners.

'I'll be glad when this opera stuff's done,' she said wearily. 'I'm like, so not getting it. . .'

Neither was I, if truth be told. We considered the festival's *La Traviata* in silence. I had heard enough of it drifting across the field as they rehearsed it.

'I mean, what's it all about?' whispered Bryony. She shook her head in a pantomime of bewildered distress.

'I've got no idea,' I said. We were united in ignorance. My idea of sophisticated music was ABBA. Maybe Taylor Swift. Jess was a huge fan and determined to convert me.

'Do you know anyone who's going?' she said.

I shook my head. 'I only know other chefs and the builders who come in here – none of them are going. The scaffolders don't seem to be opera buffs – oh, Esther Bartlett, she's going. Her husband's taking her.'

'Opera's not for the likes of us,' said Bryony sadly. 'We're just plebs.' Then she brightened. 'But at the least the orangutans will benefit, so it's not all bad.'

'Is it selling well?' I asked.

'Sold out,' she said proudly, 'mainly to Londoners, people from Beaconsfield and Gerrards Cross.'

She looked at her watch,

'Charlie,' Bryony said finishing her drink, 'thanks so much for your help, but I've got to go now. Could you let me know when you've dealt with Jean-Claude?'

'I'll be on to it straight away, Bryony,' I promised.

I watched her leave the pub and took my phone out. Maybe I could have a word with Cliff before he went back home to London for the night.

I texted Cliff. 'Hi, fancy a pint this evening?'

I sent the message and then sent a more detailed message to Graeme Strickland letting him know the details of what his maître d' had been up to.

I couldn't foresee the future like some of Esther Bartlett's friends said they could, but with Cliff to back me up and Strickland doubtless on the warpath, I could confidently predict that Jean-Claude's future looked far from rosy.

Chapter Twenty-Nine

On Friday, I helped Sam with some prep, had my meeting with Jess, showered, changed, put the things that I would need in a container and got into my car. Life outside of Nonna's Kitchen was still going on.

It was the last day of June. Time to meet the witches of North Bucks, as arranged earlier but not on a blasted heath, rather in somewhere called Paeony Close in that hot-bed of New Age Spirituality that was Milton Keynes.

Driving up the M1, I thought about what Bryony had told me and how it impacted on what I already knew or suspected. I no longer thought Jean-Claude had anything to do with Giorgio's death. He'd obviously had other things on his mind while that drama was being played out – and he'd certainly had his hands full – but I still liked him as a possible suspect for the blackmail. He also had nothing to do with the attempt on Octavia's life. He definitely hadn't been in the kitchen.

Who was the person who had locked her in the freezer? And why?

I turned my attention to the Feast of Litha as the motorway wound interminably on.

An hour or so later I was in Milton Keynes. North Bucks seemed a very different sort of place to South Bucks, less hilly, many more open fields, a sparser population density. Milton Keynes itself remained an elusive mystery to me. In the old days, armed with a road atlas for navigation, I'd have got comprehensively lost and doubtless seen a lot more of the town than I wanted to as I drove around and around in circles. It was like a maze whose centre I would have never reached, a town straight out of Jorge Luis Borges, but whose paths were wide tarmac roads punctuated by endless roundabouts and signs for places that you had never heard of. After a while, you lost all sense of reality. It was strangely featureless.

But now, in these satnav days, I was at my destination directly, not seeing any of the place, which only disclosed itself by peeping over the grassy parapets of the sunken dual carriageways that took me to the quarter that Chris lived in. Did I miss the romance of uncertainty of the old days, when going to a new town to find an address carried the almost cast-iron certainty of getting lost?

No, I didn't.

Following the warm, Radio 4-style tones of the satnav, I turned into Paeony Close. It was an odd choice of address for a prominent witch and ageing Goth, I thought. If we were going floral, Mandrake would have been more appropriate. Chris lived in an executive housing estate. The houses were modern, red-brick and cedar-stained wood, the lawns and shrubs well-tended. The cars parked outside were BMWs and Audis. Sensible cars for sensible people with well-paid jobs. Doubtless Chris's wife fell into this category. I wondered what Chris himself did for a living. He had never mentioned a job. Maybe he lived off his wife's salary.

I pulled up outside the number that he had given me. The medium-sized detached house was utterly respectable, a shrine to normality. I picked up my file containing my notes that I'd made on the food and walked up to the front door, which he opened for me.

'Why, hello!' he said and leaned forward to kiss me on the cheeks. Quite frankly I could have done without the kiss. He was drenched in some unappealing after shave that made my eyes smart. He was far from gorgeous.

Today Chris was wearing a black satin shirt and hipster black trousers showing off skinny white mankles. It was not a good look.

'Do come in. . .'

He led me into the living room. I looked around. It was perfectly pleasant, large, airy – there was nothing overtly occult about it, no pentagrams or druidic artefacts. I was surprised to see that Chris's lounge had a fair few items relating to motorbikes.

There was a framed *Easy Rider* vintage poster with a stoned Dennis Hopper and Peter Fonda; there was a poster advertising the Bulldog Bash (special guests Motorhead) from back in the day; there were framed photos of classic bikes: BSA, Triumph and Norton. Pride of place over the fireplace was given to a large black-and-white photo of a hefty woman, naked apart from an unzipped fringed leather jacket, large breasts prominently on show, astride a Vincent Black Shadow, arms raised pushing her hair back and pouting at the camera. I rather bitchily thought that facially you could use her to open the Bulldog Bash, she looked like Churchill in a wig.

'Do you like bikes, Chris?' I said, conversationally. He'd always turned up in a car, a Twingo.

'Not really,' he said, firmly and dismissively. The pictures remained a mystery. 'Now, sit down and tell me your plans for the menu and then we'll go and look at the club kitchen so you can get some idea of where you'll be cooking.'

I looked around. 'Is Rowan not joining us?'

Chris shook his head. 'He couldn't make it' – he smiled alarmingly – 'it's just us.'

I now wanted to be out of the house and somewhere more public. I wasn't keen on this intimacy. Chris was sitting on the sofa and giving me a smouldering look from his lightly eyelinered eyes. He pushed ringed fingers through his hair. His bracelets clanked. I received another waft of his cloying male perfume, it smelled like the moth repellent I'd been using recently in my wardrobe. It had a similar chemical tang.

He patted the cushion next to him invitingly. I had no intention of sitting that close. I smiled politely and pulled up a chair so the coffee table was between us, and opened the file. 'Canapés and starters. . .' I said, briskly.

We ran through the menu fairly swiftly, then as I closed the file and was about to suggest we leave for the cricket club, he said, 'I had a dream last night, Charlie, a prophetic dream. . .'

Oh my Lord, I thought. Well, he was a witch, what did I expect?

'What kind of dream?' My voice was nervous. Please don't say 'sexy'.

'One about vinegar,' he said.

'Vinegar?' That sounded OK. We were on safe ground there.

He nodded. 'Did you know it has magical properties?' he carried on dreamily. 'I checked it in my dream symbol book.' I sighed. It was bad enough when people recounted their dreams conversationally, let alone prophetically. I suspected this could go on for a while. 'Vinegar is under the sway of Mars, its ruling planet, and its element is fire, which as you know is vital to this ceremony, and it protects and gives energy.'

'Of course it does,' I said briskly.

'Charlie. . .' His voice rose dramatically. 'Dreams are important, they show us paths of action, I want to see you work your magic on vinegar to sanctify our Litha menu!'

'Can I use balsamic?' I asked, faintly. He nodded.

'Come with me to the kitchen,' he said, 'show me what you can do with vinegar!'

We walked into the kitchen, which was large, fitted in granite-effect Corian. I felt a bit safer here, on home ground so to speak. It was reassuringly clean. Unlike, I suspected, Chris's intentions.

Chris looked at me expectantly, so I smiled confidently at him. He indicated a central island as a workspace. I moved over to it. He sidled closer to me. I edged away. He repeated the manoeuvre, as did I. I was now facing the window. I wondered how many times we'd circle the island before he got the message. I saw a bottle of balsamic vinegar on the counter and a copper sauteuse pan hanging on a hook. It looked completely unused. What a waste, I thought. Those things cost a fortune.

'Balsamic vinegar and olive oil, three ways!' I said.

'Sounds wonderful.' He actually sounded a bit disappointed. My failing to appreciate his charms had probably dispirited him.

'Have you got any chillies and some olive oil? Can I borrow an apron? This is a good blouse.'

Chris went to the fridge and gave me a small pack of chillies. I raised my eyebrows, they were Scotch bonnet, extra-fiery.

'Sandra likes them on her pizzas,' he explained. I looked at him incredulously. They would blow most people's head off. I wondered if maybe she was Asian. I had worked with a petite Thai chef once and she could eat them like they were as innocuous as celery. Chris handed me a bottle of extra virgin olive oil from a shelf. He opened a drawer and passed me a red-striped butcher's apron.

He watched me intently while I got busy.

'So, how's your business doing, Charlie?' he asked chattily. 'I hear great things from Esther.'

'Fine, thanks.'

I de-seeded half a chilli with great care, chopped it up and let it sweat gently in some warm olive oil on a very low heat. I cling filmed the half chilli that was left and dropped it into the apron pocket. I washed my hands and scrubbed them vigorously. I was very concerned about getting chilli anywhere on my body that was remotely sensitive.

'And what's it like working with the great Matteo McCleish?'

'It's certainly an education, Chris,' I said diplomatically.

He nodded and examined his nails, then he looked up at me. 'Esther tells me you're single, Charlie? How come an attractive woman like you is unattached?'

I looked over at Chris. He had moved significantly closer to me.

'I don't know, Chris. It really is a mystery,' I said, taking a small step away. That made me think of Andrea, I really must chase him up on the Graziana business.

While the mixture was cooking away, I tipped a generous quantity of balsamic into the sauteuse and stirred as it evaporated, watching the mixture thicken.

When I had achieved a syrupy reduction of the balsamic vinegar, the consistency and colour of treacle, I turned the heat off and put it in a bowl. I added the chilli oil. In another bowl I just added straight balsamic and olive oil, then I used a spoon to create a lattice-like effect on a third side plate.

There was a breadboard and half a loaf of brown bread on the counter top. I cut two slices and put them on another plate.

Perhaps I could refocus our meeting back onto the food.

'Let's go in the living room,' I said. We carried the two bowls and the two plates in and put them on the coffee table between us.

'Try dipping the bread in the three of them, one by one.' Olive oil and balsamic, chilli-infused olive oil and reduced balsamic, and plain old reduced balsamic.

Chris didn't sit on the sofa opposite; he sat down next to me. He did as instructed with his piece of bread, nodding thoughtfully as he chewed.

'Very good,' he said.

Suddenly the quiet of the street outside was broken by the throbbing of engines. Chris turned around. He suddenly looked aghast. I wondered why.

'Damn, it's my wife.'

Thank the Lord.

I glanced out of the window. Any sense of relief at being saved by the appearance of his other half rapidly evaporated to be replaced by a sense of alarm and foreboding. Chris's wife was nothing like I had imagined. This was no quiet, mousy, Laura Ashley dressed businesswoman.

There were three motorbikes pulling up outside the house. One of the riders wearing black leathers and a denim cut-off, waved to the other two, who then drove off. The remaining rider removed their helmet, revealing long grey hair and a snout-like, jowled face and mean, piggy eyes. She swung her leg over the bike, stretched and looked over at the house.

It was the woman on the bike in the picture in the living room, twenty-five years older, looking now like some kind of Hells Angel granny.

Then she saw me at the kitchen window and her face turned to one of pure rage and she stormed towards the front door, fists clenched.

As Francis would have put it, oo 'er.

Chapter Thirty

'That's your wife?' I said, incredulously. The motorbike images certainly made sense now. I turned to Chris, who looked thoroughly alarmed. My apprehension deepened. I suddenly thought of Murdo, the livid bruising on his body after he'd been beaten up by the woman Hells Angel. That could well have been her. Walking towards me up the path.

He nodded nervously. The nervous bit was catching – I was beginning to feel it too.

'I thought she was a treasurer?' The word 'treasurer' had conjured up an image of a businesswoman in a suit, not a Hells Angel. I suppose it was my fault for stereotyping people. I remembered I had envisaged Chris's wife as a timid, put-upon woman, not this menacing she-ogre.

'She is,' he said. 'Sandra's the treasurer of the North Bucks Hells Angels.' Chris looked around desperately. 'They've started letting women in these days. . . like every-where. . . You'll have to hide – she gets jealous. I'll take her upstairs, then you get out of the house. . .'

'You're joking,' I said. 'It's too late anyway, she's seen me already.'

I remembered now what Cliff had said about Satan's Sluts, how they had joined forces with the Angels. I untied the apron and took it off, then remembered I had half a chilli in the pocket. I pulled it out and handed Chris his apron back. He twisted it in anguish in his hands. He was obviously terrified of Sandra. I wasn't sure what to do with the chilli – I was beyond thinking. I closed my fist around it. We both heard the noise of the front door opening.

'Chris?' said a gruff voice. Honey I'm home, I thought faintly.

Back in the kitchen Chris had the store cupboard door open and was pointing at it frantically. 'Inside!' he mouthed.

I shook my head firmly. Sod it, I thought. I was not going to hide in a cupboard, like I was in some sort of stage farce. Enough was enough. Chris's wife had no reason to be jealous – far from it – I wouldn't have touched him with a bargepole and my innocence would defend me. I would stand my ground. I thought again of the severe bruising that Murdo had shown me and swallowed nervously.

We heard the front door slam.

The door to the living room opened, and in she walked.

Sandra Reynolds looked less like a treasurer, even of the Angels, and more like the female version of the kind of monster that lurked under the bridge in a book I had when I was a kid – *The Three Billy Goats Gruff*.

She was a big woman, overweight, wearing a plaid shirt with the sleeves rolled up showing heavily tattooed fore-arms, a leather waistcoat, jeans and steel-toed boots. She may have held a Treasury position, but I suspect that being a treasurer for a Hells Angels chapter owes more to being handy in a fight than financial acumen.

I don't think I have ever seen a scarier looking woman. Ever. And that includes film, TV and stage as well as real life.

'Hello,' I said brightly.

She looked at me with dislike; I swallowed nervously.

'Who's this?' she said to Chris, ignoring me entirely.

'This is Charlie. She's a chef,' he replied. He gave the word 'chef' a kind of special emphasis as if Sandra's feelings might be soothed by my job-title.

'What's she doing here?' Her tone was as unpleasant as her words. Another glare in my direction. Evidently Chris's hopes that she might hold chefs in special esteem were mistaken.

I got fed up with being discussed as if I wasn't there.

'I'm doing the catering for the party,' I said. It was fair to say I wasn't warming to Mrs Reynolds but I gave her an encouraging smile to show her there were no hard feelings. She stared at me in angry disbelief.

'Sandra. . .' said Chris nervously.

'Who asked you?' This was directed at me. To say that there was a menacing tone in her voice was an understatement. Sandra was menace itself.

I'd had enough. Charm and courtesy had obviously failed. I thought that I would just leave politely. Chris was welcome to her. His remorseless pursuit of me was making a touch more sense. Compared to his wife, I was a real catch. I was human, for one.

'Well, lovely to have met you, Sandra. . .' I decided not to shake her hand. I was still holding half a chilli in mine.

187

Sandra wasn't in the mood for talking. She was in the mood for action.

'You thieving bitch! You leave my Chris alone!' she growled and swung a meaty fist at me.

I have excellent reactions. I ducked under the punch. Thank God it didn't make contact. I had time to think, she actually thinks I'm trying to seduce Chris. . . she's as deluded as she is violent.

Chis stared at the two of us in horror.

'Stop it, Sandra! She's not worth it!' he shrieked. I gave him a baffled look. What did he think was going on?

Sandra looked absolutely furious now. She took a step towards me. I backed away but was stopped short by the work-surface behind me, and her right arm shot out and grabbed me by my blouse collar.

I was now in serious trouble. She must have weighed about eighteen stone. She wasn't as fit as I was, but she was bigger and stronger. Any second now I was going to be smothered by her and her weight. Luckily for me, Sandra paused to savour the moment – not I suspect in a mindful way, more like a cat with a cornered mouse, before she went to town on me.

And I absolutely had no intention of letting that happen. The cling film had come off the halved chilli pepper and the inside of my hand was slick with its juice. It was no time for Queensberry rules. I jabbed my palm into her right eye and pushed.

Scotch bonnets measure 80,000 plus on the Scoville scale. To put that into context, a jalapeno, like you might put on your burrito, is in the range 2,500 to 8,000. So, you can do the maths – ten times hotter. At least. Once or twice in a kitchen I've had chilli on sensitive parts of me. Once, despite washing my hands thoroughly, I had touched the corner of my eye and it was excruciating. God alone knows what Sandra was feeling as I drove the chilli into her open eye. Even a dinosaur has nerve endings.

She let out a roar of agony and a string of swear words, then let go of me and clutched her seared eye. The pain must have been frightful. She staggered to the sink and put her head under the tap, running water into it, shouting and swearing.

I turned tail and fled, out of the kitchen, the hall and the front door, down the path and into my car.

I frantically started the engine and drove off. As I left Milton Keynes, no signs of an avenging figure on a Harley in my mirror, I began to relax.

I wondered if a chilli was under the sign of Mars like vinegar was. As the pounding in my heart subsided I reflected at the very least it had momentarily taken my mind off my troubles with Matteo's team.

Chapter Thirty-One

Later that afternoon I asked Jess, 'How are things going with Sam?' I was safe and relaxed, back home in the Old Forge Café. Sandra was a receding nightmare. I had received a text from Chris. 'Sorry', it read, together with some emojis redolent of guilt. There was a slew of monkey holding face in hands. 'Hope we're still on for the party.'

I shrugged. Presumably Sandra had calmed down. Business is business. At least Chris probably would no longer come on to me – I'd be spared that. Every cloud.

I sent him a thumbs-up emoji.

The last customers had left the dining room that lunchtime and I was alone with Jess while Sam and Francis cleaned the kitchen down.

'He's great,' said Jess referring to Sam, 'but he's terribly boring. I think his personality has been surgically removed.'

I told Jess about my time in Milton Keynes and she shook her head.

'You have a genius for attracting trouble – it's a weird gift. Speaking of which, I had a text from Bryony of all people saying she'd been talking to you. What was all that about?'

'She's being harassed by Graeme Strickland's maître d'. He's been bombarding her with texts and now pictures.' I told her what Bryony had told me.

'Oh well, a picture's worth a thousand words,' said Jess, heartlessly. She really didn't like Bryony.

'I said I'd have a word with him. I'm bringing Cliff along to underline any point I'm going to make.'

Jess smiled. She was fond of Cliff, which I was delighted about, since he was my best friend. I would never have predicted that my student manager and my Godfather, which is what he technically was, would have become buddies, but there you go.

'Don't do anything stupid,' Jess warned.

'I won't, I promise,' I said.

'Now why does that fail to reassure me?' was Jess's reply.

My phone rang. It was Graeme Strickland, asking if I fancied a quick drink in the Three Bells. Ten minutes later I was there.

He was sitting alone at a table when I went in. His face lit up when he saw me.

'Charlie, what can I get you?'

'Just a Diet Coke please, Graeme.'

He went up to the bar and gave his order to Malcolm who nodded impassively, silent as ever.

We were the only people in the pub again and, with its lack of windows, it could have been any time of the day or night. It was more like an underground bunker than a pub. It occurred to me that if you were stuck for eternity in an unchanging limbo it could very well be like the Three Bells.

I shuddered slightly at the thought of being in here for a lock-in that lasted forever.

'I owe you big time for telling me about that creep, hassling Bryony,' said Graeme as he chinked my glass with his pint of lager.

'So now you've got grounds to sack him?' I asked.

He shook his head. 'No need to, mate, not anymore.' He laughed happily. 'He's only effed off to France. He texted me, saying as a result of the embarrassing misunderstanding, etc etc. I think he thinks he might be done for sexual harassment.'

'So has he really gone then, gone for good?' I was both surprised and pleased. I don't really like confrontations although there do seem to be a lot of those in my life.

'Looks that way,' said Strickland. 'One of my commis chefs showed me a Facebook post he sent of him on the Eurostar. If that's not panic, I don't know what is.'

'Oh well, bon voyage. . .'

'I told you that man was getting worse,' said Strickland, as he drank some more lager. 'I hope Bryony doesn't bear any ill will,' he added.

'You'll be OK,' I said. 'She's not the kind of girl to hold a grudge.'

He drained his pint.

'Do you want another?' I asked.

He shook his head. 'No, I've had two – I've got to get back.' He yawned and rubbed his eyes.

'We got spanked at lunchtime,' he said. 'Seventy covers – there's a hell of a lot of prep work to make up for.' He shook his head. 'Another day, another dollar. Oh, by the way, you were asking me ages ago about someone who could sort your wine list out. I was talking about it to this person I know who's just setting up a consultancy, advising small businesses like yourself, do you want me to pass your name on?'

I thought of my underwhelming collection of wine. My wine menu that would not be winning any awards anywhere anytime soon.

'Definitely. He's good is he?'

'She is, she used to work for' – he gave me the name of a top London hotel and a Michelin starred restaurant.

'Didn't you used to work there?'

'Yeah, it's how I know her, she's an ex,' he added. I was suddenly excited at the thought of meeting one of Strickland's ex-girlfriends, it was intriguing.

'Give her my number,' I said.

'Sure, I'll send it you. Catch you later.' He stood up and left the pub with his habitual, energetic fast walk.

Alone now at my table in the pub, I stared into space thinking mainly about Chris the witch and the appalling woman he was married to. It had certainly been a narrow squeak. She was psychotic. She must have been the woman that Anna Bruce had warned me about. Time passed slowly. Malcolm didn't move a muscle behind the bar. My phone went. It was Cliff. Could we meet up later to talk about the Jean-Claude problem?

I texted back to say that was all resolved and that I had a meeting at Matteo's the following night and I should be free from ten in the evening onwards if he fancied a chat.

I'll tell you about the jealous wife!

Do what mate? he replied, then: *Sorry, got to go. Later. . .*
I texted, *Speak to Jess, she'll explain.*

The next day was Saturday. I was back working for Matteo, another tiring day in the pop-up kitchen. Charlotte came over to me while I was helping Tom to send out lunch to the orchestra. In the next few days we would have the full dress rehearsals and then the first night at the beginning of the following week. I gathered from Tom that everything was going smoothly with the production, although that was none of our concern.

Charlotte asked if I would be free for an evening meeting.

'If it's after seven it's fine,' Tom said. So at 8 o'clock I drove the short distance to the Old Vicarage, Matteo's house. Charlotte's Audi was in the drive, but there was no sign of Matteo's Maserati or Graziana's Range Rover. I walked up to the front door and rang the bell.

Douglas opened the door. He looked thinner and more stressed than usual, his eyes tired behind his glasses. They were red-rimmed and it looked like he'd been crying. I hoped he wasn't having a nervous breakdown. I felt sorry for the man, he so obviously didn't enjoy life, his only friend the rifle he owned.

I hadn't spoken to him that much since I'd started work for Matteo. But even 'not that much' was quite a bit compared to most. He was like an extra in a film, often in shot but always on the periphery of what was happening. Just about everybody seemed to take him for granted, to ignore him, as he wandered around clutching his sleek laptop like a security blanket. It never seemed to leave his hand.

'Hi, Douglas, how's it going?'

'Fine thanks, Charlie.'

He didn't look fine, far from it. He had brightened when he saw me. I guessed I was the only one who didn't treat him like a nobody.

'Do come in,' he said. 'Charlotte's in the living room.'

'No Matteo?' I asked.

He shook his head. 'No, he and Graziana were invited to an opening night of a new restaurant in Covent Garden.'

All right for some, I thought, before I remembered that of course, Matteo's life was far from all right. He was being blackmailed and someone was killing his staff. That's not all right in anyone's book.

I followed Douglas through into the living room where Charlotte was sitting on the sofa. There was a laptop open on the coffee table in front of her. I could see that she was working on a spreadsheet.

She pulled a face. 'Matteo's earnings,' she said ruefully.

I couldn't imagine why she was pulling a face. 'Pretty healthy, I should imagine.'

'You might imagine that,' she said, 'but it takes an awful lot to keep the show on the road. I mean, the restaurant only just about breaks even – despite everything the rent in central London is crazy. Staff wages, keeping Matteo in the style to which he is accustomed.' She indicated the room we were in. 'It all adds up. It's why I need this black-mail thing shutting down pronto. Matteo can't concentrate properly. He earns a lot, but we spend a lot.'

She closed down what she was working on, shut the laptop then looked at me.

'The problem I have at the moment is that now two deaths in his entourage have attracted the media. I've been contacted by a really high profile freelance journalist who's doing a feature on them. I want this thing over, Charlie,' she said. 'I want it buried. I don't want *Nonna's Kitchen* rebranded as *Murder in Nonna's Kitchen*.'

'Two deaths?' I was confused.

She nodded. 'Octavia died earlier this evening.'

Chapter Thirty-Two

'Oh my God. . . Octavia. . . I can't believe it.'

'Oh, yes,' said Charlotte grimly.

Jesus, I thought. I sat down. I felt sick. Octavia dead. I felt overwhelmingly sad at the thought of her life being ended just like that. A wave of misery washed over me. She was so young. I thought of the way that she had smiled at me as she had pulled Tom's hoodie on. Her last smile. I'd thought that she was bound to pull through. I guess that had been based purely on my native optimism. The news came as a dreadful shock. I really did think I might throw up, I was feeling her death viscerally, like I'd been punched in the guts really hard.

'The thing is,' said Charlotte, blithely moving on from dropping that bombshell and returning to her beloved Matteo, 'public acclaim is all well and good, but the public is fickle. One minute they love you and you can do no wrong, the next. . .' She shrugged and made an expressive gesture. 'The next you're history. Tastes change; people want someone new. Matteo's ratings for his last show were down. You can't rest on your laurels.'

Shut up, I thought miserably. Stop wittering on about his career and your part in it. I might as well not have bothered. As far as Charlotte was concerned, Octavia was dead, time to move on. I suppose that's part of what made her such a good agent. A relentless focus on career to the exclusion of all else. Heaven help Matteo if he ever let her down.

'So I'm firefighting,' she said. 'I've got the BBC dithering about whether or not to offer us another contract. Something like this could easily cock it all up. I've got to try and keep Matteo's eye on the ball for the next couple of weeks, on the opera fortnight. He's distraught, as you can imagine. Graziana wants to go back to Italy. Jesus.'

She looked at me fiercely. 'Find me that blackmailer!'

'I'm sorry, Charlotte, I can't help thinking of poor Octavia.'

I knew that she believed the first murder and the blackmail were not related. I think for Charlotte if Matteo were not directly involved then she simply would not care. I assumed she would feel the same way about Octavia. Charlotte pushed her hair back in her trademark gesture. 'I can't afford the luxury of grief, Charlie,' she said severely. 'Someone's got to keep the show on the road. I need you focused on discovering the blackmailer.'

'And you won't go to the police?' I asked.

She shook her head. 'No, it'll get out if I do. People talk.'

'So Tom, Murdo, Douglas, Attila. . . one of them is the blackmailer,' I said, doing what she asked of me and returning to the job in hand. Other suspects were dropping like flies. 'It has to be one of them.'

'Yes,' she said. 'It has to be. I had thought that it was Octavia, but now. . . well, it can't be her.'

'Why did you think that?' I asked, surprised.

'Because she made a pass at Matteo and was furious when he said no. Tom told me about it; Matteo had told him. And Douglas told me too – he got it from Octavia. She confided in him a lot.' She sighed. 'So it came straight from the horse's mouth. He's in a bad way with what's happened. He loved that girl.'

So that's why he was looking so morose.

'We really should go to the police. DI Slattery will keep his mouth shut,' I said.

'Absolutely not – we've been through this. You know why.' She sounded angry now.

'But the blackmailer might be the murderer,' I pointed out despite myself. As I had suspected, she shot the idea down immediately.

'Don't be silly,' Charlotte said scornfully. 'If you're black-mailing someone you're not going to compromise your scam, not when it's working successfully, by going around killing people. It's blindingly obvious.'

She stood up and paced around the room. 'You've got two different crimes, two different people. And, come to that, very different crimes. One is sneaky; the other couldn't be less so. I'm concerned about both – of course I am, I'm not insensitive,' I snorted in derision, mentally of course. She carried on: 'But murder is for the police to deal with. Let them deal with that. Your job is the blackmailer. Now, do you have any plans?'

I wasn't so sure that she was right but it made sense for

me to concentrate on the blackmailer. Besides, I didn't feel like arguing, I'd seen Charlotte's temper and it had been frightening.

'OK,' I said, 'what I suggest is I go back to the porn shop and ask the owner who Greg or Mick is and show him the picture of the other chefs, see if he might be helpful.'

I had held back on this until now. My main reason was that the guy in the shop was bound to just deny everything, and I had no leverage on him I could apply. That, and I don't enjoy confrontation. If it happens, well, I'm hard to intimidate, but I don't actively seek it out in my life. However, Octavia's death was a game changer. I felt I owed it to her to find out who had killed her. I knew I wouldn't be able to live peaceably with myself until I had done everything possible to avenge her.

Charlotte said doubtfully, 'Well, you can try, but even if the shop guy is innocent – and that's a contradiction in terms if ever there was one, an innocent porn shop owner – he's not going to tell you anything.'

'But I can try?'

'How are you going to get him to talk to you?' she asked.

'I shall use my legendary charm,' I said, with a hint of bitterness. The truth was, I hadn't got a clue, but I felt the need to do something.

She shrugged. 'It's fine by me. Do it on Monday. Then what I want you to do, is to carry on working in the kitchen the day after, until the end of the opera fortnight, that's a maximum of three weeks. We'll keep funding the agency guy who's at your place. Does that sound reasonable?'

'Absolutely.' I nodded.

'And at least, if you don't find the blackmailer, having you around more or less permanently in the kitchen, well, it might just stop any more killings. That is, *if* Octavia's death was murder.'

'How do you mean?'

Charlotte shrugged. 'It could have been an unpleasant practical joke gone wrong. I'm sure you've come across instances of people being locked in freezers for a laugh in your time in kitchens.'

I nodded. That had been Graziana's take on things, Tom's too, come to that. It was unfortunately the truth. I had seen people trapped in freezers as a cruel prank. But not padlocked in.

Charlotte and I shook hands. 'I'll see myself out.'

'Fine,' she said and bent her head over her spreadsheet. Money never sleeps.

Chapter Thirty-Three

I sat in the driver's seat in the darkness outside the Old Vicarage and scratched my head thoughtfully as I took in all that had happened. Poor Octavia. She might have seemed self-obsessed, potentially rude, but hell, who isn't at that age? I looked back to my own arrogant twenty year old self and shuddered. I'd certainly had a high opinion of myself. As Cliff would have doubtless put it, I'd thought I was the dog's bollocks, the mutt's nuts. And my opinion of her had improved massively – I had been about to offer her a job!

Still lost in thought, I pulled my seatbelt on and clicked it to. As I did I suddenly became aware of a movement outside the car. A large formless shadow looming in the darkness. I had got as far as thinking, 'What the f. . .?' when the passenger door was brutally yanked open and a huge shape leapt in beside me. The car rocked on its wheels and sank a little under the sudden increase in weight.

I turned in shock.

A mass of grey hair, the smell of cigarettes and a vicious-looking knife inches from my face.

'Hello, remember me?' said Sandra, unpleasantly, her piggy eyes boring into mine.

How could I forget, I thought.

There is something very unnerving about a knife being held to your face at eye level. It would have been bad enough if it had been a child menacing me with what looked very much like the blade of a flick-knife, but this was no child. This was an irate, eighteen-stone Hells Angel woman who was convinced I had been having an affair with her husband. Not only that, I had added insult to injury by inflicting agonising pain on her, someone far more used to dishing it out than taking it.

It was clear that in Sandra's mind, I owed her. I owed her big time.

'Hello, Sandra,' I said, weakly. I actually wanted to say, 'Please don't stab me, I'm too young to die.' But something about the woman – maybe the angry, hate-filled expression – made me feel like the plea would fall on deaf ears. I also wanted to avoid the terms 'stab' and 'die'. There was no need to give her any ideas.

Part of me also wanted to say, 'So, the eye's better, then . . .' But that would have been tantamount to suicide. Instead, I stammered out, 'How did you. . .'

She finished my question for me '. . . know you were here? They told me up at the big house. I said I was a game supplier, that I'd got a load of rabbits for you. . . they said I'd find you here.'

Bloody Tom, I thought. Trying to be helpful.

She said, gruffly, 'Now, keep yer mouth shut and drive.'

It wasn't a request I felt I could refuse. My heart beating

like thunder in my chest, guts churning and my mouth dry, I put the car in gear and we moved off down the pea shingle towards the gate at the bottom. Out of the corner of my eye, close to my face, I could see the gleam of the knife unmoving in Sandra's meaty paw.

My mind was frantically trying to come up with some form of credible plan for escape. The best thing I could think of was suddenly accelerating, flooring it, ramming the car into a tree and hoping for the best, but that seemed quite dumb. All I could do was follow instructions and hope.

Perhaps she had no intention of actually using the knife that she was holding, maybe she just wanted to scare me.

If so, she was doing a bloody good job.

The powerful headlights of the Volvo washed over the lush, verdant shrubs that lined the drive which, in my heightened state of awareness, seemed almost hallucinatory in its length. The driveway was long but not that long. I guess I was so keyed up that it seemed to go on and on forever.

We rounded the final bend and there, finally, was the gate.

'What the. . .?' growled Sandra.

I stopped the car, the engine idling as we both stared.

The gates were open but in front of them, sideways on, blocking the way, was a large Harley Davidson with ape-hanger handlebars. Her bike.

I assumed that this wasn't where she had parked it, but there it was. We looked at the obstacle, both equally puzzled.

Then a figure marched out of the bushes into view.

I felt relief wash over me. It was as if God Himself had plucked an unlikely guardian angel out of heaven and sent him to rescue me.

Sandra twisted in her seat, the knife unmoving from my face, and used her left arm to sound the horn.

It was amazingly loud in the fraught darkness of the night.

Cliff Yeats, my guardian angel, more beautiful in my eyes than if he had been painted by Michelangelo, stared placidly at the car. Unhurriedly he picked something up from beside the Harley. A jerry can. He leisurely unscrewed the lid and doused the motorbike in liquid and tossed the can aside.

You could smell the petrol from the car. The reek of it washed towards us like a wave.

Sandra pressed the button and lowered the passenger window. The fumes from outside were almost eye-watering.

'What the hell do you think you're doing?' she snarled. Her face contorted with rage.

Cliff smiled pleasantly at her. 'It's your unlucky day, darling. . .' he said conversationally.

Another volley of abuse from Sandra, none of which seemed to worry Cliff at all. She was effectively trapped in the car. If she got out, I'd drive off or run. She shook her head in baffled rage.

Cliff reached in his pocket, walked a couple of steps towards the Volvo, put a large, fat blunt in his mouth and unhurriedly lit it with a Zippo lighter. As the light flared it illuminated the tattoos on his knuckles in heavy gothic script that spelled out his name. The smell of weed joined the smell of petrol. He looked at Sandra, gestured with the lighter in the direction of the Harley.

'OK, Mrs Catweazle! Get out of Charlie's car or your bike's toast. . .'

It was no idle threat. Cliff's brutal face, revealed by the flash of his lighter, said more than words ever could. She could see in Cliff's face, as clear as looking in a mirror, the reflection of her own predilection for violence. None of us doubted that Cliff would most certainly incinerate Sandra's Harley. If anything, he'd enjoy it.

Cliff sang 'Firestarter' by the Prodigy, loudly, out of tune.

I looked at Sandra. I could see indecision playing across her face. This was obviously not how she was expecting the evening to go.

'I'm the Firestarter. . . the Twisted Firestarter. . .'

The end of Cliff's spliff glowed red as he took another lungful of smoke. 'I'm not known for my patience. . .'

I wondered how much the bike was worth. Hopefully more than my life.

She swore and got out of the car, slamming the door behind her with all her might.

Obviously it was worth more than my life.

She walked past Cliff, pointedly refusing to look at him, took a helmet that had been hanging unseen by me on the far handle of the bike, pulled it on, mounted the petrol-soaked bike and turned the ignition. My heart missed a beat. I momentarily imagined a huge fireball erupting. Nothing so dramatic happened. The engine started and Mrs Reynolds roared off into the night.

I undid my seatbelt with shaky hands and got out of the car. My legs felt like jelly.

'Cliff, you old bastard!'

I threw my arms around him as I embraced him. They didn't meet behind him, due to the combination of the size of his stomach and the width of his back.

'Hello, Charlie mate!' Cliff took his spliff out of his mouth and coughed, then he grinned at me. 'You been banging her hubbie?' he asked innocently.

I shook my head wonderingly. 'How about I buy you several pints, Cliff, and I'll tell you all about it.'

'Lovely jubbly,' Cliff said. 'Lead on!'

Chapter Thirty-Four

'So I was in Wycombe looking at this pub who'd contacted me, obviously 'cos they needed a bouncer and I had Barry in mind for it, but I wanted to see what the gaff was like.'

Cliff had a small business providing doormen for pubs and clubs. He had three brothers and several nephews whom he employed and contacts in the boxing clubs around Bethnal Green and Bow. The Yeats name was almost a brand in that part of London, but nowadays he was expanding westwards down the M4, M40 corridor.

'Which pub was that?' I asked.

'The Coal Porter, near the station.' I nodded. I knew of it. It looked fairly grim from outside.

'So I was in there, having a chat with the landlord; anyway, my mobile goes and it was that girl who works for you. . . the pretty one. God, I'm getting terrible with names. Clever.'

'Jess?'

He took a drink of his lager and nodded. The pint glass looked very small in his enormous hand.

'That's right, the one who keeps saving your arse,' he said. The remaining lager disappeared down his throat. He looked at me expectantly.

It was certainly true that Jess had saved my life before, not to mention the Giorgio incident – and probably my business too with her front-of-house skills and organisational abilities. I owed her a lot.

I stood up and fetched Cliff another pint. The Three Bells looked lovely tonight after my near-death experience with Chris's wife. I felt euphoric at having survived, and profoundly grateful to Cliff.

'So, why did she call you?' I wondered how on earth Jess had known that trouble was on the way.

'Because she was worried about old bag Sandra. The jealous wife as you put it to me. Jess told me about it. Anyway' – he took a huge gulp of lager –' that bloke Chris phoned your restaurant, wanted to speak to you, said his old lady had gone loopy and was after your blood. You weren't answering your phone so Jess called me. I was only twenty minutes away, luckily for you, so I came over.'

He went on to explain that when he had seen the Harley parked at the bottom of the drive he had guessed who it belonged to.

'I suppose she left it down there 'cos you might have heard it coming up the drive, so I knew she was still on the premises. I moved it and blocked the way with it. Bike like that costs a fortune – I knew she'd see sense.' He laughed. 'No oil painting is she!'

I tutted at his comment but, to be honest, my heart was not set on defending her. He finished his new drink and put the empty pint glass on the table. Cliff had an amazing capacity for booze.

'She's always digging you out of the shit, that girl of yours, isn't she?'

'She is indeed Cliff, as are you, thank you very much,' I replied and kissed him on the cheek.

Cliff looked at me uncomfortably. He rubbed his bald head for comfort and tugged at his double chin. Then he studied the rings on his right hand, the sovereign ring and the amethyst signet ring. He was a bit embarrassed by my thanks. I don't think he liked heartfelt talks of any description. In Cliff's world, men grunted at each other or talked about football and boxing. I knew that because that's what he used to do with my dad. In my world I didn't really know anyone except other chefs. I don't like football and Cliff knew nothing about food.

But we liked each other enormously. And that was the main thing.

'Don't mention it, Chazza.' He was the only one who ever called me that, and only when he was really emotional, that is, not that often. The subject was closed.

'Can I get you another drink?' I asked.

He shook his head. 'No, I've got to go back to that pub in Wycombe. I want to see what it's like near closing time, get some idea of the unwanted clientele. See whose heads I'll be cracking on Saturday night. See you around.'

I watched his broad back leave the pub, which now had a respectable dozen or so people in it. Malcolm behind the bar gave him a kind of bow as he left and I heard his hoarse, faint, 'Goodnight, sir,' drift across the pub.

It was unusual for Malcolm to say goodbye to his customers. I guessed it was because Malcolm, in the way that pub landlords have, recognised a fellow pub worker.

Cliff wouldn't be needed here. I'd never seen any trouble in the Three Bells.

Alone at my table, I reflected on tonight. Jess had been her usual, wonderful self. I took my phone out and texted her, told her I was fine and thanked her for sending Cliff. I thought a little longer. Two people had gone out of their way to help me when I was in trouble and I had signally failed to do anything to help Octavia.

I felt angry with myself. Images of me working with her in the freezer, having insisted on helping her, cascaded around in my head. Then she'd still be alive. Or possibly I'd be equally dead. Should have, could have, didn't. . . the tired old worn-out clichés of pointless regret.

I thought then of Sandra. Well, as I'd wondered before, Anna Bruce had warned me of a violent woman, this had to be her. Face it, I thought, they don't come much more lairy than that one. It almost made me feel sorry for Chris. Then I laughed out loud, almost, but not quite. Face it, nothing would make me feel sorry for Chris.

I finished my drink and stood up. Time to go home and to bed. I had a busy day tomorrow.

Chapter Thirty-Five

Two days later, on Monday morning, I was back drinking tea in the café opposite the adult book store. The waitress recognised me from before and smiled at me warmly. She guessed I'd be good for an unfeasible amount of Earl Grey and a big tip. I knew the EROS SHOP, so good for porn it was fully capitalised, didn't open until half past nine so I had arrived at the café about half past eight to await the owner.

There would be no chance of meeting any of the brigade today. It was the first day of the opera fortnight, the culmination of all that preparation, all those rehearsals both for the musicians, performers and the kitchen.

He had to be in on it, I thought. I was sure that Charlotte was right, that the owner/manager would deny all knowledge of everything, but I was going to try. I still had doubts about the Per I Tifosi story. However, I could hardly go up to my employer and tell him I thought that he was telling me a pack of lies, that although I believed he was being blackmailed, I didn't believe it was for the reasons he gave. Neither could I tell him one of his employees, that is

Octavia, had accused his wife of sleeping with and possibly murdering, his sous chef.

The manager or owner arrived at quarter to nine. He was of medium height, tubby, his brightly coloured Hawaiian shirt straining over his paunch, and he wore cheap-looking slip-on brown shoes and blue polyester trousers. His thinning, very black hair was combed over a bald patch. He did look exactly like I imagined a porn shop owner to look like. Soon, I guessed, he would be an ex-porn shop owner – they'd all be out of business. How could they compete with online sales and downloads? The EROS SHOP's elderly clients with their DVD players would die out eventually.

He bent down and unlocked the metal screen that protected the shop doorway and pulled it up to reveal the door. He fiddled with his bunch of keys and slipped inside. I slipped off my stool and paid the girl behind the counter, left the café and crossed the road.

I opened the door and went in.

The owner was behind the counter staring at the screen of an old, battered monitor. He looked up at me in surprise. I don't suppose many women came into the store. I certainly wasn't dressed like any of the women I could see on the DVD cases. For one, I was fully clothed and normally clothed at that. I wasn't dressed like a schoolgirl, or naked except for a pout, or wearing bondage gear or brandishing a whip.

'I'm sorry, darling, we're not open yet.'

'I know,' I said. I gave him a winning smile. 'But I was wondering if you could help me?'

The owner looked at me sceptically. He had quite hard eyes set in his chubby face. They were not full of the milk of human kindness but neither were they on fire with a mad desire to kill or maim me as Sandra's had been, so I felt comparatively relaxed.

'And how might I do that?' he asked. His tone warned me not to hold out any hope.

I took my phone out and brought up a picture of Matteo on the screen and showed it to him. 'This is a friend of mine,' I said. 'For the past few months, once a month he's been coming in here and giving you an envelope for "Greg" for "Mick" to collect. Does that ring any bells?'

I received a calculating stare rather than a reply, then: 'Not really, now you come to mention it. Sorry, love. . . Now, I'm a busy man. . .'

The shopkeeper looked meaningfully at the door, suggesting I might want to make use of it.

I nodded understandingly. 'OK, have a look at this group of people.' I swiped along to Matteo's team. There they all were, including Jean-Claude. His face, not the picture he had sent to Bryony, although given the surroundings it could have been more in keeping. 'One of these is the person who collected the envelope. Would you care to enlighten me?'

He drew himself up to his full height – he didn't have to do that much drawing, he was short – and said, 'Look, darling, do yourself a favour, why don't you sling your hook and leave my shop. I don't know any of these people. Now if you don't mind, I'm a busy man.'

I'd recently survived a double dose of Sandra. I can't say

I was overly frightened of a fat porn merchant. I raised my eyebrows. 'That's a very disappointing attitude,' I said, shaking my head sorrowfully. 'Look, for various reasons I don't want to get the police involved and I'm sure that you don't either.' I leaned over the counter so my face was very close to his.

'But if you don't help me, I won't have any choice, will I?'

I wasn't entirely bluffing. I looked around his tiny shop, floor to ceiling hard-core porn titles. But all on a moribund, old-fashioned format. The owner must have been desperate for money. The rental on this shop in this part of London would be very high. I thought again about the internet strangling his revenue stream like a huge, unstoppable virtual python – powered by a torrent of online porn. Soon, I guessed, it would have to close. He could hardly adopt a bookshop-style approach to lure potential punters by putting sofas in, selling coffee and inviting his clientele to browse.

He was probably only too delighted to act as a poste restante for dodgy customers, for a small fee. I suddenly wondered if he might be doing other shady things to prop up the business. There was a definite look of alarm in his face when I'd mentioned the police.

I would have no qualms about bringing Slattery here if necessary. Matteo, Charlotte and their fears would just have to take the risk of public exposure.

'It's not just blackmail that's involved,' I pointed out. 'You may not know this, but this is linked to two deaths, murders, and you're part of it, like it or not.'

'And who are you?' he asked, trying to tough it out, but failing. 'What have you got to do with any of it?'

'I'm a concerned citizen,' I said.

I looked at him politely. I could see indecision etched on his face. He looked like he was squirming. He really could do without the police. It confirmed my suspicions that something else was probably going on.

The door opened and a man shuffled in, his mouth fell open when he saw a real woman in there as opposed to a digital one faking orgasm – he turned away, blushing, and started inspecting the titles, his face pressed against them so I wouldn't be able to see his features. Then another man came in, saw me and immediately turned on his heel and left. I was obviously bad for business.

I could see another middle-aged man hovering around outside uncertainly. The owner noticed him too and clearly made up his mind that he had to get rid of me.

'I've got all day,' I said. 'I'm happy to wait until you remember something.'

'Look,' he eventually said, 'come back at seven tonight, when we close, and I'll speak to you then, OK? We'll have more privacy.'

'Fair enough,' I said, 'I'll see you then.'

I left the shop and headed back to the café opposite. I didn't believe a word he had said, but I had shaken the tree so to speak.

I resumed my place at the window of the café to see if he would do anything. And eventually he did.

An hour or so later a stocky, bearded guy in a tight T-shirt, the better to show off his muscular arms, strolled up to the shop and went inside. He was so different from the furtive others that I sat up and took note.

Sure enough, almost immediately afterwards, the fat owner left and headed along the street. I had been right – stocky guy was his replacement. I slipped out of the café, dropping some money to the girl behind the counter, and followed him.

I had obviously flushed a pheasant, now all I had to do was land the salmon – to mix metaphors in a very Francis way.

We walked through the quiet streets of Soho, restaurant capital of London, and along Great Marlborough Street which led down to the Palladium and Liberty's. I wondered who he was going to see, which of my suspects he would meet. At least I wouldn't need to return to his sex shop down a dark alley at night; I suspected that he might have arranged a little reception committee.

He took a left at Liberty's and we wandered down Carnaby Street then he disappeared into a Starbucks.

I was wondering what to do when a voice said, 'Charlie! What are you doing here! What a wonderful surprise.'

It was Graziana.

Chapter Thirty-Six

I travelled back home on the train, thinking about my morning and what I had learnt. I didn't know what to do with my newfound knowledge. All I could think was that the person behind the blackmail was none other than Graziana or at the very least, she was implicated in it.

Graziana had expressed surprise and delight at meeting me there in Carnaby Street. What was she doing there? Shopping of course, let's go and have a coffee, she said. I noticed that she steered me well away from the café that porn guy had gone into. To me it was clear that Mr Eros, spooked by me, had arranged an impromptu meeting with her. In these days of mobile phone intercepts, the old-fashioned face to face meeting seemed a safer bet. It could hardly be a coincidence that of all the streets in central London they should both be here at the same time. I mean, why else would porn guy have gone to Carnaby Street? It was unlikely that the result of my threatening him with the police had impelled him to pop out and freshen up his wardrobe.

I thought about Anna Bruce's prediction. The violent

woman, the existential threat, had already come to pass, in the unsavoury form of Sandra, Chris's Hells Angel wife. So there was the deceitful, malignant person to think about and the web of deception. All of those looked horribly applicable to Graziana.

It also made me wonder about her and Giorgio. I had thought he could well have seen the tattoo on the Per I Tifosi website, but now I did wonder if maybe they were lovers. A woman who could surreptitiously blackmail her husband was surely capable of anything.

My head was full of confused thoughts. I seemed to lack the clarity I could bring to food-based problems. But one thing seemed obvious, it was definitely time to find out more about Matteo's wife. After all, it couldn't do any harm. Had Graziana locked Octavia in that freezer, I suddenly wondered. I couldn't remember if she'd been around in the kitchen at the time. Well, I thought, at least it would be coming at things from a different angle. I texted Andrea to see if he had got any info back from his finance director friend. I should have chased him a while ago on this but the pressure of events had caused me to forget. He replied almost immediately to say that he was in a meeting in Milan but was having dinner with Roberto that evening and would let me know. I thanked him and put my phone away. Well, that was the Per I Tifosi angle covered as much as humanly possible.

I thought about telling Charlotte what I had seen but I couldn't. I didn't want to drop Graziana in it without more definitive proof. Charlotte wanted action taken against the blackmailer. I didn't want to be responsible for the fallout if I happened to be wrong, and I suspected that the future of any blackmailer at the hands of Charlotte would be less than rosy.

That night, I had a call from Milan. It was Andrea. We were on FaceTime; it was the first time I had seen him for a while. It's always strange to see the features of an ex-partner, someone who has figured strongly in your life.

He was in his hotel room in Milan, it was 9 o'clock my time, 10 in Italy. He was wearing a white shirt and dark trousers. In the background I could see his bed and the open door of the bathroom; I wished I could see more. I love Italian bathrooms, they tend to be so stylish. Bathrooms and lights, table lamps, these are areas in my view that the Italians really excel.

He looked tired. I noticed there was a touch of grey in his dark hair, that hadn't been there when we had been together. He was classically good looking in an Italian way. I compared him to Matteo. Matteo was more beautiful than handsome. He was, and it wasn't just his longish hair and jewellery, androgynously attractive. Andrea was more masculine. I felt a breathtakingly sharp stab of desire for him.

'Hi, how are you?' I said. 'Thanks for calling. . .'

'Hi, Charlie. I'm fine, tired.'

'How's the weather in Milan?' I asked, I don't know why. I had zero interest in the weather there. He frowned, maybe puzzled by the inane question.

'It's very hot, but y'know, Milan is not nice in the summer, very humid.'

'Oh.' I so wanted to be with him in Italy, humidity

notwithstanding; maybe we could look at lamps together, that would be nice. Or bathrooms.

'Anyway,' Andrea said in that brisk way he had. He wasn't keen on idle chit-chat. 'I spoke to Roberto, he said that there was no record of her whatsoever on Per I Tifosi. None. Niente.'

I frowned. 'But there has to be?'

'No, there doesn't.' He shook his head. 'He said not only did he try searching for her by her real name, then by her porn name – he even tried her maiden name,' I was impressed, I didn't know that, 'then he got an AI to scan the records – he gave it several images of her to compare against, again – nothing. I think that they've been lying to you. About that anyway. All along.'

'I wonder why?' I said. It was more or less what I had always suspected. I knew Charlotte's views, believing the story implicitly, believing that it would ruin the brand that was Matteo, but I had always been less convinced. Maybe partly because British people are, I feel, reasonably broad-minded, and partly because Graziana had always projected a very sexy image. Regardless of whether Charlotte or I was right, it now looked as if she had never been on the books of the website.

'Sorry I couldn't be of more assistance,' Andrea said.

'No, on the contrary.' He looked down the camera at me. I wish I were with you, I thought. The silence prolonged itself.

'OK, I'd better not keep you,' I said. Andrea liked to go to bed early.

'OK, well. . .'

'Maybe I could buy you dinner, to say thank you. . .' I hurriedly blurted out, 'or I could always cook it. . . couldn't I?' I was a chef, I did have a restaurant.

He smiled, it was an enigmatic smile. Less of the Mona Lisa shit, I thought.

'Maybe, allora. . . ciao, Charlie.'

'Ciao. . . *alla prossima*. . .' I think that means 'until the next time', which I devoutly hoped would be a thing and I terminated the call. So, once again, Graziana had been caught lying, although in fairness, this time Matteo was implicated too.

I thought, what the hell is going on. Then I thought, Oh, Andrea, I miss you.

Chapter Thirty-Seven

The following day, I was back in Matteo's kitchen.

Despite everything, a semblance of normality had returned. Today was the second day of the opera fortnight as it was called, itself. Rehearsals were over, the psychological hurdle of the first day had been surmounted, and work had begun in earnest. It was almost a relief. Lost in the whirl of the kitchens, it was, at times, hard to remember that Octavia was dead. I was supposed to be working ten until three then six until eleven, but the reality was, as I had suspected all along, that I would be working nine until midnight without a break. And I didn't mind working flat out. I was desperate to impress, keen to make the most of being with a top chef like Matteo.

From a selfish point of view, I knew that the kudos I gained from working with a household name like Matteo McCleish would stand me in very good stead locally. All too soon, the opera fortnight would be over, and, win or lose, things would move on, one way or another. In fact, working with him really was inspirational. He was one of the best chefs I had ever worked with. I hadn't appreciated how good he was until I had actually seen him in the flesh, actually in action – as opposed to on the TV.

Matteo did very little hands-on cooking. He stood at the pass and arranged the cooked and prepped food as it became ready, on plates. This sounds ludicrously easy, but he was more like a skilled conductor in an orchestra, calling out to Tom and me what he wanted and when he wanted it. Occasionally he would step into one of the sections and help out where necessary but without breaking the other person's concentration. Needless to say, he was better than anyone.

Tom was on fish and seafood; I was helping out on meat; Murdo on starters, sauces and desserts. The gangly Scot also was in charge of the pasta, which unsurprisingly featured heavily on the menu.

When you watched Matteo cook it was with the effortless ease of a true master. Like Roger Federer playing tennis. I was open-mouthed with admiration.

It was a dream team to work with. I had cooked in a Michelin place before, but I had been far down the kitchen hierarchy. Now I was working with some agency guy, the two of us filling Tom's shoes, with him stepping up to what the deceased Giorgio used to do.

Tom was a very good chef too. I'm not bad, but it's hard to keep track of how long things have been on a grill or a pan or in an oven, when you have twenty to thirty pieces of meat and fish cooking, all for various lengths of time, all simultaneously.

I have a tendency, a bit like a computer system, to crash under pressure. My mind goes blank, staring at the stove wondering what was what, and trying to match food with cheques. Tom just powered along, faultlessly, without missing a beat. I was impressed.

Considering the volume of food, it was just as well that we were working so efficiently. It was more or less three hundred meals that were going out to the hungry, critical opera-lovers. Admittedly it was a limited menu – five starters, five mains and five desserts, and done on a pre-order system – but the quality of cooking was exemplary. I guess it had to be – it was a showcase for Matteo's talents.

I was relaxing after service on Thursday, the fourth day of the opera festival, when Tom invited me out for a beer. *La Traviata*, which opened the festival, was in full swing and going well. Not that I cared. I was focused on the case and on the lookout for some revelation or insight into Graziana's behaviour or character, but I was realistic enough to guess that this wouldn't be forthcoming. I could always hope though.

I said yes, and where else would we go but the Three Bells? We arrived just in time for the nightly lock-in.

Malcolm's pub paradoxically was never busier than at ten to eleven. Because he often had a lock-in, quite a few young people who had been pre-drinking at home would drift in, then there were the chefs from the King's Head and a smattering of seriously heavy boozers. As eleven approached, the pub would mysteriously get full and Malcolm would suddenly appear almost energetic. He had even been known to smile on occasions.

There is a comforting feel to a lock-in. The knowledge that you were one of the select – that you had somewhere you belonged, a kind of a club even if it wasn't the Groucho or White's, and that frisson you get from doing something faintly illegal.

Tom brought our drinks back to the corner table where I liked to sit. The young chefs from Graeme Strickland's restaurant played pool and drank heavily, the air heavy with their profanities, their adrenaline still hanging off them as pungent as their Lynx body-spray after a heavy, tumultuous service.

'Ah, youth. . .' sighed Tom with a grin from his thirty-year-old vantage point.

We chatted about how the evening had gone, then: 'How long have you been with Matteo?' I asked.

'About three years now. He had just opened up a restaurant in Kings Cross, well, it was in a pub, not like it is now, and he bought the use of the kitchen for six months, so it was make or break time.' He drank some of his beer and stroked his short beard thoughtfully. 'Those were the best days. Nobody knew who he was, but he was cooking like an angel and he had that, well, you know, that sort of star quality. . . We were rammed from the off.'

I knew what he meant. I had worked in some places where the cooking was exemplary but the place failed to catch on. To cook really well and be really popular is a hard thing to do, the one doesn't necessarily mean the other.

He talked dreamily of those months, working mad hours, sometimes not going home, sleeping on the floor of the restaurant, going out clubbing with Matteo and Graziana. . .

'God, we were so close then, it was like being in a family but better, you know. . .'

I could imagine. The bond between chefs who work such crazily long hours together can get really intense, and after a while you develop an almost psychic connection, so attuned do you get to the moods and thoughts of the other.

'What's Graziana like?' I asked. In other words, was she the kind of girl to massively betray her husband?

'A great girl,' Tom said simply, 'always up for a laugh, and Christ, isn't she sexy. . .'

Yes.

'Did you and she ever. . .?' I asked in a kind of 'we're all guys together' sort of way, which is kind of foreign to my nature. I wanted to know if she really was the kind of person who would cheat on her husband. Betrayal, like most things, gets easier with practice.

'No,' said Tom with an air of disappointment. 'I tried to, a couple of times, you know she looks so, so up for it. . .'

He took a big drink of beer.

'Well, I thought she was up for it.' Tom nodded emphatically. 'But no, she's absolutely devoted to Matteo. She told me so, after I'd made a pass at her, my second one. I was obsessed with Graziana, I couldn't stop thinking about her: the way she looked, that smile, her sexy accent. I was crazy. I wanted her to leave Matteo for me.'

Well, I thought, so much for devotional loyalty from your staff. If Tom was prepared, as I had now established beyond any reasonable doubt, to betray his employer with his wife, would he be equally happy to blackmail him?

I evaluated Tom in terms of attractiveness. He was facially reasonably good-looking, nothing special, but he did have a good body. He was wearing a T-shirt and jeans and the muscles in his arm swelled and balled as he mentioned Matteo's name, as if he were rehearsing ripping his head off. He really looked phenomenally strong. And he was certainly a damn good chef, much better than me.

'And what did she say?' It was a stupid question really. They were still married obviously.

He smiled bitterly. 'She let me down gently.'

I nodded faux-sympathetically.

'I heard she was having an affair,' I said, casually.

'I don't believe that,' he said, 'I don't think that she would do that.'

'How about Giorgio?' I was desperate to know.

Tom laughed incredulously. 'Him! The only women who went out with him were either paid for or absolute mingers.' He drank some more beer. 'He was a weirdo. He had this huge porn collection, all on DVD.'

Well, that explained his EROS visit, I thought.

'I was round at his flat once and I saw it. You couldn't not see it. I collect cookery books – it was a bit like that. In shelves. Lots of shelves. Like a humongous porn library. I asked him why he didn't go online. He said he liked to own it, that is, own a physical copy of the film and keep it all in alphabetical order and categorised according to subject, Schoolgirl, Secretary, that kind of thing. I wonder what will happen to it now. . . bit of a loss really. . . perhaps it'll end up in a charity shop.'

He laughed at the thought of someone taking that lot

to Sue Ryder or Age Concern.

'Maybe he left it to Douglas in his will,' he added.

'I'm sorry?' My ears pricked up.

'Yeah, Douglas likes porn too. They discussed it quite a lot when they thought nobody was listening, well, that was Douglas not wanting anyone to know, Giorgio was in your face about it. I think it was Douglas's way of trying to bond with Giorgio, to suck up to him. . . Giorgio could be really nasty to him at times.'

He looked at me with a hint of suspicion. 'Why are you asking about Douglas?'

'Oh, no reason,' I said, 'but I am curious about Giorgio, he worked in my kitchen, remember. . . he was a good chef but a nightmare. Why did Matteo employ him?' I asked. I had heard one theory, I wanted another. And I was genuinely curious. Giorgio was indeed a good enough chef but at that level there are a lot of good chefs. Matteo could have his pick of skilled labour, someone like Sam, the reliable chef who was working at the Old Forge for one, but for some odd reason he had gone for Giorgio.

'I don't know,' said Tom. 'It sounds stupid, but I think he had some kind of hold over Matteo. I don't know what it was but it was like he knew something. Once or twice, in an argument, he said something in Italian and Matteo's face just kind of froze. You know the way you do when something is said that you don't want to come out – I think it was that. It was like Giorgio was taunting him with it, y'know, like "if Tom knew Italian think what he'd make of that!"'

He smiled. 'But I could be wrong. He was a great

organiser, not just of porn. And of course, he was a useful attack dog if Matteo wanted to give someone a bollocking. He could make grown men cry. I've seen it happen.'

He had another mouthful of beer. 'Giorgio liked company when he had sex. I think he had threesomes with Jean-Claude. What a bloody horrible thought, but there you go. He won't be doing any of that wherever he is now, bless him.'

Well, that was a surprise. Not the Jean-Claude thing but the hold over Matteo. What could that have been? Was it even true? Tom, by his own admission, couldn't speak Italian.

Was Graziana part of the price? Was that why Giorgio was killed?

I bought Tom another drink. He was getting surprisingly drunk. His voice was louder, his words slightly slurred. I think that maybe he was unused to heavy drinking, which is unusual in a chef. But the kind of attention he paid to his body was of the sort that borders on the obsessional. I knew that he worked out before he came to work and in the afternoon when he was on a split. Alcohol didn't play much of a part in his life and I was keen to capitalise on this. Tom's tongue was unguarded, his defences down.

'How long has Murdo been around?' I asked. I didn't suspect him of anything but you never knew.

'He came when Octavia did. She was shit really, didn't have a clue. She said that she'd done some stages for Heston and Sat Bains and Galvin's, but it was all complete and utter bollocks. I called her out on it, and she more or less admitted it.'

Deceitful? I thought back to Anna Bruce. But so many

people in this brigade were.

He drained his glass. I think he had realised that he was getting drunk and decided to leave. 'I'd better get back. I'll see you tomorrow, Charlie. It was good having a drink with you – I feel better now.'

He shook my hand and I watched him walk slightly unsteadily out of the pub.

I checked my phone, a couple of missed calls from a number I didn't know, then a message from Graeme Strickland. 'Gave Cassandra (wine woman) your number, she said she'd be in touch. xx' That must have been her, I thought. I'd call her in the morning. I put my phone away.

Chapter Thirty-Eight

Tom was subdued the following morning. Maybe he was hungover, maybe he was ashamed of himself or maybe he felt that he had revealed too much, regretting his candour. I was doing the prep for the evening with Murdo.

There were a couple of groups coming in early from London, ferried out here on coaches. After a tour of the gardens, before the first half of the opera began, *La Traviata* again, we were giving them canapés and oysters. I remember my dad used to claim that you shouldn't eat oysters if there was an 'r' in the month. Seemingly this was because in the olden days if there were increased algal blooms, it made shellfish potentially toxic. Modern ways of monitoring sea pollution have reduced this threat. Not that he would have believed it.

Anyway, I thought of him affectionately while Murdo was stuffing olives and I was making dressings to go with the oysters – an oriental-style dressing, a mignonette, which is basically shallots and vinegar, and a lime and Tabasco dressing. The oysters were sitting in big hessian sacks in the fridge, quietly awaiting their fate. You couldn't pre-open them too long before service as they were supposed to be eaten live. Yuck, in my opinion.

Murdo was pretty much out of his head, amphetamines or whatever equivalent youngsters – he was nineteen – took these days. His eyes were practically popping out. I was feeling slightly let down. I'd bailed Murdo out and here he was repeating the behaviour that had got him into trouble in the first place. I pulled myself up sharply. Murdo had never promised to mend his ways, I was in no position to lecture him – not after my own fairly chequered youth. Still, it was bloody annoying. And saving him from being beaten up had been an expensive gesture on my part.

Death metal, Murdo's music of choice, thundered from the speakers of a radio that he had synced his phone to. It was perched on a shelf just above my head. I glanced at it. It had an LED display screen so you knew what the music was: '. . . now playing. . . "Onset of Putrefaction" by Necrophagist. . .'

I'm sure it was very good, although it wasn't my cup of tea. Murdo was trying to convert me to the death metal cause but I was pining for Beech Tree FM – they wouldn't be playing Necrophagist, that was for sure. On my way over (I had driven) it had been 'And that was Harry Styles with "As it Was" and now, it's Lizzo with "About Damn Time".'

The music screamed around my ears, Murdo's head nodding along to the beat. There was certainly no mistaking it for Harry Styles. He caught my eye.

'Brilliant, aren't they!'

'They're jolly good,' I shouted over the din. Nothing cheers your day more than a bit of Necrophagist, I reflected.

Would Murdo enjoy Lizzo? Probably not.

He was working with manic, drug-fuelled intensity. The stuffing for the olives was a Le Marche speciality, a mix of pork, chicken and herbs, then the whole thing was bread-crumbed and deep-fried. Le Marche was where Matteo had grown up. When he was showing me how to make them he had cooked one for me to try; it was delicious.

It was a fiddly job. Matteo had calculated that for a hundred and fifty people we needed about three hundred of these. Murdo's fingers flew like lightning across the olives, which he had already prepped by de-stoning them. They were great olives, huge and intensely green. You slit them open, remove the stone, add filling to the centre and pack more filling around the outside, then finally you panné them. Not unlike a Scotch egg in some respects.

I finished my dressings and moved on to slicing up yesterday's ciabatta to make bruschetta for yet more canapés and one of the starters.

Murdo kept up a kind of staccato, bellowed conversation as he worked.

'I love septic flesh, don't you?' he bellowed.

I looked down at the large bowl of minced, herbed meat he was working with. It didn't look as if it had gone off. I leaned over it and smelled.

'Is it minging?' I asked. It seemed OK.

He looked at me like I was mad.

'No, you idiot, Charlie, not the meat, this track – it's by Septicflesh.' He rolled his eyes. Jesus! he was obviously thinking. Of course it was. I thought.

Thanks to the drugs, his mind was working overtime

and he was talking at a machine-gun rate. I looked at the clock; it was eleven. The morning is going to drag, I thought to myself. Murdo couldn't shut up. He had told me about his childhood and moved on to adolescence in Edinburgh. Petty theft, I guess that's where he had learnt his padlock picking skills, glue-sniffing and sex. And how he had discovered the joys of music. A discovery I was now benefitting from. Lucky old me.

Murdo, in his wide-eyed, talkative amphetamine haze, had by now filled me in on his early cooking career and life in catering. Dodgy housing estate in Edinburgh, somewhere called Pilton, college, landing a dream job in a restaurant in Stockbridge, the Stane Bothy, which won a Michelin star just after he joined. Two years there and now this job with Matteo.

'I wanted to get out of Scotland; I wanted to see more of the world,' he explained. 'Oh I love this track.'

More horrid music. Then. . .

'I love Italian food,' he added. 'It's the coming thing.'

'The coming thing?' I was baffled. It was hardly new.

'It's so adaptable,' explained Murdo, ecstatically. 'You can tweak it and everyone thinks you're being really inventive, like a ravioli of cockles and mussels in a seaweed-infused broth. Or a lasagne of. . .' he frowned as he thought of something not normally found in a lasagne '. . . pigeon and blueberry. . .'

'Yuck,' I said, with feeling.

He laughed. 'Well, you get the idea. . . anyway, give us a hand with this pan.'

There was a huge double-handled pan about the size of

a dustbin and he had filled it with water from the hot tap. Francis, I reflected, could have done it with one hand. Together, huffing and puffing with effort, muscles straining, we lifted it out of the sink and carried it across the kitchen and clanged it down on the stove where it covered nearly half the range.

He put the gas on under it and at that moment Bryony came in wearing a strappy black top, khaki combat trousers, Doc Martens, and her short blond hair pushed upwards into a kind of crest like a cockatoo's. She was clutching a large handful of rosemary branches.

She nodded politely at me. 'Charlie. . . Hi, Murdo.' She looked delighted to see him. I felt a twinge of jealousy. Wasn't I her friend? After all, I had got rid of Jean-Claude. But she had eyes only for Murdo.

'Hi, babes. . .'

They smiled hungrily at each other, both of them young and both of them completely out of their heads. They were very happy. I suddenly felt very old and worn down with care. If only, I thought, I had achieved some kind of wisdom to go with my years. But no, that didn't seem to have arrived yet.

He took the rosemary branches from her and handed them to me together with two garlic bulbs. 'Strip the leaves off these, Charlie, and chop them all small, and then finely chop the garlic please. I'm just popping outside with Bryony.'

She ruffled his hair playfully and they left the kitchen together. I shook my head and switched off 'Testimony of the Ancients' by Pestilence. I turned the function on the Roberts radio from iPod/Phone to Beech Tree FM.

'. . . *and now for something from a while back*. . .' Oh no, I thought, what if Beech Tree FM have gone all death metal too? Please, God, no Malevolent Creation. . . '*but first a question: are you good at maths? Can you count? Well, Steps certainly can. . . here's "5, 6, 7, 8"!*'

Thank Christ! I thought.

Ten minutes later I was chopping the last of the garlic when Murdo reappeared smiling woozily and smelling strongly of weed. He was obviously making hay while the sun shone in Matteo's absence.

'She's a great girl,' he said of Bryony.

The cannabis he had been smoking didn't seem to affect him as he frowned at the radio. I could see his mind wondering what that rubbish was. He looked at me, shook his head as if I'd been a naughty child and put some more death metal on. Steps were silenced, and the Fields of the Nephilim blasted through the kitchen air.

Murdo put twenty ciabatta loaves in the oven, threw ten packets of spaghetti into the boiling cauldron on the stove and while making a couple of salads, got me to make a tomato sauce with the fresh rosemary and garlic. Six minutes later, when the spaghetti was three-quarters cooked, the two of us, draped in oven cloths to protect our hands and necks from the scalding metal, heaved the pan onto our shoulders, staggered across the kitchen with it, tipped the pasta into an enormous colander in the sink, then quickly threw the parboiled pasta into a sink full of iced water.

That was the orchestra's and singers' dinner sorted. We'd be able to reheat it and feed about sixty of them in twenty-odd minutes.

We got on with prepping for the dinner guests. Tom and Matteo would be coming in at three when we had finished, to work until close of service, and we would re-join them at six.

'What are you going to do in your break?' asked Murdo.

'I'm going over to speak to a woman I know about a catering job that I've got lined up,' I said, 'and then I'm coming back here.'

He nodded. We'd talked a fair bit about the Old Forge Café. He'd been very complimentary about my menu, which was nice of him. Young, highly ambitious chefs like Murdo are apt to be a bit sniffy about old chefs (in my mid-forties I seemed ancient to the nineteen-year-old Scot, well, I was over twice his age).

'If it all goes tits up I could always come and work for you,' he'd said. Cheers, Murdo.

'And what are you going to do during your break?' I asked.

'Special K,' said Murdo.

'The cereal?' I asked, suspecting it wasn't.

'Ketamine,' said Murdo.

'Are you mad?' I said. I looked at the gangly, red-headed kid, cheerily stoned. He grinned at me, proud of his ability to shock.

I wasn't shocked; I was just worried about him.

'Isn't that stuff horse tranquilliser?' I asked.

'Aye, it's brilliant,' he replied. 'Do you want some?'

'No thanks.'

Murdo looked pleased with himself, at the reaction he'd caused. He then decided maybe he'd overdone it.

'Just pulling your leg,' he reassured me. 'Just a wee bit of Charlie to take the edge off things, nothing serious.'

I sighed and rolled my eyes.

'I used to do it a lot in Edinburgh on my breaks,' he said defensively. 'It's no big deal.'

'Well,' I said primly, 'I wish you wouldn't. It's probably very bad for you.'

No point asking Murdo how he was paying for it. He'd only have lied to me, or got huffy. You can't make addicts alter their ways, change has to come from within.

Murdo rolled his eyes. I was a stupid, old fart.

3 o'clock came. Tom arrived looking freshly showered and pumped up. Matteo arrived, driven by Graziana in their Maserati. You could hear the throb of its powerful engine over the noise of the fan in the kitchen as it pulled up outside the kitchen door.

'I'm gonna have one of those one day,' said Murdo, nodding at the car. He spoke with all the magnificent assurance of youth, an infinite number of days and opportunities ahead of him.

'See you at six.' He squeezed past me. He had changed out of his chef's whites and was now in skinny, ripped jeans and a T-shirt. His thin, pale arms were heavily tattooed in a mass of lurid colour. His face under his mop of ginger hair looked ridiculously young.

'I'm off!' he shouted to Matteo who waved at him as he buttoned up his chef's jacket.

I, too, said my goodbyes to Matteo and Tom, changed and started to walk back to Hampden Green.

Chapter Thirty-Nine

It was only a ten-minute walk across the fields. I passed by the gigantic marquee where the opera was being staged in the first field. It was a work of art in itself, built by the same people who had done the tents for the Holland Park opera. When you looked at it you began to understand why the tickets were so expensive.

In the area of the field near the marquee and the serried ranks of VIP Portaloos, I could see a couple of locals I knew who had been roped in as stewards for the temporary car park. They were busy laying out traffic cones for the two coaches that were due later that afternoon.

I looked back at the idyllic scene. The stately manor house, not a grand place like Blenheim or Chatsworth or Cliveden, but a sizeable, pleasant brick building, the manicured gardens with their trees, shrubs, parterres and the occasional grey glimpse of stonework through the lush green foliage and dotted artfully around, splashes of colour from flower beds or shrubs.

You could just make out the white fabric of the smaller

marquee below the house that was used for the dining room.

Later on this warm summer evening, there would be a genteel, orderly procession of guests walking between the two tents in the break between the two acts of the opera. The men in evening dress, the women in gowns.

Nobody looking at this picture of tranquillity could have any idea that the kitchen supplying the gourmet food had suffered two deaths. And the strange thing was that, like everything in catering, it carried on regardless. The show had to go on. The band played on as the ship slowly sank. The orchestra had to be fed, the customers had to be fed, the contracts had to be maintained. Meanwhile, a high level of weirdness – murder, blackmail, drugs and sex – was being played out in Matteo's kitchen.

Five minutes later, I was back in my own kitchen. Sam was nowhere to be seen. I wondered what he'd be up to. Hopefully not doing drugs or sleeping with someone else's wife, like Matteo's brigade.

I found Jess in the restaurant talking to a dark-haired woman. They were looking at Jess's laptop while Jess was indicating some charts. She stopped what she was doing and smiled at me.

'Hi, Chef,' she said, 'this is Cassandra Jenkins.'

'Nice to meet you,' I said. I looked with interest at Strickland's ex. She stood up to shake hands. She was tall and very slim with long dark hair and a beautiful, mournful face. She was wearing a dark, skater dress that emphasised her slender build and boots. She looked like she had stepped out of a religious painting – like she was a mediaeval saint, she had that soulful look, tinged with melancholy. Mind you, that could have been the result of going out with Graeme Strickland rather than innate spirituality. He'd drive anyone nuts.

We sat down and talked about my existing wine stocks, sales, what did and didn't go well, the possibility of introducing wine flights. Cassandra seemed intensely knowledgeable and extremely nice. I gave her my budget and she said she'd email me a list of suggested wines with mark-up and margins. Her consultancy fee was high but not excessive; in all honesty I would have paid her a lot more. When she left, I turned to Jess.

'Well. . .' I said.

'God, she's good.' Jess seemed enthusiastic. 'My dad might even start coming here.'

I let that one pass. 'Well, we're agreed. She's a find. How was today?'

'Quite busy, thirty covers, lots of compliments,' she said. 'How about you, how's life in the fast lane?'

I told her.

'How quickly the gloss wears off,' she said with mock-sadness. 'So what are you doing this afternoon?'

'I'm off to see Esther. She's got some comments from Chris on the NoBWic menu – want to come?'

No surprises for the fact that Chris was slightly shy these days when it came to talking directly to me. Well, if he preferred to filter his communications via Esther that would be fine by me. Jess had already agreed she would be helping me out at the party. 'I would indeed.'

I was delighted that she was coming. She had a knack for asking questions that I would never think of, including important questions like when I'd be paid.

We drove over to Esther Bartlett's house in my car. I half-expected to see Sandra emerging from the shrubberies that lay on each side of the tarmac of the drive, hell-bent on revenge. I was getting paranoid.

Esther welcomed us and led us into the lounge. There was a man in there, not Chris I was relieved to see, but the Wizard Doctor as I thought of him, Dr Rowan Herne.

'Hello, Rowan,' I said.

'Good afternoon, Charlie.' He looked at me gravely and stroked his chin. He was wearing a black leather jacket, despite the heat, and looked more than ever like a bank robber. An old school bank robber. I hadn't noticed before he had the physique of a man who works out a lot, the jacket was covering what looked like very muscular shoulders. 'I've been giving a talk at the surgery in Frampton End. I'm just going over The Ritual with Esther then I thought I'd stroll over to the Manor and have a look at the tent, she says it's really something.'

'It is,' I said, 'but I'm afraid all the tickets have gone. It's sold out.'

Rowan frowned. 'I'm not remotely interested in opera, Charlie,' he informed me. 'I'm more of a Thomas Tallis man, no that's not the reason. . . I'm an Outdoorist.'

'Sorry? Is that a branch of Wicca?' I asked, proud to show off the fact that I knew what Wicca was.

'No,' he said with a hint of exasperation. 'The Great Outdoors. I'm an outdoorist, I'm interested in tents.'

'Oh,' I said. Silence fell. I felt remarkably stupid. Rowan shook his head, pityingly. I didn't know who Thomas Tallis was either. I had thought he was the singer for Radiohead, but wasn't that Thom Yorke?

'I've got the finalised menu for the NoBWic gathering,' Esther said brightly, changing the subject.

'That's good.' I said, relieved we were back on a subject I knew about. Unlike tents. Or music for that matter.

'I hope that Chris's wife isn't going to make an appearance at this do?' said Jess. Her voice was very calm but I knew her well. She was still angry about the Sandra incident, much more so than I was. I don't hold grudges. She underlined the point: 'She's attacked Charlie twice now – we don't want it to happen again.'

I thought to myself that she sounded like a mother talking to a schoolteacher about a kid in class who'd bullied her son.

'Of course not,' said Esther, decisively, 'that's why it will be taking place here, not in Milton Keynes. I have spoken to all concerned and it has been agreed. Both by the North Bucks Wiccans and Rowan's Milton Keynes Coven.' Rowan Herne nodded sternly. Esther continued, 'Sandra will not be making a scene in my garden, Jessica Turner, I can assure you.'

Esther was wearing an enormous electric blue caftan and her chins moved in unison as she shook her head. She looked very impressive, more than capable of dealing with Sandra.

'Well, that's all very well. . .' said Jess, doubtfully.

'Chris assures me that she realises now it's all a complete misunderstanding,' said Esther. 'It's all water under the bridge. She's very apologetic.'

'It'll be fine, Jess, it'll be fine,' I assured her with a certainty I didn't feel. I wasn't a hundred per cent confident. Sandra did not seem like a woman amenable to reason and I was pretty sure she was not going to come and say sorry, but neither did I think she would create a scene in front of over a hundred people at a large party.

'Words have been spoken,' intoned the Doctor. He looked at me reassuringly. There was something about the Wizard that made you feel reassured if he was in your corner. He looked more than capable of dealing with Sandra at a physical level if needs be, which gave an idea of his presence. 'Sandra will not be attending, even as a guest.'

Jess shook her head mistrustfully and pushed her dark, curly hair back from her face in an aggressive way.

'She had better not,' she said darkly to Esther.

The four of us sat down and went through the menu, just in case there were any misunderstandings. Jess went through exactly where and how the food would be served and what quantities of plates, glasses, crockery and cutlery would be needed. Then she moved on to the quantity of wine and other beverages. My mind glazed over.

I thought of how lucky I was to have Jess overseeing the details. God, how I would miss her in the autumn when she went back to Warwick for her second year to work on Python, Prolog and machine programming skills. Whatever they were. She had told me but my attention had wandered.

Then she would go somewhere for an internship. Please God, let it be local, I prayed.

I could understand why Matteo had more or less handed over the running of his life to Charlotte. There was a lot more to being a successful chef than the ability to cook and write menus. That was the easy bit. Handling life outside the kitchen was the hardship.

'So,' said Jess, wrapping things up, 'that's that.'

'Indeed,' said Esther, 'and how's Jane?'

Jane was Jessica's mother whom I had never met.

'She's fine. She and Dad went to see *Traviata* at the festival last night.'

'I saw it two days ago!' Esther clasped her hands together ecstatically. 'We ate there too – the food was delicious, thank you, Charlie!'

I smiled. 'Thank Matteo.'

'Mum's a huge fan of Matteo,' Jess said. 'She was thrilled when Charlie got him to sign that cookbook for her.'

'There we go,' I said modestly, 'me and my celebrity connections. . .'

'Well,' said Esther, 'I think we're jolly lucky to have Charlie cooking for us tomorrow!'

And on that happy note we parted.

We said our goodbyes and Esther led us to the door.

We walked back to my Volvo and I took Jess back to her parents' house on the outskirts of the village. I dropped her at the gate (all these people seemed to have driveways) and drove back to the restaurant.

It was now nearly 5 o'clock. The restaurant dining room had that hushed and expectant air that it does when it's waiting for customers. I walked back into the kitchen. It was beautifully tidy. I opened a couple of fridges, and everything was neatly labelled in an unknown hand; it had to be Sam's. I felt oddly unsettled, like it was no longer my place. I was being usurped by Sam, the Reasonable Chef.

I couldn't complain. Matteo was paying me twice what I would make on my own and he was supplying Sam for free and what had I achieved? Very little, it had to be said. Maybe reassurance. The only person in his kitchen team, besides the Poles, who he knew was definitely not trying to blackmail him or kill anyone was me.

I decided to go back to the Earl's house and join Tom and Matteo. If I was unable to relax, I might as well help with the prep. I walked back across the fields.

Murdo would be sunbathing somewhere out of his mind on coke or horse tranquilliser (I wasn't entirely convinced that he wasn't going to take any ketamine) listening to his dreadful death metal. Doubtless he'd perk himself up with something for the evening shift, more coke probably.

The day was drowsily quiet in the late afternoon heat. The colour scheme was muted and quintessentially English, the various shades of green of the trees and ferns and grasses, the blue of the sky, the lacy white blooms of the elderflowers and the distinctive yellow flowers of agrimony and meadow buttercup. The countryside seemed to be holding its breath. The only noise was the occasional high-flying jet – Heathrow was only a few miles away, maybe about twenty as the crow or Airbus flies – and the occasional clatter of a helicopter and the squawk of the few pheasants that had survived the shoot earlier in the year.

The footpath I was using to approach the field where the opera was being held was overgrown; the dog walkers didn't use it much as it led through a meadow with sheep and they had to put their dogs on a leash. As I drew nearer to the field, through a copse of trees I could hear tinny, faint music. Not the kind that you associate with the country. Not folk. It was death metal. I had come to recognise it by now. It had to be Murdo. I sniffed the air for the tell-tale scent of weed but nothing. That was a surprise.

I walked off the path, skirted a bush and saw him.

He was lying face down on the grass at the edge of the field, arms stretched out before him. His phone was pumping out the music, the earphones still in his ears but no longer connected to the phone itself. He had been using old-fashioned cable connected earphones, the jack had come out of the socket on his phone and the speaker was playing to the wide world rather than his ears.

I felt a prickle of unease. I went over to him. What was going on?

'Murdo?'

He didn't move. I was now very worried. I bent over him and touched his thin shoulders gently. Nothing. I rolled him over. His eyes were closed and his pale face now looked even whiter than normal but with a bluish tinge. His breathing was faint, his chest barely moving.

Christ, I thought, the ketamine, he'd OD'd. Or was it cocaine? God alone knows what the idiot had been up to. I suddenly felt sick with worry.

'Christ,' I said aloud, followed by, 'don't die, Murdo, you cretin!'

I got my phone out and I phoned 999.

No signal. I stared angrily around me for inspiration. That didn't work.

Shit, I thought, I'll have to run for help. Then I thought, he could be dead by then, maybe I could carry him to the road and flag a car down. I was about to try to get him in some kind of fireman's lift when in the distance I saw a familiar burly, black jacketed figure making its way across the fields.

'ROWAN!' I screamed. He must have been inspecting the tent and was on his way back to Esther's. He didn't hear me. Dear God, don't let him be wearing ear-buds, I prayed.

I leapt in the air trying to attract his attention, 'ROWAN!'

He looked around, puzzled, I shouted again, jumping up and down and waving my arms. He must have realised something serious was happening, he ran over to me.

'What's happening?' He looked very cross, red in the face from running, then he saw Murdo.

He knelt by him, looked up at me.

'Do you know him?'

'He's one of the chefs. . . I think he might have taken some drugs. . .'

He was bent over him now, checking his pulse. 'Do you know what?'

'Ketamine, I think, no, wait, coke.'

He shook his head. 'Doesn't look that way. . .' Rowan rolled back one of Murdo's eyelids, the pupils were like pinpricks. 'Miosis. . .' he said to himself '. . .slow breathing. . .' he squinted up at me. 'Does he do heroin?'

'I have no idea. . . probably.' Murdo would do anything if it was available, I thought.

Rowan unzipped his backpack and took out a syringe and said to me, 'Call an ambulance.'

'I can't, no signal.'

'Shit.' He tried his own phone, then barked, 'Run, get an ambulance out here, say suspected opioid OD, tell them there's a doctor with him and I'm injecting Naloxone. Hurry. . .'

He didn't need to tell me to hurry. He was now giving him CPR.

I was off at a pace that wouldn't have shamed Laura Muir. As I sprinted across the field, I thought – thank God for Outdoorists.

Chapter Forty

'It looks very much like attempted murder,' said DI Slattery to me.

It was nearly midnight and we were sitting in my restaurant drinking whisky. Murdo had been rushed off to hospital where he was still in intensive care.

'A massive opiate OD,' said Slattery. He rubbed his jaw reflectively with a large hand padded with muscle. 'You were probably the last person to see him before he overdosed – what do you think?'

I sipped my Scotch. I had already given a statement to the police, so Slattery's visit was off the record. He just wanted to see if I had any insights. I had spoken to Matteo and Graziana. Matteo was grim-faced, Graziana in tears. Her eyeliner had run.

'He was just a kid,' she had sobbed.

I had offered my resignation. 'I'm sorry, Matteo, I don't seem to be doing very well at all. . .'

Graziana had butted in. 'Please don't go, Charlie. . . If it hadn't been for you finding him, he'd be dead.'

'Well, that was mainly Dr Herne,' I said. But what she

said was undeniably true. If I hadn't found him, Murdo would have been, to quote from an album he'd made me endure by a band called Children of Bodom – a Skeleton in the Coffin.

This latest incident confirmed to me that I would have to act. I would have to confront Graziana. It was my job, after all, to uncover the blackmailer. It was a task I had little enthusiasm for. I knew how much Graziana meant to Matteo, I suspected that the truth was going to hurt.

Matteo laughed bitterly. 'Don't worry about it, Charlie. At least with you there, I've got someone in my kitchen I can trust.'

So there we had left it.

Back in my own kitchen, I now looked at Slattery. 'He told me he was going to spend his break taking ketamine and/ or coke. I'm not sure about the ket. When he saw my face he told me he was winding me up, but God knows. . . I can't see it being an accidental overdose. I think Murdo probably knew what he was up to when it came to taking drugs.'

Like many drug users, Murdo had been keen to impress upon me how reliable his dealer was, how wonderful his wares. For this reason, I thought any chance that he would have been sold a batch of unusually strong stuff, or drugs cut with something lethal, seemed unlikely. As I told Slattery, he almost certainly hadn't bought it off the street or from one of the other chefs in the Three Bells.

'Then, I suspect, his plan was to do some coke or more speed to perk him up for the evening shift. I guess that's when he OD'd.'

Slattery nodded.

'He did have ketamine in his bloodstream. But it can stay detectable in your blood for up to three days I believe. It's not wholly clear at the moment. But that's not what nearly killed him. The lab – I had a word unofficially – think it's fentanyl.'

'Fentanyl?' I didn't know what that was.

'About a hundred times more powerful than heroin. I don't think even someone like Murdo would have taken that before going back to work. Someone got to his drugs and spiked them.'

'So, someone tried to kill him!' I said.

'And would have done, if it hadn't been for that witch doctor friend of yours.'

'He's not a witch doctor,' I said, defending Rowan, 'he's a doctor who happens to be a witch. There's a difference.'

Slattery shrugged. 'Whatever.'

I raised an eyebrow.

'So whoever spiked Murdo's drugs would have to have had access to a fairly connected dealer.' Presumably you can't buy the stuff as easily as you can cocaine, which seems to be everywhere these days.

Slattery nodded. 'My money would be on Tom,' he said. 'Those muscles look assisted to me – if you can get a supplier for steroids, why not fentanyl? Also, he's got a record for Class A drug possession. He was busted with three grams of Charlie a couple of years ago.'

I nodded. Colour me shocked. The thought of a young, successful chef being busted for cocaine possession was not exactly surprising.

But why would Tom want to kill Murdo?

I remembered Octavia, how she was so full of life just before she had gone into that freezer. A moment frozen in my memory like the food in that minus eighteen environment. What was it she had said? Something like, Tom's gone out, got to meet a supplier, bet I know what kind of supplier it is too. Yes, that was it. She had sniffed loudly, tapped her nose and winked.

'Octavia had hinted that Tom was meeting a drug dealer before she died,' I said. 'If that's of any relevance?'

'I'll certainly bear it in mind,' said Slattery. 'Can you be any more specific?'

I shook my head. 'I'm afraid not.'

I wasn't going to tell Slattery about my bailing Murdo out, I didn't think it relevant.

'Well,' Slattery stood up, 'thanks for the heads up on Tom, I'll see you around.'

'I'll let you out.' I got up too.

As I opened the door for him, he turned and said to me quietly, 'You take care of yourself, Charlie, I don't want to be investigating your demise.'

'I'll be fine,' I promised.

I watched his broad back disappear into the darkness of the night. I smiled to myself. There was something very reassuring to know that Slattery cared about me. I closed the door thoughtfully and locked it.

Chapter Forty-One

I got up early the following day, about half past six, and went for a short four kilometre run hoping to clear my head from the various cobwebs of self-doubt and speculation. After I'd showered I went down to my kitchen at about half seven and made myself a coffee. As I was standing sipping my espresso and staring at Sam's mise en place list for the day there was a knock at the kitchen door.

I opened it, thinking I might be expecting an early delivery. Framed in the doorway was the imposing figure of Earl Hampden. Quite frankly, the last person I would have expected.

Although it was a Saturday, the Earl was dressed for a day at the office. He had a beautifully cut dark suit on and a yellow paisley tie. His iron-grey hair was slicked back, his silver military moustache precisely cut. The creases in his trousers looked as sharp as my Japanese Shun knife. The polish on his expensive black shoes was like a mirror. Murdo could have chopped a line of coke on them. His presence filled the room. It wasn't just that he was very tall, he had such a forceful character it created a kind of magnetic field around him, in short, he radiated charisma.

His cold eyes ran over me appraisingly. The expression on his face was that of a powerful man viewing the world with utter disdain. That was only partially true; the Earl's scorn was reserved for people. He was an ardent ecologist and a committed misanthropist. His interest in the human race seemed to be purely recreational. Sex and drugs and opera. He certainly cared little for what anyone thought of him. In the village he was regarded, paradoxically, as practically a god. His chequered, sometimes criminal, past was spoken of in terms of reverence. He could do very little wrong in the eyes of Hampden Green. We're very feudal down here in the country. The thing about the Earl was, if he had access to a nuclear button that would destroy the human race and allow animals to flourish undisturbed, I very much feel that he would have pressed it without a moment's hesitation. Sometimes I wondered what had caused this misanthropy. Maybe an unhappy childhood. If your character is formed by your schooldays, I don't think he'd enjoyed Eton very much.

'And how are you this morning, Charlie?' He smiled icily at me.

'Do come in,' I said.

He walked in and glanced around. I never really knew what to make of the Earl. He was undeniably extremely charismatic. He had that rare quality that leaders of men have. I have seen it before in a couple of executive chefs that I have worked with. If they said 'Jump!' the automatic response was to ask how high. They never had to raise their voices and a glance was enough to either cut you dead or make you feel that you were something very special. You would do anything to bask in their golden approbation.

My own dealings with the Earl had shown him to be amoral, uncaring as far as people went, and a hard-core womaniser. In Jess's opinion which I shared, he was far too old for Bryony but then again, Bryony was over twenty-one and old enough to make her own decisions.

So here he was. In all fairness, he had helped me out of a very tight situation not that long ago, and I owed him for that. He also treated me with, for him, an unusual degree of courtesy. And I wasn't even an orangutan, so I shouldn't really complain. I do have unusually long arms, and there is red in my hair, maybe that spoke to him at an unconscious, visceral level.

'This Matteo McCleish business,' he began, 'I take it that he hired you to get to the bottom of some trouble in his kitchen, rather than your cooking abilities?'

Well, he was spot on, much as I hated to admit it.

'Yes,' I said. I shrugged nonchalantly to show I didn't care. The Earl's eyes flickered with malicious amusement. I knew I hadn't fooled him.

'And now people are dying.'

'That's true,' I said.

'Well? Have you come to any conclusions as to who is responsible?' he asked.

Again, I saw no reason to beat about the bush, no reason to equivocate. 'No.'

The Earl frowned and stroked the corner of his moustache with his thumb. 'Personally, I don't like TV chefs,' he said, decisively. 'No particular reason, I suppose I don't like anyone who would want to be on TV because I think they are vain.' His eyes narrowed and his nostril flared slightly. 'Vanity. . . Not a quality I admire.'

He paced up and down my kitchen. You're not really allowed to walk into a commercial kitchen without changing your footwear, for obvious reasons – you could be tracking God knows what all over the floor – but I meekly allowed the Earl to do it. Maybe generations of plebeian deference had been bred into me.

I looked at the Earl, his beautiful clothes, the shoes. Are you wholly free from vanity, I wondered? Pot, kettle? I kept my mouth shut. I knew my place.

'You know something,' the Earl said. He stared down at the top of my range as if the cooker held some odd fascination for him.

'When McCleish's troubles at my place started, when that girl died. . .'

'Octavia,' I said, my voice now as cold as the Earl's. I wasn't going to have her so cavalierly dismissed, as if her death was of no account.

'What?' He turned and looked at me, his eyes narrowed in annoyance.

'Her name was Octavia,' I said, angrily. It was important to me that she shouldn't be referred to as 'that girl.'

He shrugged. It was obviously a matter of indifference to him.

'As I was saying,' he carried on, 'when Octavia died, I can't honestly say that I was particularly concerned. If it had wrecked the catering I wouldn't have had to pay

McCleish, and I would have made a lot of money from the insurance.'

He paused, thinking doubtless of the money. Those orangutans would certainly have benefitted, and the dormice of Bucks, another beneficiary of the Earl's pocket-book. Glis glis, they're called.

'You'd have needed to find somebody at very short notice,' I pointed out.

He made a contemptuous sound. 'You have a very exaggerated sense of your own importance,' he said. 'Good chefs aren't hard to find.'

I looked at him irritably.

'Oh, I've hurt your feelings – I am so sorry,' he said in mock apology. 'Let me rephrase that, they're easy to find if you're prepared to spend money. They're replaceable, unlike say' – here he took a step aggressively towards me – 'the white rhino or the coral of the Barrier Reef or any one of a few hundred species I could mention. When they're gone, they're gone forever. So don't try and get me feeling guilty about the death of someone I don't know.'

I could have said, sure, there are nine billion people on the planet, but there was only one Octavia. Would Octavia's parents have been comforted by the thought that there were still sixty-seven million Britons left minus one, when that one happened to be their daughter? I rather doubted it.

'And what brings you here?' I asked.

'To find out if you knew who put Murdo in hospital.' His tone was impatient.

'But I thought you weren't remotely interested,' I said.

'Someone spiked Murdo's drugs,' said the Earl grimly, 'drugs that he might have shared earlier with Bryony; that could be her lying dead in the hospital.'

'I see,' I said.

The Earl's face darkened with anger. 'They could both be dead.'

'So it's personal,' I said. That was the reason.

'Exactly.' He nodded. 'It's personal.'

Well, I thought, at least the Earl was honest. No messing around with abstract notions of justice for him.

'So, do you want my help?' he asked.

'How do you mean?' I wondered in what sense.

He sighed. 'Do you want my help to find out who is killing McCleish's team?'

'How would you do that?' I asked.

He said just two words, but they were enough. 'Anna Bruce.'

I looked at him and nodded.

'Anna Bruce, absolutely,' I said.

Chapter Forty-Two

'Anna says she can fit you in at quarter to twelve on Wednesday, if that's OK with you,' said the Earl.

My face fell – that was only three days away, but it would have been nice if it had been earlier.

'Nothing sooner?'

He shook his head. 'Anna's abroad, in Berlin advising clients. You're lucky it's me who's asking – a few days is short notice for her.'

I sighed. Well, it would have to do. I just had to pray nobody else died in the interim. I certainly seemed powerless to prevent things happening.

'Wednesday it is.'

The Earl nodded. 'I'll tell her.'

He walked out of the kitchen. He didn't bother saying goodbye.

Anna Bruce, medium extraordinaire. If anyone could sort this mess out, it would be her. I thought back to my last meeting with her, a couple of weeks ago. Then she had warned me of a dangerous woman, and that I would be facing a web of deception. Well, both of those had certainly come to pass. If you had said to me before I moved to the village and met her, that I would believe in stuff like, precognition, I would have laughed in your face. I would have said it was superstitious nonsense.

Anna Bruce, though, had been remarkably, almost scarily, accurate.

Maybe it was nothing whatsoever to do with psychic ability. Maybe she was just very, very good at reading people and situations. Maybe she was just very lucky. Maybe it was a Jungian thing, some kind of synchronicity – or a proof of the existence of pan-psychism. The how really didn't matter, what mattered were the results. If it works, it works.

Thanks to her, I had uncovered a killer before, and obviously I had hopes that she would help me again. To be honest, without her I felt I had very little hope of a breakthrough.

Chapter Forty-Three

At eight on Sunday morning I was downstairs in the Old Forge Café to begin getting things ready for lunch. We had sixty booked in and there was quite a bit of prep to do. Matteo had given me the morning off. I had said that I needed time to investigate a lead. That meant, in reality, scratching my head over the Graziana situation. While I was doing that I would help Sam with the prep. He wasn't expecting it, it would be a delightful surprise for him – like in a fairy story where the elves have secretly arrived and made all the shoes for the kind cobbler.

I put the radio on.

'Another hot Sunday here in Bucks – don't forget the sun cream. . . My it's so hot let's have an old Euro disco hit, from 2013 – here's O-Zone with Dragostea din tei. . .'

For some reason, if only because he would have hated it, that made me think of Murdo, who thankfully was on the mend.

For amusement's sake, I made a whole load of gnocchi the way that Matteo had shown me and some aubergine pesto to go with them. The gnocchi dough, a mix of egg, flour and potato that had been put through a ricer, was one of those things that was incredibly pleasing to the touch. I sang with O-Zone, or as best as I could since it was in Romanian, but I did know the chorus, 'Hiyyaa hoo, hiyya hei', or at least that's what it sounded like to me.

I finished making the pesto and was scraping the last of it out of the Magimix blender, when there was a knock on the kitchen door. I glanced up at the clock – it was just nine. Too early for Sam the chef, I thought as I opened the door. It couldn't be the Earl again, could it?

'Hello, Douglas,' I said looking at him in surprise.

'Hi.' He was clutching his laptop again. I thought, not for the first time, how the wretched thing was like a security blanket for him. I couldn't remember ever seeing him without it.

Although it was so early in the day, the sun was blazing down from the heavens and my yard was extremely hot. Douglas's hair was plastered to his scalp with sweat and his white shirt was sticking to his thin body. His Adam's apple bobbed up and down in his throat as he swallowed nervously.

'Would you like to come in?' I asked, noticing he was wearing chinos and had matched this outfit with socks and sandals.

'Thanks.' He walked nervously into the kitchen, clacking in on his Birkenstocks and looked around suspiciously as if he'd been followed. He was on the waiter's side of the pass so I forgave him the outdoors footwear.

'I'm going over to the house to go through some admin stuff with the Earl,' he said. 'Then there's a kind of do with the opera promoters and the conductor and some of the singers. Could I leave this laptop here with you and collect it later? I don't need it for the meeting and I'm worried in case someone nicks it at the tea party.' He shook his head sadly. 'You can't be too careful these days.'

I thought of Murdo trying to steal Attila's money. He was right.

'Sure,' I said. 'You can put it in my office.' I pointed to the cubbyhole at the back of the kitchen that was the space under the stairs that ran up to my flat above the restaurant and kitchen.

'I'll be back later to pick it up, if that's OK.'

I watched him thoughtfully as he walked away and then I promptly forgot about it as the morning progressed.

'Whose laptop is that in your office, Charlie?' Jess appeared. She'd changed out of her shorts into trousers, something more demure and appropriate for my restaurant.

'It's Douglas's.' I thought of Tom's remarks about Giorgio and Douglas. 'God, I wish I could see inside it.'

Sam disappeared to the storerooms outside and Jess moved further into the kitchen with a furtive look over her shoulder, watching him leave.

'My goodness that man is boring.' She shook her head disapprovingly. Then she looked at me conspiratorially. 'Do you really want to hack into Douglas's laptop?' she asked quietly.

I looked at her. I suddenly thought, that's exactly what I do want. 'Sure do.'

'Come on then.' She motioned with a shake of her curly,

dark hair towards my office just as Sam reappeared carrying a box of fish he needed to prep.

'I'll be with you in a minute, Chef,' I said. 'Jess is showing me something in Excel.'

That sounded plausible. Sam nodded. 'I'll crack on without you.'

In my office Jess connected Douglas's laptop up and switched it on. Then she rummaged in her handbag and produced a memory stick, which she put into the port on the side.

'Can you really do this?' I marvelled.

Jess rolled her eyes and didn't bother answering such a stupid question.

Her nimble fingers flew over the keyboard. She could touch type, which I couldn't. I was a slow one-finger woman.

It was a joy watching Jess work. Her calm, intelligent face concentrating on the screen, answering prompts which might as well have been in Chinese for all I understood.

'Just loading these files. . .' Various menus appeared.

'What's that, Windows?' I asked, I don't know why; I hadn't got a clue.

She smiled. A slightly malicious, knowing smile. 'A very weird variant – truly weird, funky. It's what is going to let me in.'

A couple of dropdown menus appeared on the screen. 'Create new user.' Jess was talking to herself, her eyes narrowed in concentration, chanting the instructions like an incantation that Esther Bartlett might use. 'Yes please.' Click.

'Create new password. . .' She shrugged. 'Pasta1 – that'll

do. . . OK, close, remove hardware. Restart, username. . . password. . . there you go.' She turned to me and smiled. 'You're in.'

'Right,' I said. I couldn't believe how easy she had made it seem.

'I'll leave you to it,' she said. 'I don't want to see what's in Douglas's head – his face is more than enough.'

She went back into the restaurant and I hunkered down at my task.

Going through Douglas's laptop was a weird experience. As Jess had suggested, it was very much like entering some-one's mind. I had never really given any thought as to how much of our personality lies stored and encrypted in these files that we keep.

Memories in the form of photos, correspondence, search history information.

In Douglas's file explorer, in a folder named 'Douglas pictures Graziana McCleish', I found hundreds of images of Graziana he had collected from social media, taken himself and wheedled out of the employees of the Matteo empire, all captioned and dated. He was a meticulous person.

The names he used for the folders were revealing: 'Graziana-bikini', 'Graziana-breasts', 'Graziana-hot dresses', 'Graziana-wet'. . .

He had even followed her to Italy although not her directly. It must have been some kind of kink pilgrimage. There was a folder labelled, Graziana – Le Marche. This had pictures of various bars and restaurants, one bar in particular seemed to have taken his fancy. There were several pictures of it. Maybe it was part of her history that he was snuffling after like a repellent bloodhound.

Even worse than this was 'Graziana out and about'. This was what it held: images of her in the street, walking into Waitrose, going into a café, down by the river Thames. The images were innocuous, what wasn't was Douglas following her with a long lens, the better to document his unhealthy attraction for her.

He was obsessed with her. I had an image in my head now of Douglas, hunched over his laptop, late at night, his thin face lit by the glow of the screen, fantasising over the pictures of this beautiful, unobtainable woman.

It was very disturbing.

I was beginning to feel very grimy, looking at these intimate pictures, and I was thankful that Jess wasn't here. It felt voyeuristic – it was voyeuristic – obviously a feeling that Douglas actively enjoyed.

Interestingly there were no pictures of Graziana with another man, or another woman, come to that. If she had been having an affair with Giorgio as Giorgio had bragged to Octavia, it would not have surprised me to find photo evidence of the two of them together.

Also, conspicuous by its absence, was nothing from Per I Tifosi. If there had been a history of her with that porn site, I was sure he would have managed to track some images down, for Douglas it would have been like the Holy Grail. There were also no pictures of the hidden tattoo. If he'd shared these files with Giorgio (which I kind of doubted, they weren't hardcore) he wouldn't have got the tattoo info from them.

I had a quick look through the folders again. I clicked on one labelled 'personal'. My eyebrows raised into a more or less perfect arc of surprise like I was an emoji come to life. Here was a photo of Douglas with Porn Shop guy, both of them smiling at the camera. Douglas was holding a CD that looked familiar, it was *Schoolgirl Supersluts 1 – Barely Legal*. Giorgio had Volume 3 on him when I had confronted him.

I sat there a moment, processing what I had learnt. Douglas was obsessed with Graziana. He was also an avid porn fan, an enthusiasm he shared with Giorgio. He obviously knew Porn Shop guy and was almost certainly part of the blackmail.

Where did this leave Graziana I wondered. I had a sudden thought. I took my phone out and called Matteo. I asked him where Charlotte's offices were. They were in Marshall Street, just off Oxford Street. Thanks, I said and terminated the call. Marshall Street was near Carnaby Street. Graziana could well have been there seeing Charlotte for business, Porn Shop guy was probably on his way to see Douglas.

Things looked brighter for Graziana, darker for Douglas.

I was hoping that Anna Bruce might shed some light on it when I saw her, but I still ran through Douglas's documents on the off-chance there was one labelled, 'Blackmail Notes'. But there wasn't.

I heard the kitchen door bang as Francis arrived. I got up and gave Jess a shout.

'All done?' she asked. I nodded. I told Jess about my regrets that there were no files labelled blackmail.

'Have you checked his Word documents?' I shook my head.

'We'll just have a quick look.' There were hundreds of files. My heart sank.

'We can't look through all of these on the off-chance.' I was disappointed, it would have taken forever.

'No,' she said, 'we can't now, but I'm going to copy them onto the memory stick,; I'll look through them later. I'll create a program to search them for the phrases, key words the blackmailer used in the note to Matteo. You've still got copies?'

'Yeah.'

Good.' She added, 'I'll also check for any other images. It could be that there are locked image files elsewhere that contain illegal pornography. If there are,' her voice was grimly confident, 'I'll find them.'

'Thanks, Jess.'

'Well, let's clean our footprints,' she said, turning to the laptop and taking the reins.

'And he won't know we've done this?' I asked.

She shook her head as her fingers ran lightly over the keys.

'There,' she said, shutting the laptop down, 'now he'll never know you've been here.'

Chapter Forty-Four

So, on Wednesday morning, I drove along the roads through the beech trees to High Wycombe. At the traffic lights near the station, I thought of the stalker, Douglas, and his creepy photos. Douglas and his friend Porn Shop guy. Douglas and his friendship with Giorgio. Andrea's friend had been sure that there was never any involvement between Graziana and Per I Tifosi. If she had been on that porn site, I was a hundred per cent sure that Douglas would have had the photos neatly filed with the others. So, no official record, and no images. The blackmail related to something else. I had been lied to. The web of delusion.

I thought of Douglas's pilgrimage to Le Marche, Matteo's and Graziana's place of origin. I thought of those photos. Was it there that the heart of the secret lay?

I parked in the multi-storey carpark near Anna's flat. Her apartment was in a brutalist, post-modern block over-looking the station, the kind of place that lawyers and architects live in, all glass and concrete and exposed steel joists. It shone and gleamed where it wasn't looking expensively distressed. Raw concrete was a major feature. I rather liked it. It seemed an odd place for a psychic to live – the first time I had seen it I had been surprised, expecting something more chintzy, Laura Ashley rather than Bauhaus – but then Anna Bruce was no ordinary psychic.

I rang the intercom and was buzzed in. I took the lift to the top. She opened the door at the end of the short corridor and we walked up a flight of steps to her penthouse apartment. It came with a roof garden with views across Wycombe that, despite it not being the prettiest of towns, still managed to look impressive from the seventh floor. And from up here you could see the greenery of the Buckinghamshire countryside on either side of the looping grey ribbon of concrete and brick.

'Have a seat and I'll bring you a drink,' Anna said gesturing to a bench on the terrace. Her voice was cool and slightly mocking, as always, but her smile was genuine. Anna liked me.

'Diet Coke if you've got it.'

I sat down and enjoyed a break from the heat of the day, as the wind was cool and refreshing up here. A red kite glided effortlessly in the sky above on its enormous wings.

Anna brought me my Diet Coke and sat down opposite me. She was in her late fifties, I guessed, maybe older, with a commanding, striking face. You wouldn't mess with Anna Bruce; she didn't suffer fools gladly. Her short white hair was sharply cut and she was wearing a tailored white shirt and black trousers. Around her neck was a very green jade necklace. She looked wealthy, confident, very much in control of her own destiny. Why shouldn't she? She was well paid, her clients were mainly corporate and mostly from the Far East. She was in great demand.

'How are you? You're looking well,' she said. I smiled at her. The last time I had been here I had been wanted for murder. I imagine I had looked fairly harassed.

'And you,' I replied.

She did. Above all she had an air of confident calm, a quality I really wish that I possessed. Sometimes I was capable of it, but not nearly enough in my opinion. Certainly not at the moment.

'I'm just back from Berlin; I had to do a reading for a captain of industry. Things are not looking good for him, unfortunately.' I was impressed. Anna's reputation crossed continents. I was getting her for free – presumably the Earl would pick up the tab.

She looked at me quizzically. 'So,' she said, 'let's get down to business.'

She produced her pack of Tarot cards and handed them to me.

'Shuffle please.'

I did so, looking at the heavy old cards with their strange illustrations. I remember her telling me that the Tarot as a system had been in use for some seven hundred years. But so what? Age is not necessarily a guarantee of authenticity. I did as she instructed. She was drinking green tea from an earthy green and brown oriental cup, very delicate with a beautiful glaze. It looked expensive; I wondered where it came from. I finished shuffling.

'Well. There you are, now, keep the question that you want answering in your mind as you do so and deal. . . three cards please, face down.'

'Oh, it was a gift from a client, by the way,' she suddenly said.

'What?'

'The cup you were wondering about. It was given to me in Osaka, by a grateful Japanese businessman.'

How the hell had she known what I was thinking? I tried to concentrate on my question as she'd told me to.

'Who is responsible for the blackmail and the murders?' I thought silently to myself. Faces shuffled through my mind much as the cards had done: Douglas, Graziana, Tom and all the others, everyone connected to Matteo. The cards, their designs as enigmatic as the face of Anna Bruce, seemed almost to select themselves as I dealt them out in front of me.

'And shuffle and repeat,' she said.

I now had six cards face down in front of me. Anna Bruce looked at them and then at me. I had the feeling that something momentous was about to happen. The traffic noise had died away. The sounds of the town had vanished as if we were in a kind of noise-cancelling bubble. There was a sense of heightened reality, like I was high or something. One by one she turned the cards over. The beautiful images, powerful, archetypal seemed to glow like they were living.

A seated woman between two pillars.

A man on a throne with an air of being very much in command. Some kind of king, a monarch.

A woman pouring water, above her head seven stars, one of which was brighter than the others.

Mixed with these picture cards were the ten of Wands, the eight of Swords and the nine of Coins. I stared at what lay before me. Was this truly my future, so clearly laid out? It seemed unlikely.

'You only get partial glimpses,' said Anna. 'It's like looking out of a plane window as you fly over a city, say London. . .' She sipped her tea, from her Japanese cup gifted by a grateful Japanese client.

'Here's a view of the river, then clouds, then the plane banks and you see the city, then it circles, you see sky, then Staines reservoir. None of it necessarily makes any sense, it looks random, chaotic. It doesn't seem to fit together, but sometimes it does. You're seeing the bits but not the whole. You just need to know how to interpret it.'

'What do you see here?' I asked.

Anna studied the cards. 'Well,' she said, hesitantly, 'it's confusing to say the least.'

She tapped the first card with a very red fingernail. 'This is the High Priestess; she's very enigmatic' – she smiled at me – 'like all women. And of course there's a wealth of meanings, but we'll move back to her later. You have to read the cards as a totality, rather than singly. Here she's next to the Emperor. He holds earthly power. The sceptre is a symbol of that and the globe you see in his other hand, that's the world as it is. It's an interesting juxtaposition.'

I looked at the calm face of the Emperor, the tranquil look of one who is all-powerful. Easy to be calm when you're rich and the world belongs to you. I immediately thought of the Earl.

'Now we have the nine of Coins, *le neuf denier*, wounds, a quarrel.' She frowned. There'd certainly been a lot of those, I thought, as Anna continued '. . . sudden events?'

She pointed to the next card. 'Moving on, the eight of Swords, that's an upset, a disorder, and it's strongly linked here with the ten of Wands, which symbolises a very heavy burden, and has strong links with travel. It's beginning to make sense.'

Maybe to you, I thought.

'And this last card?' I pointed to it. The image was particularly arresting, a kneeling woman pouring water from two vases, one in each hand. One was being emptied into a lake, the other onto dry land. Above in the heavens were seven stars, one much brighter and bigger than the other.

'The Star of the Magi.' Anna nodded. 'A very interesting card, the realisation of Hope.'

She looked at me.

'Well, what does it all mean? That's what you need to know, and particularly in relation to the business with Matteo McCleish.'

I said, 'Yes, please.'

We looked at each other. Why couldn't she just say she saw a scrawny man with a bobbing Adam's apple and horn-rimmed glasses? Or a beautiful woman with a swan tattoo? Life would be so much simpler.

'. . . but there are all sorts of loose ends that could do with tying up.'

Who was the killer? Who was the blackmailer?

'OK then,' she said briskly, folding her arms and looking me in the eye. 'The last time I saw you, I warned you of a woman.'

'You did,' I said. I told her about Sandra. She nodded. 'I don't think the danger is over yet,' she said, 'but in order to find the answer you need to go to where it all started.'

'And where's that?' I asked. Kings Cross? That's where his restaurant started, the beginning of his path to fame.

'Italy,' said Anna, firmly, 'where Matteo came from – that's where the answer lies.'

So, not Kings Cross then.

'You're sure it's not London?' I said.

Anna looked at me. 'The cards say Italy. You also had two questions.'

Who was the killer and who was the blackmailer? I looked at her in astonishment. How could she have known?

'The answer lies in Italy,' Anna said firmly. 'That's where you have to go. The why and the who is for you to discover.'

So, Italy it would have to be.

Chapter Forty-Five

'So, you're off to Italy then,' said Jess sceptically, 'to find the answer as to who has been killing Matteo's team and blackmailing him as well. Two birds with one stone.'

Charlotte, who was the real power behind the throne, had approved my absence for a couple of days.

'Provided we're not paying,' she had said darkly.

I could afford to do it myself from the money that they had already given me. I had told them that I was chasing leads around London and would be away from the village. It didn't seem wise to say I was going to Italy.

I felt nettled by Jess's tone. 'Yes, yes I am actually. I need to try to discover what actually lies behind the blackmail, I'm ninety-nine per cent sure this Per I Tifosi business is a smokescreen.'

'And how is going to Italy helping?' Jess was sceptical.

'I want to see where his career began, see the village where his nonna taught him to cook. Anna said to me, way back when all this began, that there was a web of deception surrounding things. Well, I want to blow away the cobwebs. . .' I shrugged, 'and if I fail, I won't have lost anything and I'll have eaten some pasta. I'll even bring you back one of those giant Toblerones from the airport.'

Jess was wearing her slightly pugnacious look. Maybe she didn't care for Toblerone. Her hair looked thicker than ever. I had noticed that when she got angry it seemed to increase in size and volume. Maybe it was like a dog with hackles. She looked sweaty and tired. I guess it had been a busy service. *That's great, you just swan off to Italy and leave me here, I'll be fine*, I could imagine her saying in her head.

The kitchen bore the hallmarks of a frazzled lunchtime.

Sam was a neat and efficient chef but there was an unusual amount of mess and the sink was piled high with just about every plate in the place. It had obviously been an uncommonly busy Wednesday, that's not generally a busy shift.

It was half past three and my agency chef was sitting in the kitchen yard with a beer, accompanied by Francis who beamed at me through the window like a good-natured Labrador.

Jess said, 'So you're flying to where?'

'To Ancona, there's an airport there.'

'Come and show me where you're going in Italy,' said Jess, pointing to the office. She had obviously accepted the inevitable – I was definitely going. We crouched in front of my laptop.

'Le Marche,' I said.

Pulling up the map of Italy, both of us stared at the boot-like landmass. There was Le Marche, one of the regions of Italy, about halfway up on the right.

'Can you be a bit more specific? It looks quite a sizeable area. Where exactly did he grow up?' she said.

'I seem to remember Matteo's village was called Monte Salvia.'

The Latin name for sage is salvia. God knows how I knew that, but I did. Synchronicity, I thought, an auspicious omen. I could do with some sagacity.

'Well, that's a good start,' she said, her fingers moving over the keyboard as she looked at me. 'Now we've got something to work with. . . ah, here we go.'

We both looked at the map, and there it was. In the middle of nowhere by the looks of things. I'd definitely need a car.

'Are you going to tell Matteo?' she asked.

I shook my head. 'No. If Anna says that all of this is because of what happened long ago in Italy then it's more than probable Matteo is mixed up in it. . . I'm just going to tell him that I'm off investigating leads elsewhere.'

Jess changed the view from map to satellite and down we went, zooming in on the actual place. There was not a great deal of habitation around there.

'It's quite off the beaten track,' she observed. The village appeared to be surrounded by countryside. 'How good is your spoken Italian?'

It was a rhetorical question, she knew damn well I didn't speak any languages.

'Not good at all,' I admitted. 'In fact, it's non-existent.'

But she did have a point. A total inability to speak Italian might impede my investigation – that was definitely true.

Jess was still looking at me expectantly. 'How are you going to cope?' she asked.

'I shall rely on charm and ingenuity,' I said.

'Ha!' she said. It was not a 'Ha!' of emphatic agreement. There was more than a hint of sarcasm in her tone.

'Oh, ye of little faith,' I said. 'The Italians appreciate charm and politeness, I've got both.'

'You should take someone with you who speaks Italian, that'd be easier than relying on charm,' she said, innocently. I suddenly had an uncomfortable inkling as to where this conversation was heading.

'Jess. . .' I said warningly.

She scratched her head for effect and stared wonderingly at the ceiling, saying in a faraway voice, 'If only we knew someone who spoke the language like a native, maybe someone who was actually Italian even. . . someone who was intelligent. . .'

She turned to me. Her eyes were gleaming.

'I don't. . .'

Jess was remorseless. 'Someone trustworthy who cares for you. . . Do we know anyone who fits that description?' She recapitulated the qualities, counting them off on a finger. 'Intelligent, trustworthy, speaks Italian, actually likes you for some reason despite the way you treated him in the past. . . maybe someone who gave you his phone number not that long ago. . .'

'It's a bad idea,' I said firmly. 'It's not going to happen.'

Jess was not to be deterred. 'We do know someone, don't we, Charlie? Someone who fits all those descriptions?'

'He won't do it, Jess,' I said firmly, 'and I'm not going to ask him.'

'Then I will.'

'Over my dead body!' I said.

My tone was flinty. I had made my mind up. It was not going to happen.

I was not going to Italy with my ex-fiancé and that was final.

Of that there was no doubt.

Chapter Forty-Six

'Just like old times,' Andrea said.

Anna Bruce might have put it down to the planets being correctly aligned, but whatever the reason, three days later on Saturday morning, I found myself where I had not expected to be, with someone I hadn't expected to be with, when I'd woken up in the morning.

'Welcome aboard this Lufthansa flight to Munich.'

The Lufthansa flight attendant had finished her announcement in German and had switched to excellent English.

We were in the front row. We were flying Lufthansa to Ancona, with a stopover to change planes at Munich. There were other carriers who flew direct from the UK but they were sold out. Jess had booked us Economy but Andrea, through some alchemy, frequent flyers maybe or name-dropping or sheer force of personality, had got us upgraded. The conversation had been in German, one of his four languages, so I hadn't got a clue as to what was being said.

I contented myself with trying to look sophisticated. I

was wearing shorts and a blue short-sleeved blouse. I thought I looked quite good.

I looked wonderingly at Andrea di Stefano, my ex. It really was a conjunction of opposites. Dr Rowan Herne would have been impressed with the alchemical imbalance, the Coniunctio Oppositorum as the alchemists put it. The Union of Opposites.

He worked in investment banking, doing something incomprehensible with mergers and acquisitions. Or maybe he was doing something else these days. He had once or twice explained to me what his job entailed – it was along the lines of complex financial valuations – but I didn't really understand. My mind glazed over at the details. Money has never been my strong point. Either making it or under-standing it. Bit of an Achilles heel that. So, he did something financial, I was a chef.

There were other differences. He spoke several languages fluently, I spoke only English. He was effortlessly elegant; well, I had my moments, but I'm not usually complimented on my poise. He was rich, I was perpetually hard up.

Today in designer jeans – I didn't know the brand but they looked fantastic on him, a grey, V-necked T-shirt and virginally white training shoes, his dark hair beautifully cut, he radiated sophistication and charisma.

I had noticed quite a few women in the Lufthansa lounge eyeing him surreptitiously. He was, quite simply, gorgeous. Some of the women in the lounge had been eying me too, but in a more speculative manner. I had a feeling they were wondering what a man like him was doing with a woman like me. I was obviously not a trophy bride.

I discussed this with Andrea.

'Almost certainly that's the case,' he'd said.

'But they obviously don't realise I have hidden depths,' I said, 'and they haven't realised how witty and charming I am.'

He nodded. 'Me neither. But, credit where credit's due, you are very good at making bread, and cakes. . . your bavarois in particular are to die for. . .'

'And let's not forget how good I am now at pasta and gnocchi,' I said proudly. 'Matteo's taught me.' I paused, 'But you're right, men love my bavarois, rightly so, moist and utterly delicious.'

He patted me on the knee. 'Of course,' he said in a patronising way.

The flight to Ancona took a few hours including our stopover. Munich airport was a pleasant place to while away an hour with a coffee and some multi-layered Prinzregentorte. I admired Andrea surreptitiously, as he caught up with some work on his laptop. Spreadsheets, how tedious. I was pleased to see that we were still friends. Though, it has to be said, I was surprised. Possibly his colleagues in the mergers and acquisitions world were not so exciting and glamorous as might have been expected. That led me to speculate about his fiancée. Did she work in the same field as him, or was she like me, an outsider? Did she work in hospitality and catering like I did? I couldn't ask, it was none of my business.

Anyway, here we both were. On an aeroplane, going to Italy.

Ancona was a run-down seaside town with a sizeable

port attached, where a couple of the gigantic ferries that criss-crossed the sea to Croatia were moored up. The sky was azure, the sea an oddly pale blue and the beach in front of the esplanade was covered in serried ranks of the beach umbrellas the Italians call *ombrellone*. For such a chaotic lot, Italians are weirdly regimented when it comes to beaches. There were free bits of the beach but most of it was divided up by the umbrella and sunbed concessions.

I was quite taken with the look of Ancona. There was a mysterious lack of anything to do or see in the guidebooks and I liked that about it. Sometimes places get a bit stuck up their own arse like Venice or Florence. In Ancona there was nothing particularly worth seeing and so there was none of that pressure to rush around ticking things off a list.

I would have been perfectly happy to sit around eating pasta, have some drinks in a piazza and generally do nothing. But I did have a crime to solve, and here it was surprisingly easy to forget the fact.

En route to the hotel I had filled Andrea in as to exactly why we were here and what we were doing. We had three days to find the answer to the enigma of the identity (or identities) of the blackmailer and the killer. Charlotte had agreed to two days, I figured she would be good for three. There's a lot of truth in the assertion that it's easier to ask for forgiveness than permission. Andrea could do his job, apart from a few key meetings, remotely. Try working from home if you're a chef, we're tied to our stoves. It would be hard to imagine us replaced by an AI.

He listened to my plans with polite scepticism.

'We're here because a psychic told you to come?'

'Exactly.'

'Well!' he reflexively sounded the horn at an Alfa Romeo that had cut us up and gave the finger to another motorist, swearing in Italian. He grinned, he was obviously enjoying his break so far.

'I'm glad to see you've got it all figured out, Sherlock,' he said. 'The crime is practically solved.'

We checked in and I noted that our hotel was coolly elegant and again I felt faintly superfluous as he dealt with the receptionist, in his native Italian. The bell-boy took us and our two suitcases to our rooms. I had been quite specific with Jess about booking two rooms, two single rooms. I had got her to book online because I didn't trust myself to do it in case I cocked it up. I was still smarting from a computer mistake I'd made involving goat's cheese. I had thought I was ordering five goat's cheese logs of 500 grams each when in reality I'd ordered five of 50 grams each. Instead of the sizeable blocks I'd expected, two and a half kilos' worth, I ended up with minuscule doll's house ones suitable for a child's picnic.

'As much use as an underwater aquarium,' as Francis had sagely observed.

Two single rooms.

Impossible to make a mistake.

'Here is your room,' said the bell-boy, opening the door with a flourish.

It was a lovely room, airy, a balcony with a view of the sea, a door to the bathroom partially open revealing wonderful stainless-steel fittings. As I have always thought,

Italians excel at bathroom decoration, that and lighting. The bathroom excited me unreasonably. Nice art on the walls. A complimentary bottle of wine.

And one lovely king-size bed.

Andrea looked at me. It was not the kind of look that suggested we were going to be sharing it.

Chapter Forty-Seven

'I don't know how it happened,' I said. Yet again.

The hotel had been unable to find us another room. They had shown us the booking request as filled out by Jess who had, without any shadow of doubt, booked us in together. Mentally I cursed my waitress's matchmaking intentions. She was a big fan of Andrea and was determined to get us back together.

'You belong together; you – complement each other perfectly,' were Jess's words.

This was horribly embarrassing, not helped by the fact that Andrea looked sceptical at my protestations that I hadn't been responsible.

'Do you want me to check into another hotel?' I asked. Please don't say yes, I thought to myself.

'This is very problematic, Charlie,' he said, shaking his head, exasperated, 'I'm engaged.'

'We'll top and tail,' I suggested.

'I don't think that'll work,' he said.

'Why not?' I asked. He looked at me like I was crazy and shook his head.

'Just. . . just because. . . OK,' he said. Irritably.

The two suitcases – his, a sophisticated jet black, unscratched, expensive-looking, mine, faded pink, scuffed, travel-worn and sad – sat side by side like some kind of visual aid to our broken relationship.

Andrea began to unpack and changed the subject. 'Do you have any immediate plans for today?' he said.

I shook my head. It was 4 o'clock already. 'No, I thought we'd head out to Monte Salvia tomorrow, but today, no.'

'Well, I'm going swimming,' he said, removing trunks and goggles from his case.

He turned his back to me and undressed.

When I was at catering college we had the quality points of various bits of meat explained to us. I reflected, staring at Andrea's sculpted, naked figure from the rear, that the same could be said of men. He scored highly. If he were a piece of meat, he would be a prime piece of fillet. He had a great backside, there might be grey in his hair but his derriere was still holding out.

We went down to the pool. He swam up and down for half an hour while I just sat there drinking wine, enjoying the complimentary crisps and olives and the ambience.

He climbed elegantly out of the swimming pool and joined me. We spent the rest of the afternoon chatting like the old friends we still were. The subject of his fiancée was not discussed, although occasionally she inevitably cast shadows on the sunny nature of our conversation.

We had an early dinner at a local restaurant. It was good food, Linguine al Pesto Genovese, which was linguine with potato batons and green beans in a pesto sauce (I shall put that on my lunchtime menu, I thought to myself) and a tiramisu (not as good as Matteo's). My companion had the Le Marche version of lasagne, Vincisgrassi, which contains quite a lot of offal, that was enough to deter me. We went to bed early. Andrea made himself a bed of sorts on the floor from blankets he found at the base of one of the wardrobes. I lay awake for a long time listening to his even breathing.

Chapter Forty-Eight

The following day, the Sunday, we drove deep into the centre of Le Marche. The countryside was beautiful. It was very green, by Italian standards, and hilly, not unlike parts of Scotland. Like Scotland, there were occasional outcrops of rock and stone and you were very aware of the skeleton, of the very bones of the country.

Unlike Scotland, the tops of many of the hills were dotted with small mediaeval walled towns and villages, a reminder of a more uncertain past when it was obviously wise practice to construct such places on easily defensible sites.

The villages were old, antique-looking. At times it felt like we were driving through an Italian Quattrocento landscape.

An hour and a half from Ancona, we turned off the main road that ran along the bottom of a valley and headed up into the hills.

The village of Monte Salvia was, as the name implied, on top of one of the many hilltops and was surrounded by sizeable mediaeval-looking fortifications. We parked in a car park outside and walked through an arched gateway into the town.

The walls were tall and red-brick, the streets narrow and cobbled and the small houses leaned over them as if whispering to each other, their roofs made of red earthenware tiles. Huge double doors gave way to courtyards. The atmosphere of the place was secretive and inward-looking. It was historic, atmospheric, pretty and claustrophobic all at the same time. You often heard voices, a torrent of liquid, beautiful Italian, but you didn't see anyone. It was a mysterious place, very turned in on itself. The sun beat down from above and very few people were around. It seemed an odd sort of town for a British boy to be transplanted to by his parents. Nonna notwithstanding, the culture shock must have been immense.

I contrasted it with the village that I lived in. Everything in Hampden Green was on show – the houses, their gardens, the common – it was all very open. Here things were hidden. The whole place seemed shrouded in mystery.

'What did his parents do?' asked Andrea as we walked through the streets and alleyways, attracting curious stares from the few pedestrians we passed. I suspected that from a distance with my ultra-pale skin I would be practically glowing like a fluorescent light tube. The few locals that we did meet were elderly, gnarled and as brown and lined as walnuts.

'They looked after properties that British people owned in Le Marche,' I said. 'They did things like cut the grass, kept the places in good order, arranged for plumbers and electricians, that kind of thing. Stuff that's time-consuming in your own country, but bloody difficult if you don't know the language well and if you don't know any reliable tradesmen.' I paused to let a Piaggio Ape, a three-wheeled van popular in Italy, pass by loaded with melons.

I waited until the noisy roaring rattle of the small van had subsided before I continued. It was a story I had gleaned from Charlotte and Tom. I had also gathered that the parents had passed away.

'I gather they were sort of hippy-ish. Free spirits.' I thought that was probably code for stoners, unable to hold down a steady job. 'And then Matteo got into cooking when he was a teenager. Shall we sit down over there? I could do with a drink.'

We were in a square, probably the main square, of Monte Salvia. There were a couple of cafés or restaurants with tables outside and we sat down at one of these under an awning and looked around.

There was an old fountain, a war memorial and a statue of someone from the nineteenth century whom I didn't know. The square was half full of parked cars and there was a bakery and a town hall with an Italian and an European flag.

While it was very pleasant as a tourist to sit and have a coffee enjoying the olde-worlde architecture, I couldn't help but feel that this could well be a pretty dismal place for a kid with no connections other than his granny and parents to grow up in. Particularly a foreigner like Matteo. It was a safe bet that everyone in Monte Salvia had grown up here, as had their families more or less for centuries. It was hard enough being a newcomer in a Bucks village only twenty miles from London; it would be far more difficult to fit in here.

I looked around. 'Yeah, it was round here that he grew up and met Graziana. His cooking reflects this place. It's regional Le Marche.'

'So what's the plan?' Andrea asked.

'I want to see where his parents are buried,' I said. Andrea raised his eyebrows; I explained.

'I know it sounds odd, but he lied to me about the reasons for blackmail. I just want to check what is real or not real in his story.'

'OK,' he said, 'I'll ask the waitress if she knows anything about the McCleish family and where they might be buried.'

The waitress, a pleasant-looking woman in her late thirties with dramatically thick black eyebrows, came with the bill and Andrea spoke to her in Italian. I guessed that she was probably old enough to have been around when Matteo was. I heard the name 'McCleish' mentioned.

I suppose I could have asked her myself, but I always feel there is something rude in asking in English as if you expect the non-British person to speak your language. There was some head-scratching and then a slap of the forehead – 'dawning realisation!' I thought smugly to myself, I was a master of reading body language – then a pointing of a finger across the square.

'Grazie,' said Andrea, and he stood up as the waitress left to serve another table.

'Well?' I asked eagerly.

'Follow me,' Andrea said, nonchalantly.

We walked in silence down the narrow streets. It was all downhill and I realised that we were leaving the village. I hoped it wouldn't be too far.

Fairly soon, in maybe under ten minutes, we were outside the walls of Monte Salvia and still walking downhill along a narrow lane with cypress trees on either side.

The funereal shade of the trees and their stately planting indicated our destination. The cemetery was small and enclosed by a high, white marble wall. The tall, black, ornamental iron gates were open and we went in. The walls of the graveyard on the inside were lined with rows of what looked like drawers in a filing cabinet, again made of the same white marble as the rest of the graveyard. They had an ornamental handle, as well as a kind of clip, which could hold a vase for flowers, and the names of the deceased in an elegant uniform lettering. It was a rather magical place, orderly, quite beautiful and incredibly serene. It was a nice place to be buried, or interred.

We walked slowly along the walls, reading the family names, until Andrea stopped.

'Here we are,' he said pointing to one of the boxes. There were two names on it:

Magnus McCleish 1950–2016

Shona McCleish 1951–2010

'Matteo's parents,' he said, 'they died young, a shame.' I nodded, then he said what I was thinking, 'I wonder where his nonna is buried?'

'It is strange,' I said. 'She should be here, in the family vault so to speak.'

I reflected on this, as we headed to the village.

'Where now?' asked Andrea as we navigated the silent, mysterious streets.

'Let's go back and talk to that nice waitress,' I said. 'Ask her if she knows of anyone who knew the McCleishes.'

We went back to the café and Andrea spoke to the girl again. More Italian that I didn't understand and then she nodded and pointed then she disappeared back inside her café. Andrea turned to me.

'The waitress told me that someone called Tommaso might be worth speaking to. He's the head chef at that other restaurant, across the square,' Andrea said. 'Seemingly, he's local.'

Catering in this part of the world would be quite a small pond, and as he was presumably from around here there was a very good chance he had come across Matteo in the past.

'So this guy Tommaso maybe knew him, if Matteo's story checks out.'

'Exactly, but I wouldn't get your hopes up,' warned Andrea. 'He's *molto brutto* by all accounts.'

'What does that mean?' I asked.

He looked at me. 'Take a wild guess.'

We arrived back at the main square. It was Sunday and the Osteria Bianca, Tommaso's restaurant, was closed and shuttered, the chairs stacked neatly, waiting to be placed around the dozen or so tables that fronted on to the fountain. I wondered if it was maybe his day off. I hadn't thought about Italian opening times.

The al fresco restaurant dining area that was outside in the square was delineated by rectangular planters filled with well-tended flowers. As we approached I could see that the place was immaculately kept. Always a good sign. There was a menu in a box by the door. I looked at it. It seemed fairly pricey, double that of the place across the square and then some.

I was aware of movement and then a woman who looked very much like a waitress/manageress opened the door. She was about forty, slim, good-looking, with a brisk no-nonsense air. She said something to Andrea. I caught the word '*chiuso*'.

More machine-gun Italian. The manageress shook her head regretfully but she was obviously holding firm to some point or other.

Andrea turned to me. 'She says she's very sorry but they're closed for a function and the chef is up to his eyes in it. The other chef's called in sick and basically Tommaso's screwed.'

I could sympathise. Sunday night is usually either quiet or the restaurant is closed, but I have noticed a trend for weddings in England to be held on the Sabbath, and I've done a couple of parties myself on that day. Not many people want to close their restaurant for a private event on a Saturday night, but a Sunday is a very viable option.

'OK, we'll go – maybe we could come back tomorrow,' I said.

Andrea translated. Judging by the expression on the manageress's face it seemed unlikely that would be a wise move.

'Tommaso is a busy man,' she said.

Just then a figure in chef's whites appeared from inside

the restaurant. He was tall, maybe six three, burly with a black beard streaked with grey, and angry eyes. Doubtless he was searching for his manageress. Flour coated his muscular hairy forearms, and he glared at us for having the temerity to interrupt his frantic work schedule.

A torrent of Italian. I didn't need Claudia to translate.

'Tell him,' I suddenly said to Andrea in a moment of inspiration, 'that I'm a chef and if he wants I'll help him out until after service if he agrees to answer some questions afterwards.'

'Are you sure?' he said, looking at me as if I were mad.

'Just do it.' I was confident. 'Tell him I'm a good one.'

He shrugged and did. I heard the word Michelin being deployed. Well, it was true, I'd done time in a starred place during my life in the kitchen environment.

Tommaso looked me up and down. At least I had the optimum number of arms and legs to be of use to him.

'You're a chef?' he said in English, slowly.

'*Si*,' I replied, exhausting my stock of Italian.

'And you want to know about Matteo McCleish?'

'*Si*.'

'*Si, va bene, affare fatto*,' he nodded. '*Andiamo*.' Let's go!

As I followed him into the kitchen I felt that the end was in sight.

Chapter Forty-Nine

A commercial kitchen in Le Marche was much the same as in England. Steel tables, large, metal versions of familiar kitchen implements, scaled up as if for a giant's use. A massive eight-burner range, a walk-in fridge.

I couldn't speak Italian but I could speak kitchen or 'la cucina' as I gathered it was called here. Andrea had accompanied us in and, while I washed my hands with ostentatious thoroughness, rolled my sleeves up and put an apron on, Tommaso, frantically hand-kneading pasta, eyes glaring, explained what he wanted doing and he translated.

Two hundred people, 7 o'clock, canapés, bruschetta, arancini, crostini, *bignè ai funghi* (mushroom puffs). First course, *ravioli di Branzino* (seabass ravioli). Or for those who didn't like fish or meat, a vegetarian lasagne with homemade spinach pasta sheets. Then as a main, a chicken stew, Pollo in Potacchio. This one had a line through it, at least that had been done.

Times that tasks had to be accomplished by were written on a whiteboard, the jobs listed under the names Tommaso and Giancarlo. Giancarlo was presumably the AWOL chef.

I could see at a glance that he was woefully behind. I looked at the prep list. Most of it was meaningless, but I seized on a word that I did know. '*Soffritto*'. It was 'the holy trinity' as Matteo had said: celery, onion and carrot. Chopped into fine dice. What Matteo had shown me. What I'd done with Octavia. A very time-consuming job. These were listed under Giancarlo's tasks. I could see a stack of these three vegetables, enough for two hundred, that is, a lot of them, on a table together with a chopping board and a knife.

I walked over.

'*Soffritto?*'

'*Si.*'

God alone knows what the words for 'fine dice' were. I picked up the knife. I noticed the tension in Tommaso's posture. He had no idea if this pale, female intruder with no word of Italian and a weird interest in some English kid, long since departed, knew what on earth she was doing. Could I even handle a knife?

Was this a joke?

I picked up a head of celery, cut the base off, dropped it in a container for use later if he wanted it (you never know) and got to work.

I've cut a lot of vegetables in my time and, as a one-man band in my own place, I've never had the chance to get rusty. I am very fast and accurate. And now I worked as if my life depended on it. The knife was a blur in my hand. I pushed the board over for him to look at. I'd only done a few stalks, but it was enough of a demo for Tommaso. He grinned at me, gave me a very nice smile, and clapped me on the back.

'*Va bene.*'

'Do you need me?' asked Andrea.

'Not really,' I said. 'I think I won't need a translator as Tommaso's bitch.'

Andrea winced at the brutal kitchen expression and translated that for the chef's benefit.

'Ho, ho, ho!' He had a booming, slightly unhinged laugh. Tommaso put the radio on. 'Music,' he said, a trifle unnecessarily. I wondered what Euro horror we would have to work to.

'*Rock me, rock me. . .*'

Blimey I thought, Falco and 'Rock Me Amadeus'.

As often featured on Beech Tree FM.

I'd been working the previous week to classical music, *Rigoletto* and Verdi's *Traviata* drifting across the Earl Hampden Estate, the week before to horrible death metal, and now I had Falco's take on Mozart.

I knew which one I preferred.

'You like?' asked Tommaso.

'*Si*,' I said, using one of my two words of Italian.

'See you later,' said Andrea. He seemed both amused and impressed. It had been a long time since he'd given me a look like that and I felt a huge surge of confidence. I knew then that everything would go well in the kitchen.

'After ten.' I didn't even look up from my veg. I was in the zone.

Andrea left and Tommaso pointed at the door as it swung closed behind him.

'*Amico?*'

Presumably that meant boyfriend. I shook my head. 'Ex.'

'*Che peccato*,' he said.

I guessed that meant, 'shame'.

He was right. A crying shame. I cracked on with my veg prep. I thought of me and Andrea, of what we had had together.

The tears in my eyes weren't entirely due to the sulfenic acid produced by the onions.

Chapter-Fifty

'So how did it go?' asked Andrea. Above us in the night sky, the moon hung high. It was one of those velvety nights that you get in warm countries where the air is still heavy and warm and enfolds you almost like a cloak.

I was in that zone of stupefied relief that follows an insanely busy service, when you've been physically and mentally pushed to the utmost, your concentration keyed to crazy levels as you desperately try to get everything out on time, cooked to perfection, nothing burned or under-cooked. And then it all stops and you can relax.

I was sitting in the yard outside Tommaso's kitchen with the chef and Andrea, the three of us on upturned beer crates. Old-school, I thought with approval. Tommaso was drinking red wine by the glass from an unmarked bottle. I got the impression – we'd established a rudimentary conversation via Google Translate on my phone – that it was his own vintage, made in the commune winery from his own grapes. It kind of tasted that way too. I had a beer.

Tommaso lurched to his feet and patted me affectionately on the head.

It had been quite a day. The main issue had been the sheer volume of prep needed. Luckily, the cooking had been self-evident. First, we got everything prepped. Tommaso had rolled out the pasta dough then expertly ran it several times through the adjustable rollers of the pasta machine, while I chopped, filleted and sautéed as if my life depended on it. Luckily for me, it was all simple work that was blindingly obvious. We didn't need speech.

When we'd finished on the stroke of six, I had taken over the actual cooking, leaving him to plate everything up. The ravioli had been the biggest problem. He'd made them and I had to cook them for five minutes in three gigantic pans, fishing them out with a spider – not the animal but an enormous flat sieve that we use in catering. It would have been no problem at all except that there were about 300 of them.

The logistics were simple but daunting. You could get about 50 in each pan so that was 150 at a time, multiplied by two at five minute intervals. So ten minutes or so to get it all cooked, and they couldn't be held for more than a few minutes beneath the lights under the pass before they would start to toughen up.

It was a very fraught 20-odd minutes, Tommaso swearing non-stop in Italian as he ladled lemon butter sauce over them, garnishing them with tomato concasse (I had blanched, skinned, quartered and diced a hell of a lot of tomatoes) and chopped parsley. (I had chopped bushels of parsley). Five waitresses ran them out to the customers.

Then lasagne time which was incredibly stress-free compared to the ravioli. Then the chicken stew. Finally, dessert, a stroll in the park with 150 panna cotta, forest fruit puree garnish and 50 tiramisus. Easy.

We had also listened to umpteen David Guetta mixes, 'Ace of Base', 'All That She Wants', 'Barbie Girl', 'Don't Cha', 'Oooh Ah Just A Little Bit', 'All The Things She Said' and basically just about everything that Roxette had ever recorded, which was fine by me. I felt that Roxette's 'The Look' was a perfect song, an ideal accompaniment for stirring 30-odd kilos of chicken and veg in a huge stockpot (oh for the Earl's Bratt pan).

And now Andrea was here.

'So,' he said, translating Tommaso's words, 'you want to know about Matteo McCleish and Nonna Bonini.'

So that was her surname. '*Si*, his grandmother Nonna Bonini.'

Tommaso frowned. 'Nonna Bonini wasn't his grand-mother. . .' he said, then carried on in a cascade of Italian.

'Whoa,' I interrupted, and turned to Andrea.

'Get him to explain about his Italian granny.'

Andrea listened carefully to the chef, providing an almost simultaneous translation for me. The story that unfolded was very different from the authorised version. There had indeed been a Nonna in Matteo's life, but she was no relative. Nor was she a simple Granny, teaching him her home cooking.

'Matteo worked with me at Nonna's,' was how he started. The story led on from there. The reality of Matteo's cookery odyssey was more or less as he had said, but with this crucial difference.

The McCleishes lived in the village with Matteo. As I had suspected, the family weren't terribly popular.

Small places in the country are not usually too enamoured of incomers, particularly foreigners, and Monte Salvia was no exception. Magnus's (Matteo's father) job too, looking after expats' properties, meant that he was doing jobs hitherto done by locals (or at least left him open to that accusation) and he tended to favour expat British workmen – plumbers, electricians et cetera – who had moved to Le Marche, over Italian ones.

That added to the underlying local hostility to the foreigners who were unjustly suspected as being the advance party of a horde of British invaders. So there was that to contend with, the country dwellers' suspicions of incomers, particularly those from another country.

Then, of course, Matteo had obviously struggled in school. A ten-year-old boy with presumably not that much Italian, even if his mum had spoken it at home, it would have been a far cry from his classmates' linguistic competence. Then there was the challenge of an unfamiliar curriculum in an unknown language in a place where he had no friends. It must have been a lonely childhood. Although he was startlingly good-looking and with his exotic – to a Le Marche girl – background, he had been popular with the opposite sex.

Then he got a job at Nonna – 'Granny' – Bonini's restaurant as a dish-washer. 'It's gone now,' Tommaso said sadly, 'the Ristorante Bonini was both born, and died, with Nonna Bonini. She was a wonderful woman, a fantastic cook back in the day when you just didn't get top-class women cooks. They say that as a girl she was taught by a master chef who was so old he'd actually been taught by Escoffier.'

307

So Matteo didn't have a granny who had taught him how to cook at home at all, she was as fictitious as Mr Kipling. He had learned his trade from an expert.

'But he was exceptional,' said Tommaso, via the medium of Andrea, pouring another glass of wine. 'He was amazingly good at cooking – it was instinctive and effortless. He was fourteen when he started there, working after school twice a week washing up. In a month he was doing the desserts. Two months, starters and desserts, three months, the grill section. By the time he was fifteen he was better than the sous chef. Nonna adored him, wanted him to stay, and he would have, if it hadn't been for that *troia* Graziana.'

I was sitting next to Andrea on a beer crate, and our knees suddenly touched. It sounds tame, particularly as we had lived together in London and shared a bed for a couple of years, but it had the same effect on me as touching a live wire. It was like the completion of an electric circuit that detonates a bomb. He didn't look at me; he was still looking at Tommaso while he translated. I stared at my ex's head, his slightly large nose in profile, one wonderful, sculptural arched eyebrow, his strong, elegant neck, the beautiful hair.

I was high as a kite on adrenaline, a chef's high, hysterical after the unremitting pressure of the last few hours, and now the blissful release, the beer, the cool night air after the heat of the kitchen. And the presence of Andrea. Now a tsunami of erotic desire.

He paused every now and then to get Tommaso to explain dialect words or expressions that he used. *Marchigiano*, it was called, he later explained to me.

My heart was thundering, my throat dry, my mind racing. This was partly to do with the revelations from Tommaso, partly down to Andrea's presence, almost wholly due to the pressure on my knee.

'She was obsessed by him.' I know the feeling, I thought to myself., 'And I will say that he was a popular guy. He was only sixteen, maybe seventeen, very good-looking, girls adored him. Then he met Graziana. She was a looker too. I tried, I must say.' He laughed and shook his head ruefully. 'She was like the cool, bad girl that all the boys wanted. Her mum was divorced, her dad in Ancona. Divorce, that was unheard of in this village. . .'

I pressed my knee against Andrea's and felt an answering nudge.

'She wasn't interested in Nonna and her restaurant, nor in Le Marche. She wanted bright lights, then she started getting tattoos. Anyway, Graziana's dad had a bar, Roberto's, down by the fish market in Ancona, in the old town. That's where she moved Matteo to, to live, not to work. It didn't do food. The last I heard he was working in some restaurant there, but until you asked about him, I'd forgotten about him. I've got plenty to think about other than those two.'

He drank some more. 'Nonna was heartbroken. He was like her son, she had taught him everything and he just walked away, no gratitude, no nothing,' sighed Tommaso. 'I think it killed her, when he left. She gave him all that knowledge, all that love, and he just walked away. I think he might have killed her.'

No wonder he changed the narrative, I thought. Inventing

a charming story involving a fictional Nonna, rather than the reality of breaking an old woman's heart. Was this what he was being blackmailed over?

He drank some more. 'And that's the last I saw or heard of Matteo until you two turned up today. Why the interest?'

Behind Tommaso I could see into the kitchen via the door that had been propped open to allow fresh air to circulate. I could see one of those magnetised strips on the wall that you can use to hold knives. He used it for holding skewers. There were ten of them in a row. They reminded me of something. I suddenly recalled Anna Bruce's comment on the Tarot card, the ten of Wands. What had it meant, a heavy burden. Maybe that described the guilt that Matteo could well be feeling when the blackmailer had forced him to confront his past, a past that he had neatly re-invented. Guilt and shame, often the prime movers in a person's life.

'Oh,' I said, airily, 'the McCleish family were friends of a friend. He asked us to find out what had happened to them in Italy. It's nothing important.'

Tommaso nodded and yawned and stood up, as did we. It was obvious that our interview time was over.

We had heard enough now; the rest we would piece together the following day.

'Charlie, my friend. . .' I got up and he flung his arms around me and kissed me on both cheeks. I felt the wire-wool scratchiness of his beard rubbing against my skin.

'Charlie,' he said again, holding my elbows as he looked into my eyes, 'thank you, and if you ever want a job. . .' Then he said, 'Go and see Roberto, Graziana's dad. He'll know what Matteo is up to – he knows everything in Ancona. Ciao, my friend.'

Andrea and I left his restaurant and walked into the main square. Somehow, by the time we reached the car, we were holding hands.

Chapter Fifty-One

On Monday morning we found Roberto's bar easily enough. It was tucked away in a small street near the main harbour in Ancona. The area was quite rough-looking, the kind of place where there are groups of kids on street corners, up to no good – and men sitting at tables outside, smoking, running their eyes up and down you in a reflective way. The bars that you find near docks are not usually the most genteel of establishments and Ancona was no exception. Ancona, hilly and slightly grotty (although infinitely nicer than Wycombe), is not an attractive town. Roberto's was more upmarket than its neighbours. It was more a bar/café than a purely drinking establishment, with tables outside on the pavement, a small menu selling panini and ice creams. I remembered Tommaso saying that Matteo had worked in a restaurant in Ancona, not in a bar. I guess he had just been staying there.

I had a sense of déjà vu when I saw it, then I realised why. I'd seen it on Douglas's laptop. My heart started beating faster, I felt that something momentous was going to happen.

It was 11 o'clock and we ordered coffees – a macchiato for Andrea, espresso for me. He was wearing ripped jeans, a white T-shirt, a checked shirt and sunglasses that looked so good they must have been ruinously expensive.

I guess I was wearing an expression of dazed happiness. I didn't know what last night meant. I didn't know what position Andrea was in, in terms of relationships. I knew he was engaged but that can cover a multitude of things. The truth was, I didn't want to speculate or do anything that might detract from the moment. Andrea had not spent the night sleeping on the floor.

Now he smiled at me and leaned over and, as if to reassure me, put his hand on top of mine. He took his sunglasses off and our eyes met.

'It's good to be with you again, Charlie.'

'I'm glad you feel that way.' I think I'd been expecting something along the lines of: 'Charlie. . . about last night. . . terrible mistake. . . Don't know what came over me. . . We can still be friends. . .'

I'd more than settle for 'good to be with you'.

'So what do you make of what Tommaso told us last night?' he asked. Maybe we were both relieved to be skirting around the subject of 'us'. It was, as they say, the elephant in the room.

'I think we now know that Matteo does not want the true story of Nonna Bonini aired,' I said. 'He's a household name. Lots of people would be interested to read a story headlined "How Matteo McCleish broke Nonna's heart".'

I glanced at the bar behind me. Douglas had thought it worthy of a photo and the only images he was really interested in were porn. There had to be a reason. To be honest, I didn't really want to conduct yet another laborious conversation with an old bar owner, via an interpreter, even if he was Graziana's father. I wanted to sit in the sun and look at Andrea. But I couldn't. Perhaps the dad wouldn't be there anymore; for all I knew he had sold the place long ago and the new owner had just kept the name.

I walked inside. It was cool and shady after the glare of the sun. There was a curved bar, a couple of those big glass-fronted fridges that Italians seem to love in their restaurants, framed black-and-white photos on the wall.

The pleasant waitress who had served us was behind the counter. She said something to me in Italian.

I smiled and said ruefully, 'I'm sorry, do you speak English?'

She smiled. 'A bit.'

'Is the owner in?' I asked.

'Why?'

'Tommaso from Osteria Bianca in Monte Salvia told me to look him up.'

She grinned. 'Tommaso, mamma mia. . . how is he?'

'Very well, I was working with him last night.'

She looked suitably impressed. 'No, I'm sorry.' She shook her head regretfully. 'Signor Salvini, he's away at the moment.'

'Oh.' I was leaning against the bar and looking idly at the framed black-and-white photos. Jolly Italians fishing, a jolly Italian holding up a very large fish while beaming with pride at his catch. She followed my eyes.

'Yes, that is Signor Salvini.'

And then, there he was again, with a very young Matteo, outside a restaurant in the village square where I'd been last night, and a spry old lady with white hair, holding a copy of a book, jacket facing out: *Mia Cucina* A. Bonini.

I asked although I knew the answer.

'Who is that with Signor Salvini?'

'That's Alessandra Bonini, with her cookery book.' She smiled at me. 'You must be a chef. Would you like to see a copy, it was quite the thing fifty years ago. . . we have one behind the bar.'

'Yes please.'

She handed me a copy of the book. It was seriously old. The colours had faded on the hardback jacket and the font was really old-fashioned, the pages slightly yellowed and musty.

'Can I take it outside? To show my friend.'

'Of course.'

I looked again at the photos on the wall. Roberto Salvini holding his fish, it was a swordfish, *un pesce spada*, a very common menu item in Italy. I was reminded of the card Anna Bruce had turned over, the eight of Swords. What had it indicated, upset, disorder? I looked down at the book in my hand. That would be about right.

I walked outside and sat down.

'What's that?' Andrea asked.

'A cookery book.' He rolled his eyes.

I opened the book, looked at the list of contents. I don't know Italian but I didn't need to.

And then everything clicked into place, just as Anna Bruce had said it would.

I knew why he was being blackmailed.

I knew Matteo's dirty little secret that he very much did not want the world to know.

Chapter Fifty-Two

Night was falling as I drove up to Matteo's house. I had spoken to a grim-faced Jess when I had got home. After she had shown me what she had found on Douglas's laptop I felt pretty grim too.

I parked my car and when I got out, I noticed that Graziana's Range Rover was nowhere to be seen. Good, I thought, it would be easier if it were just him.

I rang the bell and Matteo answered the door.

'Charlie,' he said, 'do come in. . .'

I gave him that kind of tight smile you give to people that you've either had a terrible row with or are about to have, and I noticed him look at me curiously. There had been a dramatic shift in our relationship and although I hadn't yet said anything, it was almost tangible. He obviously felt something was different.

He led me along the hall into the gangster-style living room. I looked around at the chrome-and-glass coffee table, the huge desk with the clicky chrome balls and the out-of-date intercom, the black furniture, the white carpeting, and I repressed a shudder. The nudes simpered at me from the walls. You could tell they were good pictures by the way their nipples seemed to follow you around the room.

At least they weren't Sandra Reynolds'.

'Drink?'

'I'll have a beer,' I said.

He went over to the globe drinks cabinet. It had lost its charm for me. It now seemed tawdry and faintly ridiculous. Not unlike Matteo. He returned with a Nastro Azzurro. I poured the bottle into a glass and studied Matteo over the rim.

I think it was the first time I had looked at him really closely, and I guess it was because now I knew the truth about him. He brushed his long hair away from his eyes.

Matteo was very good-looking, regular features and a strong jaw and chin. A determined face, with brown oval eyes in a kind of Modigliani way. His skin was brown and Italian-looking, dusted with stubble. Despite everything he was quite beautiful.

'So, you said we needed to talk,' he opened his hands in a very Italian way. 'Let's talk.'

'I've been to Italy,' I said, looking steadily at Matteo. 'I went to Monte Salvia and I met Tommaso. I went to the graveyard. I went to Roberto's bar, Graziana's father's bar, in Ancona.'

'Oh.' It was the kind of 'oh' that carried a hundred shades of meaning: resignation, relief, the knowledge that you would have to face up to things. That kind of 'oh'.

'I read the book, Alessandra Bonini's book,' I said.

'The book?' he said innocently, as if that were going to deflect me.

317

'Can you please tell me what's been going on?' I asked. I think it was at that moment he realised that the game was up.

'Where do I begin?' he said, half-whispering.

I had lost patience with Matteo and his evasions. 'Begin at the beginning, Matteo, and work forwards. . .'

He nodded. I suddenly realised it had cost two deaths, nearly three including Murdo, to keep a secret that wasn't really terribly important outside of catering and publishing.

'OK,' he said. 'Here goes. . .' He poured himself a large glass of wine and drank a mouthful.

'I'm thirty-eight,' Matteo said, and pulled a face. 'Terrible isn't it! And I started working in a kitchen when I was fourteen – that's twenty-four years, my God, nearly a quarter of a century.'

He stood up and walked restlessly around the large study. He gazed up at one of the lurid nudes, and continued speaking.

'My maternal grandparents were from Le Marche, by way of Scotland. But my mum always wanted to live in Italy. I was born in England, where we lived at the time, so my Italian was quite poor as a child, even though she spoke Italian to me at home, when she remembered.' He smiled bitterly. 'Their parenting skills left a lot to be desired.'

I nodded.

'We moved back to Italy where her family were originally from, back in the day. I was ten. My parents were looking after holiday homes for British owners. When I was four-teen I got a part-time job when I was at school, after school

318

hours, as a pot-washer, my first kitchen job. And then I got promoted. You can understand that.'

'Indeed I can,' I said. That's more or less how Francis had ended up being a chef for me. The big difference of course being that he had no talent and Matteo was a genius.

'Now,' said Matteo, tearing his gaze away from the painting and looking at me, 'the thing was, the restaurant that I was working in was amazingly good.'

'Ristorante Bonini?'

He nodded. 'Exactly. Though I didn't know how good it was at the time. Who knows anything when they're a teenager?' He told me how skilful she had been. He confirmed Tommaso's story about her having worked with the chef who had known Escoffier. The mind boggled. Escoffier had died in 1935. 'She had an amazing pedigree. Ristorante Zeffirino in Genova, the Trattoria della Pesa in Milan. . . Then she got sick of the hours and the stress and opened her own quiet place in the country. . .' he smiled at me, 'not unlike you, Charlie. But I was young, I had other things to worry about. . .'

He waved a hand to indicate a fraught childhood as a foreigner in a village, a perennial outsider. 'And I rose through the ranks. Well, it was a small place, thirty covers max, and great regional cooking. Nonna Bonini adored me, I was the son she never had. But I had to get out of the village. She begged me to stay but I couldn't. Village life was killing me. . . You know what it's like, you live in one.'

I nodded; it could be claustrophobic at times. The thing was, I was old enough that I kind of had ceased to care.

He continued: 'I moved to Ancona, worked in the best

restaurants there. That was not a large pool. Ancona's a bit of a hick town but I had Graziana. She's always backed me up, from day one. Then I outgrew Ancona. I was sous at a couple of Milan's best restaurants. The one head-hunted me from the other, and then when I knew enough I came to England. And when I got my place in London, I re-created her menu.'

'That wasn't all you re-created, Matteo, was it?' I said, quietly.

'No.' He had the grace to blush. 'No it wasn't.'

'You re-created her book, didn't you?' I noticed a slight tremor in the hand that held the wine. 'In fact you plagia-rised it. You took all her recipes and you passed them off as your own.'

'Yes,' he was almost whispering, 'she was dead by then and it's true, I stole all her recipes. The book was long out of print and when I worked for her in the restaurant I was unknown. But I always lived in fear that someone would find out, that someone would discover the truth and expose me as a thief and a fraud and the kid who broke Nonna's heart.'

He paused as the last sentence sank in. I guessed that this was the first time he had ever vocalised the truth. He knew it, but he'd hidden it, and now it was finally out. He repeated the sentence softly, almost wonderingly, 'I stole all her recipes,' and stared into space.

I sighed. 'Like I said, it's called plagiarism, isn't it, Matteo. I spoke to someone I know who works in publishing, they said it's taken very seriously in those circles.'

He nodded. 'I know. It was a calculated risk. The book

was old, she'd been off the radar for a while even when she was alive. . . and face it, Charlie, a lot of people don't read cookbooks, they just look at the pictures. . . fortunately for me.' He sighed. 'I stole everything. I mean all of them,' he confessed. 'That first TV series, that was all her stuff, and I passed it off as my own. My signature dishes, the *zabaglione*, the *saltimbocca* with a twist, they're hers. And my first cookery book. . .' He shook his head sadly, got up, went to the safe in the corner (of course, there had to be a safe, here in the lair) and spun the dial this way and that. It clicked open and he reached inside and returned with a paperback book.

I examined it. It was a copy of the same edition that I had seen the day before in Ancona. *Mia Cucina* by A. Bonini. It was hard to believe that behind all the glossy footage on TV of Matteo making gnocchi, twirling the crank handle of the pasta machine as he turned pasta dough into lasagne, chopping onions with amazing speed (he was incredible with a knife and I should know; I was good but he was awesome), lay this long-forgotten book.

I flipped through the pages, which were heavily annotated in biro and pencil. There was hardly any white margin left.

'That's her book. Long since out of print, the publisher no longer exists.' He pulled a face. 'If you look at *Matteo Does Italy*, the book that made me – it's pretty much the same book. I just translated it. More or less the same recipes in the same order.'

'And that's what the blackmail's about, isn't it?'

He nodded. 'Yes. Obviously I couldn't tell anyone, so Graziana suggested that she take the heat to give a cover story as to why I was being blackmailed. Charlotte bought that. If the blackmailer had gone public with this, I'd have lost the TV show, aside from maybe being sued. No reputable British publisher would ever touch me again with a bargepole. And, of course, I would have looked like a total fraud. That would have been even worse.'

'Did Giorgio know any of this?' I asked, suddenly. I remembered Octavia's theory that Giorgio had some kind of hold over Matteo. He shook his head.

'No, at least I don't think so.'

'Why did you hire him?' I asked. 'He was so horrible.'

'I worked with him in Milan,' Matteo said. 'You must have noticed what a good chef he was. And in Italy he was really supportive of me. He was different back then. Then he got his own place in Vicenza, it was a disaster. He could follow orders faultlessly, but there was no creative vision. He put everything into that restaurant, and came out bankrupt, morally as well as financially. And he lost his wife. He lost the lot. It made him bitter, but. . . but I felt I still owed him and everyone was shit-scared of him and I'm terrible at disciplining people who work for me.' He sighed. 'He did it for me, kept the troops in line.'

'I understand now,' I said. That confirmed Attila's guess.

'And I could sympathise with him. I stole my creative vision from Alessandra Bonini, Charlie, like Prometheus stealing fire from the Gods.' He paused and then said, 'That's the problem, I'm not just a chef. . .'

'Aren't you?' I was confused momentarily.

'No,' he said firmly, 'I'm also a brand. And the brand is all about integrity.'

I looked across at Matteo who smiled sadly at me. I began to feel a bit sorry for him. At least I was my own person, I didn't need to measure my actions against the expectations of others.

'Most of the people who watch me are never going to cook what I'm showing them.'

'They're not?' I felt somehow disappointed.

'No,' he said, shaking his head, 'they like what it repres-ents. These are people who haven't got the time or the inclination to cook, but they like watching me do it. For me it's like having sex in public when I cook and they're the voyeurs.'

'Is that where you got the idea of the OnlyFans thing, because you felt like a sex performer, that your audience are almost perving on you?' I asked.

He stared at me. 'My God! I hadn't thought of that. . . you're very perceptive aren't you, Charlie. Anyway, if my public thought I had stolen some old woman's heritage, it would be terrible for me, a real game changer and not in a good way. The TV public are like piranhas, if they catch a whiff of a celeb's blood, they'll tear him to pieces.'

Silence fell.

He refilled his glass. 'So, is that what you found out? The real reason I'm being blackmailed?'

'In Italy, yes, but I know who the blackmailer is.'

'Who's that?' he asked. Almost wearily.

'Douglas.'

'Douglas! I don't believe it.' He looked shocked and then relieved. It hadn't been one of his team after all.

'It's true.'

323

'Do you have proof?'

'Yes, the blackmail letters are still there on his laptop. I'm sure the police forensics can confirm that they were created before you received them, then I'm sure they'll discover the cash; lastly, I think he'll break down under police questioning.'

That was a safe prediction. Douglas was not exactly made of stern stuff. There was a lot more to him than met the eye. Including the images from the staff toilets. Thanks to Jess's computer skills I had seen not only the blackmail letters, I had also seen Graziana's secret tattoo, a secret no longer thanks to Douglas and his micro-cameras. That was how I imagine Giorgio had seen it. I decided not to share this with Matteo, he'd got enough to process for one evening.

Matteo shook his head. 'Absolutely not. I, we, do not want the police involved, nor the media.'

I shook my head; I knew he would say that.

'It's out of your hands, Matteo. After I leave here, I'm going to Slattery. Douglas didn't just blackmail you, he's responsible for two deaths. I don't care about Giorgio but someone has to pay for Octavia.'

He nodded. 'I understand.' He sighed. 'Oh, well,' he said, '*che sarà sarà.*' He looked with a hint of pleading in his eyes. 'You do know that this will finish me, don't you?'

I nodded. 'Two people are dead,' I repeated. 'I'm sorry, Matteo, if it could be some other way. . .'

'You won't change your mind, please Charlie. . .'

I shook my head.

'Yeah, you're right.' He blinked back a tear of self-pity;

he gave a wan smile. 'Well, Graziana wanted us to go back to Italy, she'll be happy.' He laughed bitterly, 'Charlotte's not going to like it, she'll be furious.'

There was a heavy silence and then the door to the study opened. Charlotte walked in. Speak of the devil.

As Matteo had predicted, she looked very cross indeed. But that wasn't what caught our attention.

In her hand she held a rifle. I recognised it immediately. I'd held it myself not that long ago, I could still remember how heavy it had felt.

It was Douglas's rifle, the CZ 457. It was also pointed directly at us.

Chapter Fifty-Three

Charlotte advanced on us, the gun unwavering in her hands. I had never been held at gunpoint before. I couldn't say it was an experience I was enjoying. I sat motionless, barely breathing.

What was even more frightening than the matt-black barrel of the gun in her hand was the expression on her face.

It was one of pure rage. It rose from her like steam. I had seen her angry before, but that was nothing compared to this. The word 'furious' failed to do her justice. Her eyes behind her glasses were incandescent. Her face was red; stray bits of brown hair stuck up from her bun like warning signals. Warning signals. . . 'A violent woman possibly, or maybe a deceitful one. Either way, she is malignant, more than that, she poses an existential threat.'

Anna Bruce's words. I had thought they applied to Sandra, the biker woman from Hell. Maybe they did, but I knew an existential threat when I saw one, and I was looking at one right now. She's the High Priestess Anna had mentioned, the figure behind the scenes who is the gateway to the mysteries. She was the one who had pulled the strings on his career and was now set to bring the curtain down on it.

'Calm down, Charlotte,' said Matteo. He put his hands up in a placating kind of way.

'Calm down!' she spat out. 'I've been sitting out there listening to everything that you've been saying on that. . .' She pointed to the intercom on the desk. Oh Jesus, I thought, now we're in trouble. I cast my mind back to what Matteo had said. His confession of plagiarism had obviously gone down terribly badly with his agent. Then there was the little matter of me ending his career for him.

'And you're telling me to calm down!' Her voice rose to a near scream. 'I killed those people for you Matteo, to stop them blackmailing you and Graziana, and now it turns out it was all for nothing!'

So it was Charlotte, not Douglas, who was the killer! How wrong had I been. But I didn't have time to brood on this. She carried on:

'You're a thief and it's going to get out and end your career, all that work I did, and you're going to flush it down the toilet. We're going to get our asses sued over intellectual property theft, all the TV will go. . . we'll be left with nothing. You asshole.'

'You killed them?' It was Matteo's turn to shout now. 'Giorgio and Octavia. Why? Are you crazy?'

Oh, God, I silently willed him not to provoke her.

'Crazy, am I?' I saw her knuckles whiten as she tightened her grip on the gun. 'Well, we all thought it was Giorgio bleeding you dry, didn't we, so I went round to his place to tell him he was busted and he laughed in my face and so I killed him to stop the blackmail. If anyone's to blame for that, it's you. You told me he was the blackmailer when Charlie saw him leaving the porn shop and I believed you!'

'Oh, so it's my fault now is it!' Matteo didn't seem fazed now by the gun. Maybe he didn't believe his agent was prepared to pull the trigger. I certainly did.

'Yes, Matteo, it's down to you.' She looked a bit calmer now, but the gun never moved.

'And Octavia? You surely didn't suspect her?' he demanded.

'I thought it was Tom in that freezer, not her,' she said, irritably. God, I thought, she must have seen that Iron Man hoodie from across the kitchen and thought it was him disappearing in there – they were the same height.

'Tom?' he stared at her in disbelief. 'Why the hell did you want to try and kill Tom? What did he have to do with anything?'

'Because he was the only one with enough balls and brains for blackmail, so I had a second go when the first one failed. That's why I spiked his coke.' She frowned angrily. 'Only he sold it to Murdo.'

I remembered Slattery telling me that Tom had been in trouble before for supplying coke. I suppose old habits die hard.

'In a way,' mused Charlotte, 'it was Tom who nearly killed him, selling him drugs. Nothing to do with me when you think about it.'

Matteo shifted in his chair; the gun barrel followed.

'So none of this is your fault?' he said bitterly. She

ignored the question. The tell-tale red spots returned to her cheeks.

'And now I learn it's all been for nothing.' Charlotte was almost shaking with rage. 'I made you – you'd have been nothing without me, you and your shit Italian food. . . nothing, you ungrateful bastard!'

I might as well not have been in the room. Neither of them was paying me any attention. I wondered if it might not be a good time to try and slip away. I shifted in my seat and Charlotte's gun moved direction to cover me. I froze where I was.

'Stay where you are, you smug slut.'

Why am I a slut? I didn't ask. Or smug, come to that. I just sat there. She was a very efficient manager. She was a very efficient businesswoman. She was a very efficient organiser. She had proved herself a highly efficient murderer. I had little doubt she would be a highly efficient shot. She had been in the army after all.

Oddly, now it was Matteo's turn to get angry. He jumped to his feet.

'It's all about money, for you, isn't it, that's all it's ever been. You money grabbing, fat-faced b—'

He never got as far as the word 'bitch'. Charlotte had heard enough and she pulled the trigger. The noise was very loud in a horribly emphatic way. The gun kicked in her hands and propelled by the force of the bullet, Matteo collapsed back in his chair.

Chapter Fifty-Four

I stared at the scene in front of me in frozen horror. Matteo was not dead. He had been shot in his right arm, in the bicep. I don't know if she had meant to just wing him, probably she had. He had his left arm clamped around the wound. Blood seeped through his fingers and stained the black-and-white zebra fabric of the chair a deep crimson. Time seemed to stand still, the way it does when you have a car crash. A small metal bowl on the surface of the desk in front of Matteo caught my eye. He used it to keep money in. I could see some notes, euros and sterling and fifty and twenty pence pieces. I suddenly remembered Anna's predictions, le neuf denier, the nine of coins – a quarrel, a wound. . .

Charlotte looked at her work with satisfaction. 'That's right, Matteo, and now you're worth a lot more dead than alive. None of this will come out. Graziana will be your executor and I will stand loyally by and turn your memory and your story into cash.'

Matteo slumped back in his chair, the loss of blood weakening him.

'Get up! Both of you!' she ordered. Her voice was like a whip crack. No wonder she was so effective in negotiations, I thought, as I stood up and Matteo struggled to his feet.

'You!' she ordered, pointing the gun at me for emphasis. 'Take off that belt you're wearing and tie it round his arm. I don't want him dying here.'

I did as I was instructed, pulling the belt from my jeans.

'Now' – she motioned with her gun – 'outside. We're all leaving.'

I put my arm around Matteo. He leaned his weight against me as I supported him.

We made our way down the hall. The front door was open and I could see the cars outside. My Volvo. The Maserati. The other one was Graziana's Range Rover, their country car. It hadn't been there earlier. Matteo looked at it and then at Charlotte.

'Where is she?' he whispered.

'Oh, she's fine,' said Charlotte, 'she's in London. Asked me to deliver the car back here for her.'

I felt Matteo's body sag against me in relief. I let him slide down slowly until he was on the gravel of the drive. Charlotte glanced at us, took a key out of her pocket and unlocked the Range Rover. She opened the door and chucked the key inside, leaned in, retrieved her handbag and walked back towards us.

Matteo had obviously fainted. I felt a twinge of jealousy. At least he was no longer aware of this nightmare scenario. I thought about jumping Charlotte, but I was too scared. She would just shoot me and I didn't want to die. I was so frightened I could hardly breathe.

331

Run for it, said my brain, *run. She'll shoot, but she might miss. If you stand around here, she'll kill you. That's for sure.*

I stayed rooted to the spot.

Charlotte had another key fob in her hand. She pressed a button and the boot of Matteo's Maserati yawned open.

'Pick him up and put him in it!' she ordered.

'In the boot?' I asked, stupidly. Would he fit?

'Yes, in the boot.' Her voice was testy, impatient.

I did so, holding him in my arms like a religious painting, La Pietà. Matteo's head lolled back. He looked like a sexy Christ with his long hair hanging down and his rather beautiful face. No wonder he'd been such a hit on TV. No wonder Graziana found him so attractive.

I laid him gently in the boot, as instructed. He was an awkward shape but years of lifting heavy pans and hard manual work in kitchens have given me a rock-hard core. It was a tight squeeze but I managed to fold him in.

I turned around to face Charlotte.

'You won't get away with this,' I said. I wanted to snarl, in a kind of tough, devil may care way – but it came out as a whimper.

'Why not?' she sneered. 'The police will think Douglas did it. It's his gun after all. He won't have an alibi for tonight, he'll be alone, at home, as always.' She said point-edly, 'Your waitress will tell them about his laptop. They'll arrest him and go through his computer, they'll assume he's moved on from blackmail to murder. And I'll be assisting them with their inquiries. I have a lot of dirt on Douglas.'

'What kind of dirt?' I asked, both genuinely curious and

hoping to delay whatever she had planned on the off-chance of someone turning up and spoiling her plans.

'You know why he got the sack from his last job?' said Charlotte. 'He's a voyeur, a peeping tom, quite a hi-tech one.' After what Jess had told me I was not remotely surprised. 'I know for a fact he's got indecent images on his phone. This gun,' she nodded at the rifle, 'I'm going to put back in his flat. It'll be found there.'

She smiled at me. 'It's all there. Hard evidence, circumstantial evidence, my testimony. . . He's screwed. By the time they find you and Matteo you'll be too damaged for them to put a definitive time on when you died. They'll assume he did it, and if not,' she shrugged, 'well, no one will suspect me. Why would I kill the golden goose?'

Charlotte's phone started ringing in her bag, which was on the ground next to the Range Rover. 'Don't move,' she ordered, pointing the gun at me.

Momentarily she disappeared from sight behind the great bulk of the car. Charlotte was short, the Range Rover high. I should have taken this moment to run. I knew though that my feet on the gravel would alert her and she'd shoot me in the back.

Mind you, I knew she was going to do that anyway. She'd only made us walk out here so that she didn't need to drag our bodies through the house.

That was the efficient way to do it.

I stood where I was, miserably, and then I frowned. I have a keen nose and standing there in the cool night air, taking what I imagined might well be my last few breaths on this earth, I could smell the faintly ferrous tang of

Matteo's blood, the smell of the roses in the shrubbery and then, weirdly, a faint smell of weed.

I frowned, perplexed. . . maybe I was hallucinating. . . hope leapt in my breast, could it be Cliff? Then, a rustling in the bushes and. . .

'THERE YOU ARE! YOU BITCH!'

Sandra Reynolds burst into view from behind one of the huge rhododendron bushes.

Sandra had obviously decided, upon sober reflection, that I needed to be taught a lesson. In her view I had seduced her husband, half-blinded her with a chilli, causing her a great deal of agony, humiliated her, and then I had been responsible for the near incineration of her beloved bike. It was a lengthy list. She would probably kill for less. She hadn't realised though she would have to join a queue.

I stood stock still. Caught between a rock and a hard place. Two women, both prepared to kill me. What were the odds?

'Not so tough without your boyfriend around, are you!' Presumably she meant Cliff.

Sandra was taking no chances with me. She had come prepared. She had brought what looked like a Samurai sword with her and she held it in both hands. This was certainly not one for show – it gleamed like a weapon from a martial arts shop, which is doubtless where it had come from.

'I'M GONNA. . .'

She raised the sword above her head. Rather uselessly, I raised my forearm to protect myself and then Charlotte stepped out from behind the Range Rover, rifle in hand.

Sandra stared at her in disbelief. Charlotte stared back at her for a moment, and then she calmly and dispassionately shot her in the sizeable area of her midriff.

If Charlotte imagined she had taken care of the Sandra problem, she was sadly mistaken. Sandra was not the kind of woman to take defeat lying down. Mrs Reynolds never knew when she was beaten.

I could testify to that.

She staggered back. One hand let go of the sword and went to her stomach. She stared at it, red with her own blood, but she was far from dead. Surrender was not in Sandra's lexicon, even with a .22 bullet in her.

With a roar of anger, ignoring me, she hurled herself forward at Charlotte, all eighteen stone of her, the sword now held with two hands again, aimed at her in a kind of downward stabbing motion. Charlotte worked the bolt on the rifle to chamber another round but she wasn't fast enough. Sandra was on her. She had thrown her entire weight behind the point of the sword and as its tip descended towards Charlotte she fell onto it, driving it downwards with all the force of her body behind it.

I thought, I bet they didn't cover that at Sandhurst, Charlotte.

The tip of the sword drove down through her chest and skewered Charlotte to the ground. She died without a sound. Sandra was now on top of her, Charlotte invisible under her great, leather-clad body, and then Sandra rolled to one side.

'Jesus Christ,' I said

Charlotte was obviously dead. Her eyes were open, her

arms by her sides. Even in death she had achieved neatness. An efficient and speedy departure from this life. Sandra's sword was planted in her like Excalibur in the rock.

Sandra looked much less decorative. She had been shot in the stomach and there was a lot of blood. She was unconscious, her eyes closed.

I stripped my blouse off and wadded it up, and crouching over Sandra, pulled her T-shirt up, wincing at the sight of the vast, pallid, flabby apron of her belly, now covered in blood. It was everywhere and cascading out of her at an alarming rate. I pulled her belt off out of her jeans, slid it round her and used it to secure my shirt as a pressure bandage.

I called for the police and the emergency services and then I sat down heavily on the ground.

There was nothing more to do other than wait.

Chapter Fifty-Five

'It's DI Slattery to see you,' said Jess. She'd been putting away the bottles of wine that had arrived to start the new wine list that Cassandra had put together for me. The list included several from the Le Marche region in Italy. I'd specifically asked her to source me some from there in Matteo and Graziana's honour. He'd given me a large bonus for my help; that had funded my new wine list.

I put down the strawberry bavarois I was making. The bavarois is like a piece of sponge cake topped with a jelly, to put it crudely. But oh, so much more! I hadn't been lying to Andrea when I had told him that my bavarois was a thing of splendour. Now I needed to perfect it, just in case. . .

I straightened up, yawned and stretched. It had been the Feast of Litha the night before. All had gone well. There was no chance of Sandra bursting in on the scene; she was still in Stoke Mandeville hospital.

Slattery looked at me and then Jess. 'Mind if I have a word alone?'

It was nine in the morning and my other two co-workers had not yet arrived.

'I'll get you a coffee,' offered Jess.

'Double espresso, please,' said Slattery.

Jess nodded and left us to it.

'Have you arrested Douglas?' I asked.

'Yes,' said Slattery, 'for possession of indecent images.'

I looked up from what I was doing. 'What kind of indecent images?'

Slattery leaned his powerful frame against a fridge.

'He'd got photos of girls. Girls, I would guess, in the ten to fourteen age bracket – well over a thousand or so pictures on his phone.' I suddenly thought that is probably what Octavia had meant when she'd said Giorgio had told her that someone in the team was doing something illegal. 'There were also images of mature women that were obviously taken without their knowledge or consent. We found several of those tiny micro-cameras you can get these days at his flat. Judging by the photos, he'd installed a few in the ladies' toilets at the restaurant in Marylebone and at the Earl's place.'

Slattery continued: 'He's pleading guilty to that. He says he knows nothing at all about any of the killings relating to Matteo McCleish but says that in his opinion, Charlotte was the murderer.'

I felt with the death of Charlotte, Octavia had been avenged.

'What's going to happen to him?' I asked.

'A lot of those images are Category A,' Slattery said. 'I imagine he'll get between three to five years.' I hadn't mentioned blackmail to the police, neither had Matteo, nor had Douglas. Let sleeping dogs lie, I thought. So Matteo's definitely going to get off with things, I thought to myself. I was pleased for him. I liked Matteo. Despite the plagiarism and the lies. The DI added, 'Douglas is definitely going down, that's the main thing.'

Good, I thought. I wondered if Douglas had guessed at the time that Charlotte was behind the killings in her attempt to nail the blackmailer. I think he probably did. No wonder he looked so nervous, knowing that if she suspected him, the axe would fall. On his scrawny neck. I should have worked out earlier Charlotte's office was just behind Carnaby Street and that might be why Porn Shop Guy was there. My own feeling too was that Porn Shop Guy was probably one of Douglas's paedo chums, possibly the source of his indecent images. In good time I would suggest this to Slattery.

Porn Shop Guy had obviously been on his way to Charlotte's office to warn Douglas about me, when I'd bumped into Graziana. She had also been visiting Charlotte, and I added two and two together and made five.

'How's Sandra Reynolds?' I asked.

Slattery laughed. 'Recovering.'

I was obscurely glad she was still in the land of the living. I doubted if Sandra would be sending me any flowers for saving her life. Hopefully though some vestige of gratitude would stop her from having another go at me in the third-time lucky stakes.

'It's incredible she's still alive,' I said.

'The bullet deflected off her brass belt buckle and was still in her body. She's a very lucky woman, really.'

'I'll say. The devil looks after his own, she was a Satan's Slut let's not forget.' Thinking of Satan's Sluts made me think of Murdo. He'd never repaid the money I had lent him, not that I'd really expected him to. But at least I was still alive, and still feeling euphoric as a result. I wasn't going to hold any grudges.

'Very true, Charlie.' The DI smiled, an unusual sight. 'I'll go and get my coffee, leave you to your cooking.'

He turned to leave the kitchen. I glanced down at the table by the outside door. Someone had put the post down there. There was a leaflet from a company that did Christmas puddings. 'Be prepared' it said, 'think ahead.' I sighed with irritation, it gets earlier every year. The flyer showed the Three Wise Men heading towards a stable where the Star hovered. My phone buzzed; I glanced down at the message. It was Andrea.

'Have called off engagement.'

I looked down at the ad, the Star of the Magi. Anna had said it represented hope.

I wondered where this left us. Time would tell, I suppose.

I turned my attention back to the bavarois.

About the Author

Photo credit: Alex Coombs

Alex Coombs was born in Lambeth in South London and studied Arabic at Oxford and Edinburgh Universities. *Murder on the Menu* was his first book in the new series: the Old Forge Café Mysteries. Alex lives in the Chilterns.

www.alexcoombs.co.uk

Bedford Square Publishers

Bedford Square Publishers is an independent publisher of fiction and non-fiction, founded in 2022 in the historic streets of Bedford Square London and the sea mist shrouded green of Bedford Square Brighton.

Our goal is to discover irresistible stories and voices that illuminate our world.

We are passionate about connecting our authors to readers across the globe and our independence allows us to do this in original and nimble ways.

The team at Bedford Square Publishers has years of experience and we aim to use that knowledge and creative insight, alongside evolving technology, to reach the right readers for our books. From the ones who read a lot, to the ones who don't consider themselves readers, we aim to find those who will love our books and talk about them as much as we do.

We are hunting for vital new voices from all backgrounds – with books that take the reader to new places and transform perceptions of the world we live in.

Follow us on social media for the latest Bedford Square Publishers news.

🐦 @bedsqpublishers
𝐟 facebook.com/bedfordsq.publishers/
📷 @bedfordsq.publishers

https://bedfordsquarepublishers.co.uk/